A FAITHFUL SON

A FAITHFUL SON

—

Michael Scott Garvin

Facebook: Michael Scott Garvin Author - A Faithful Son
Website: MichaelScottGarvinBooks.com

ISBN: 1519414730
ISBN 13: 9781519414731

Dedicated to C. A.

.

PROLOGUE

I KNOW LESS THAN I did, but of this I'm certain: a journey best begins at the start. So my story will begin there—before Dad left, before I spotted Doug's crooked grin across the nightclub. My tale begins before I understood this old world is held together with twisted baling wire and rusted penny nails.

If I were to retrace my steps, I'd find my way back to those warm summers in Durango, where I first heard the echoes of the Silverton Narrow Gauge whistling through the San Juans, down the familiar dusty road, just off County Road 250, winding its way to the small white house on the left with the screened-in porch, peeling gray-blue shutters, and a barking yellow dog. Back to Mom's warm waffles and itchy Sunday mornings, sitting on a pew in my starched button-down best, gazing up at a carved crucified savior suspended over the congregation like some great dying hope.

Standing behind his pulpit, Preacher Barnett stretched his arms above his head, fists clenched, warning of a day of reckoning close at hand. The ladies of the First Assembly of God choir reminded the congregation to take our souls down to the River Jordan and wash our sins clean.

After the sermon and the pastor's call to the altar, my two sisters and I would escape from God and our afternoon chores, running deep into the woods, down Parker's Path, through the meadow, and farther on to Rainbow Lake. Breathless, we'd shed our Sunday skin, clasp our hands together, and leap off Mancos Rock, splashing into the water below.

Together the three of us canvassed the mountainsides and overgrown gullies. We spent those brilliant, shining summer days exploring the backwoods of the San Juans. As we lay side by side along the shore of the lake in the warm August sun, dragonflies hovered low out across the water.

With Cousin Dell's old canoe balanced atop our shoulders, we'd stumble down the path to the mighty Mancos River and maneuver through the river's rocks and muddy, rushing rapids.

I was the swashbuckling pirate and my older sister, Laura, my able foe. The youngest, Kate, with her sea-grass green eyes and tousled honey-blond hair was the damsel in distress.

As the sun slipped behind the pines and darkness found us, tales of buried treasures turned to stories of ghosts and lost children. We'd drift to sleep in our bedrolls, circled around a crackling fire. So close were my sisters and I that I'm certain we three shared the same dreams.

When dawn's first light splintered through the trees, we'd awaken to find the forest wrapped in its own white quilt of morning mist, wet aspen leaves blanketing us, and our campfire burned to smoldering embers. Morning unfolded as we lay waiting for Mom's voice to beckon us back home.

My life bears no resemblance to those summers of my childhood. Durango's bustling Main Street is now cluttered with T-shirt shops and storefronts hawking turquoise jewelry. The First Assembly of God was bulldozed to make way for Carl's Jr. Katie is gone, and Laura married an accountant who took her far away.

My sisters' laughter is only a faint memory now, lilting through the pines when a September breeze cools the last days of August. There are no pirates, no dragonflies, and our mother is the only ghost haunting these woods.

I'm an old man now, and no matter the years traveled, I carry an aching feeling that something has been lost and that the missing pieces maybe found somewhere there—the only home I've ever known. Good or bad, right or wrong, I am left with the memories of these people and the small white house on County Road 250.

Perhaps if Parker's Path greets me once more, I will find them waiting—Laura and Katie, laughing, with their bare feet dangling off Mancos Rock. Together, hand in hand, we can jump into the clear waters below. And if the lifting of the morning mist through the aspens clears an unmarked path, and if the Colorado clay breaks easily beneath my hands, maybe I can unearth some answers and, like a buried treasure, find what is lost. In that moment, kneeling on the banks of Rainbow Lake, I will wash it all clean and, finally, leave it there. I will then rest in the shade of the pines and wait for the echoes of my mother's distant voice to hasten me home.

And so, no matter where I am, I remain exactly where I lost him.

—JOSEPH OLSHAN, *NIGHTSWIMMER*

———◆———

CHAPTER 1

Durango, Colorado, 1959.
ON A DUSTY BACK ROAD on a sunny afternoon, I was planted be-
tween Mom and Dad, straddling the gearshift of an old rusted-out
Ford. Sitting on a metal toolbox lodged between the front seats,
I watched the passing blacktop through a crack in the cab floor.
Johnny Cash's rhythmic guitar kept time with slipping gears. From
my lower perch, all I saw was dashboard beneath the wide, blue sky
stretching from mirror to mirror.

Earlier that morning Dad had woken up a poor man, and later
that night when he climbed into bed, he was still poor as Durango
dirt. The small mason jar hidden above the Frigidaire contained
his amassed fortune, but sitting between my folks, I measured
wealth by something far greater than any currency.

Driving deep into the San Juan Mountains, the pickup's jerky
shifting gears accelerated us through the countryside, coughing
gray exhaust as we started our climb up the mountain pass. Dad
shifted and released the whining clutch, powering ahead.

Momma shook her head. "Lloyd, slow down—the babies are in
the truck."

Pops took a long last drag and flipped his cigarette out the open window. "Yes, babe." Flashing a grin, he reached across me to squeeze Momma's leg.

"Lloyd, stop it right this minute!" she said, smiling and swatting his arm. "Keep your hands on the wheel. You're gonna take us right off the road."

"Babe, now don't you go workin' yourself into a tizzy." Dad grinned at her like he was conjuring up mischief.

Laura poked her head through the truck's back window. Long, wild strands of her chestnut hair whipped in the summer wind. "Look, Dad!" She pointed to a collection of clouds in front of us, just above the mountain ridge. "A duck! See it over there? Can you see its beak?" She laughed.

"Yup, I see it right there." Dad traced the shape in the sky with his finger.

Our summers were long threads of warm, golden days. The hours sitting behind school desks were forgotten, replaced with lazy summer afternoons floating on tubes down the irrigation ditches. Afternoons were spent drifting along the culverts and under the roadways, all the way to Vallecito Reservoir.

On those bright, blazing days, hotter than afternoon asphalt, we caught tadpoles in the last puddles of summer. We swung from a knotted rope off Baker's Bridge and jumped, aiming for the center of a floating rubber inner tube below. With my pellet gun, we shot tin cans, one by one, off the picket fence or took aim at the black crows perched on the wire.

Laura and I explored the backwoods, with young Kate scrambling to keep pace. Flashlights in hand, we scouted the dark, abandoned mine shafts that peppered the hillsides.

"If I catch you kids anywhere near those mines, I swear I'll take a piece of each one of your hides," Momma warned. "You'd best be listenin' to me!"

"Yes, ma'am."

Ever since the Delany kid had fallen to his death, Momma had forbidden us to venture anywhere near the dark shafts.

Later I made little Kate swear, with her hand pressed to her heart, not to tell a living soul as we ventured off in the pitch-black tunnels.

"If you open your flap to ma, you ain't goin' with us no more. You hear?"

She shook her head. "My lips are sealed tight." Turning an imaginary key, Katie locked her pink lips.

The three of us ran wild, tearing up and down the rows of cornstalks at the Bledsoe farm. Slithering like snakes, low on our bellies, we hid rotting eggs in the crawl space beneath fat old Nettie's front porch.

"You children, listen up!" Nettie hollered from behind her screen door. "Your daddy's going to swat the skin from your backsides with a switch when I tell him!"

The three of us escaped into the nearby woods. Breathless, we hid low in the scrub brush as big ol' Nettie emerged from the screen door, madder than a hornet's nest and waving her frying skillet.

"You young'uns get back here right now. These eggs are stinking like all get-out!" Shuffling her enormous frame to the edge of her porch, she huffed and puffed and yelled, "I'm calling your daddy, and your momma is gonna hear all about this."

Hiding in the deep summer grass, Laura covered Katie's mouth with the palm of her hand, smothering her laughter.

By the time we made it back home, Nettie had already phoned the house. Pops stood waiting on the porch, a green sapling switch in his hand.

"Lloyd, remember, they're just kids," Mom called out from the kitchen window, trying to save us from a well-deserved whipping.

"Alice, these children are up to no good. I will not abide such behavior."

With crocodile tears streaming down her flushed cheeks, Laura sniffled, "Pops, since it was Zach's idea. You don't suppose you could give him a few of my swats?"

"No, Laura. You've earned them."

Following after Laura, I took my turn, bent over the piano bench, and braced for a strapping while a weeping Kate was made to look on.

With a stern eye, Dad assigned all three of us chores, including mowing the Bledsoes' patch of grass for the rest of the summer.

On this day there was no talk of afternoon chores. We were heading high into the San Juans for the afternoon. Mom bounced little Kate on her knee while Laura rode in the truck bed with the yellow dog.

The pickup followed the narrow back road as it snaked through La Plata Canyon up to the timberline, where the muddy Mancos River begins. Dad pushed the old truck as fast as it could muster, traveling along the blacktop until it turned to gravel, and then a trail of dust followed us higher into a collection of aspen trees.

"Go, Daddy. Go!" Laura laughed through the open back glass.

"Young lady, sit your tail back down," Momma warned. "You'll bounce right out of this truck."

Laura rested her back against the bed, pulling her knees into her chest. As we passed through a grove of oaks, nets of sunlight and shadow were cast over her head. The yellow dog leaned precariously over the side of the pickup, barking and snapping at the wind.

"Pull on over, Lloyd. There's a pretty spot right there with plenty of shade." Mom pointed to a cluster of trees near the reservoir.

Dad took the pickup off-road, driving us across a field of knee-high grass.

Together we unpacked the cooler and picnic supplies. While Mom and Kate prepared our lunch, Dad took Laura and me into the hills to explore the remains of a burned-out farmhouse.

The old abandoned homestead teetered on crumbling footings, pushed forward by a slowly encroaching hillside. Dad, Laura, and I trod carefully through the skeleton frame of boards and shingles, searching the vine-choked ramshackle for any remains of lives lived before.

An old teapot, a few rusted tin cans, and an empty leather satchel were the last remaining treasures in the charred ruin.

I crept up the dilapidated, shifting staircase to explore the small vacant rooms. The walls, papered with a repeating pattern of tiny roses, had yellowed and peeled where they met the plastered ceilings. With one good kick of my sneaker, I busted out the last remaining glass pane from an upstairs window. The shards fell to the ground below.

"Zach!" Dad hollered up the slanted stairs. "What the hell are you up to?"

"Nothin', Pops. It's just an old window."

"Get down here right now! This old house has stood a hundred years without the likes of you coming through like some bulldozer. Haul your tail down here now!"

"Yes, sir." With my hands stuffed deep in my pockets, I trudged down the steps.

"Son, you gotta use the good sense God gave you."

"Yes, sir."

Standing in the remains of the kitchen, Dad called me to his side, placing his hand on the back of my neck. He reminded Laura and me that when folks die, some part of them still lingers behind. He told us we should honor the old house as if someone still slept in the small rooms upstairs and gathered each morning around the table for breakfast.

"Zach, treat this place with common courtesy and respect. Just like you would if you were visiting Toby's house for the night." He lightly squeezed the back of my neck with his fingertips. "Do you understand me, boy?"

"I understand, Dad."

In actuality, Toby's place was a pigsty—the squalor stunk like dirty socks and soured milk—but I knew Pops was making a bigger point.

As Dad spoke, Laura shook her head in my direction like a snotty, disapproving schoolteacher. She was only sixteen months older, but she used every bit of daylight to boss me around.

Dad disappeared onto the lopsided porch while Laura gathered a handful of wildflowers for Momma, and I took one final look around the abandoned, splintered farmhouse. Shadows filled the tiny rooms except for the slightest sliver of sunlight peeking through a decaying rafter. The last remaining shreds of linen hanging from the windows danced in the warm whisper of an August wind. Dad's story had me thinking hard, and just the notion of ghosts haunting the bare rooms was enough to send me hightailing it from the old abandoned shack.

The three of us hiked back down to the reservoir and hunted for smooth rocks to skip on the water. Dad taught Laura how to grip it just right and showed her how to throw it across the surface. With a quick flip of his wrist, Pop sent a gray stone sailing over the still water. It skimmed the surface for eight yards before skipping five times and then disappearing into the blue. I could already skip rocks like an ace on account of I'd been doing it since I was almost seven and a half. Laura's sad attempt took one bounce in the shallow water and then sunk like an anchor.

"Miss Know-It-All, you throw just like a dumb girl," I yelled.

"That's enough, Zach," Dad called to me.

Stripping down to our underwear, Laura and I raced across the reservoir and swam over to our waiting mom, who championed us on at the water's edge. Katie cheered from the banks, and the yellow dog jumped into the cold water to swim the last few strokes with us.

On a blanket spread on the ground, Mom sliced open the last of the buttermilk biscuits from our morning breakfast and filled them with pulled barbecued pork. Sipping sweet tea from white Styrofoam cups, we lunched on Mom's barbecue sandwiches, potato salad, and a bowl of green beans from her garden. Using our bare hands, we gobbled up slices of Momma's fresh strawberry pie, gorging ourselves until our stomachs ached.

"Swing me, Daddy, swing me!" Katie pleaded.

Holding tight to her small wrist and ankle, Dad spun her around. The yellow dog chased Katie's revolving course, yelping and snapping at her gingham dress.

"Lloyd, you're gonna make that child sick," Momma called. "She just ate. She's got her belly full."

"Look, Momma, I'm a carnival wheel!" Kate giggled. "Go faster, Daddy, faster!"

He spun her around until his arms grew heavy and then gradually brought her to a soft landing in the meadow.

Wobbly, little Kate tried standing upright but stumbled, falling back to the ground. She lay dizzy in the tall grass, laughing and watching the spinning world.

Since Kate was the youngest, we all kept a watchful eye on her. Laura and I shared an unspoken pact to stay vigilant with our little sis. Even the dog seemed to trail close behind her.

I was seven when Mom arrived home with little Kate. I recall Pop lifting her from the crib and placing her into my arms. She was pink and powdered and squealing like a newborn piglet. The moment I laid eyes on her, I thought she was all mine—made just for me. I suspect Laura and the dog felt the same.

While my older sis and I fussed and fought around the clock, we tended to little Kate as if she was something fragile, like one of Mom's porcelain figurines on the foyer credenza. Not an hour passed that I wasn't pulling Laura's ponytail or she wasn't snooping where she ought not, but I never gave a second thought if little Kate messed with my stuff or tagged close behind.

"Again, again! Spin me again!" Katie tugged on Pop's belt.

"Missy, you're just gettin' too big." Dad pulled her into his chest and kissed the top of her head. "Run along now, and go help your momma."

While Mom packed up the picnic, Dad leaned back in his lawn chair to smoke an unfiltered Camel. He surveyed the tranquil, green expanse of the Hesperus Valley, the old mutt resting at his boots.

Pointing to a cluster of white clouds, Dad called out, "Laura! Over there, a grizzly bear up on his hind legs. Can you make it out? See it?"

"I see it, Pops, I can see it right there!" Laura ran out toward the clouds, disappearing in the green meadow. She rested on the ground and watched the clouds pass high above her until the white bear scattered in fragments across the blue sky, lost behind the San Juans.

Reclining in his chair, Dad explained to Laura and me. "The sky gathers water from all the lakes and reservoirs, and then that same water rains right back down on our heads from the heavy clouds."

I sat in the grass at his boots, listening intently, although none of it made a lick of sense. But Laura sat upright, nodding her head up and down in agreement. Laura was a lot smarter than I was; without saying so, *everyone* pretty much agreed. I reckon her brain had more aptitude for learning. She made high marks in all her subjects and read thick, heavy books. Laura possessed a keen sense of how things work. Always scribbling something in her school binder, she understood the *whys* and *what fors* and took note of every changing wind.

Pop said Laura was part sass, part smart, and part stubborn. My bare backside was calloused over from whippings, but on the rare occasion Laura was scolded, she'd take the stern talking to, but her two small, defiant fists remained balled up tight behind her back. If my sis determined the punishment was an injustice, she'd stomp her foot almost clean through the floorboards.

———

"Zach doesn't work to his full potential."

"Zach needs to focus."

"Zach doesn't pay attention."

"Zach lacks discipline."

Year after school year, teachers repeated their disappointment at parent-teacher conferences. I sat small at Mom's side, staring down at my untied sneakers while the teacher went on and on. Momma huffed, shaking her head sharply.

On our way home, I hunched low in the backseat of the car without saying so much as a peep.

"Zachariah, I'm not sure what I'm going to do with you," she declared, eyeing my small reflection in the rearview mirror. "You've got to try harder, son."

Up front in the passenger seat, Laura's two ponytails shook back and forth disapprovingly, her judgmental ringlets begging to be jerked right from her scalp. Not to worry—she'd get what was coming to her back at the house.

Still, I plodded off to school every morning. Laura and I met the yellow bus where County Road 250 crossed Trimble Road. My best bud, Toby, saved a seat for me in the tail end while Laura sat with her friends up front.

After standing for the Pledge of Allegiance, the countdown began for the final bell to sound. I studied the hands of the small round clock above the chalkboard as they ticked off the minutes to my freedom.

Five days a week, six hours a day, sitting at my small wooden desk, I learned from a stack of big bulky textbooks meant to expand my half-baked noggin. On Sunday mornings I sat behind another desk and memorized Scripture from *the* book meant to nurture my fledgling soul.

Struggling through my homework, Laura piped in. "Zach, if you just tried applying yourself, you could earn higher marks in your classes."

"Is that so?" I said. "Well, if you keep up your yapping, you're gonna earn yourself a knuckle sandwich."

"Violence doesn't solve anything."

I gave her a hard look. "No, but it will shut your trap up."

"Zach," Mom called out from the front room. "That's quite enough."

Later, when Laura was upstairs readying herself for bed, I pulled her homework from her school bag. Away from mom's eyes, with my pencil and eraser, I rearranged Laura's multiple choice answers on her American history lesson.

I never took to learning like Laura did—I never saw the point. But not a soul dared call me lazy. No school principal, no Sunday school teacher could ever claim the Nance boy didn't work like a harnessed ox.

Dad instilled in me his backbreaking work ethic. He believed an honest, hard day's labor cleansed the mind and purified the soul. If I wasn't pushing a mower back and forth on a neighbor's lawn, I was painting fences or balancing a bike with a basket full of the morning edition of the Durango Herald.

One afternoon, Dad said, "Being poor is just the cards some folks are dealt. There's absolutely no shame in being poor—but a lazy man is hell bound."

"But when is it our turn?" I asked Pops.

"What?"

"When is it our turn to be rich?"

"Where in tarnation did that come from?" Pop cracked a smile.

"It just don't seem fair. When do we get our turn?" I repeated. "The Ellisons drive around town in a brand new Ford and Betty Pilchard has a new dress every single Sunday morning."

"We have enough. The good Lord has provided us with an abundance."

I shrugged my shoulders up to my ears.

"Son, because we live in a small place doesn't mean we're simple and small. We're decent and we love as big as anyone."

I thought on it but was still unconvinced. "It just don't seem fair."

"We have more than we need. Less than some, but more than most." He said. "We're strong in faith and kind of spirit."

"I just want my turn," I declared.

"Zachariah, you get what you get in this life. God provides."

Undeterred, I said, "Pop's when it is my turn, I'm gonna buy Mom so many new dresses that she can toss'em in the bin after one wear."

"Is that so?" He asked.

"Yessum."

Dad laughed and pulled me into his chest.

I was just a stupid kid and didn't know God picked his favorites like the prettiest flowers from a garden. In his care he tended and nurtured the chosen, blessing them with good fortune. The rest of us were left to strive and struggle.

He was a good, decent man, my dad. Built lean but strong, with an easy laugh and a quiet nature. He wore a constant grin at the corners of his mouth and spoke with an air of gentleness.

His full head of thick hair was as black as polish. A clean, ra-zor-sharp part on one side was combed and greased smooth like a movie-screen actor's. Not so with my moppy, faded-brown hair with cowlicks all around. Momma waged war with my untrained follicles every morning before school until finally, near my fifth birthday, she surrendered the fight, explaining it was simpler just to shave it smooth. After four brief minutes under Dad's buzzing electric shaver, the issue was put to rest.

His mother and father were from Northern Oklahoma. Trying to outrun the Great Depression, my grandparents had packed up everything they owned and took to the road. The aching heart-break and disappointment of losing the farm and leaving loved ones behind followed them out west. In the struggle Grandma Nance turned to her Bible. Grandpa turned to the bottle.

My grandparents settled in Southwestern Colorado, and Dad was born in the small town of Mancos. Grandpa Nance worked the ore mines up in La Plata Canyon until cancer took him at fifty-five.

My dad's thirst for spirits was the sole inheritance from his father. He and his younger brother, Leland, had supported their frail mother by working the mines until one sunny afternoon her heart gave out as she weeded her vegetable garden.

The day they laid her in the ground, Leland packed his belongings in a leather case and hitched to Nebraska, where he stayed to farm barley.

Uncle Leland found success in the fertile soil of Nebraska. Dad said of his brother, "Leland is so rich that he goes out and buys himself a new fishing boat every time the old one gets wet."

Pops stayed behind, rambling around the small farming towns of Southwestern Colorado, looking for a single reason to stay put. One afternoon he glimpsed a pretty green-eyed girl at a high school football game in Pagosa Springs.

My mom had been born and raised in Cortez, Colorado. The youngest and only girl in a family of three older brothers, she was a petite, pretty young thing with a long mane of blond hair that hung halfway down her back. Having been reared in a farmhouse full of men, Mom became adept at an early age in how to stake her ground. Just like her own mother, she accomplished this task without saying a single word more than was necessary.

Dad had first noticed Mom sitting on the top row of the bleachers at Pagosa High. At halftime he made his move, trailing her to the concession stand. After two bottles of orange soda pop, the little blonde agreed to a date at the drive-in movie theater.

Pop described how his shy date sat so distant from him in the front seat of his Chevy, her right shoulder remained pressed tight against the door panel, and her fingers gripped the handle, positioning herself for an easy escape. It was a chilly November night, but Mom insisted that her window remain cranked. She preferred to shiver through *Twelve O'Clock High* rather than be alone in a closed car with her new suitor. Dad joked that when Momma spoke, her chilled breath clouded in the cold Colorado night air.

Momma declared, "Your daddy was cocky as all get-out. He thought the sun rose every morning just to hear him crow."

Standing six foot two, Dad towered over his sweetheart, but he soon discovered the tiny, shy blonde disguised a very tall constitution. Stubborn, with a determined streak a country mile long, she didn't take any guff.

Mom came from a long line of God-fearing Christians and put a quick stop to Dad's cursing and cussing and, for a good spell, put the brakes on his drinking.

While Mom never tempted Pop's boots over the threshold of the First Assembly of God church, he admired her strong faith and wanted the same passionate belief to be instilled in his offspring.

Lloyd married the shy, green-eyed girl with long, straw-blond hair. Baby Laura arrived the following summer.

I can still recall Pop's gentle manner with Mom—the way he held her hand when she fretted, how he stretched open his long arms around her tiny waist, lifting her small frame off the floor.

She'd squeal, "Lloyd, you put me down this instant!" Dad held Momma suspended off the floor a second longer until she met his gaze.

Dad was a kind and gentle man, quick to laugh and hard to provoke. While Momma was always cooking or cleaning something, Pop invariably lingered somewhere near us kids. If we were playing in the front yard, he'd be rocking on the porch swing. If we were doing homework at the kitchen table, he was nearby fixing himself a cup of coffee. Our watching television in the front room was his opportunity to saunter in, pull up a chair, turn off the TV, and recount one of his long-winded, familiar stories. Come the weekends he'd load us into the bed of his truck and head off someplace new to scout out and explore.

Only Dad could tease away Momma's blue days. When she couldn't find her smile, he knew just where to go looking. A goofy grin or a tickle to her side with the tips of his fingers brought her back to us. If she asked Pop to fetch mail or take the garbage bin out, he saluted her like a soldier from across the room.

"Yes, ma'am!" Standing straight at attention, Dad clicked his heels together. "Officer Nance at your service, ma'am!" Crisscrossing his denim-blue eyes, he saluted and marched like a stiff-legged cadet out the back door.

A smile teased at the corners of Momma's mouth.

"Lloyd, you look like an absolute fool," she quipped as he marched on by.

We three kids rushed to tackle him. Little Katie wrapped herself around his calf, riding his boot. Laura hopped on his back as he marched out the screen door with the garbage pail in hand.

Roughhousing on the floor was a nightly ritual. We wrestled like wild muskrats, knocking over chairs and lamps. He'd pin Laura and Katie on the couch and tickle their sides, planting dozens of small kisses on their foreheads and the tips of their noses.

"Daddy, your beard is scratchy," Laura squealed with delight as he rubbed his scruffy face up against her pink cheeks.

In the palm of his big hand, he gripped a basketball high above my head. I jumped, trying to snatch it away, but he managed to keep it just out of my reach.

"Lloyd, you take the ruckus outside, or you're gonna break my porcelain dolls," Mom hollered from the kitchen.

"Yes, babe," he'd respond but then continue to play on.

At the end of a summer day, Dad and I sat fishing on the dock in the fading light. He told me about his father, the grandfather I'd never known. As the sun slid behind the San Juans and the surrounding pines were all at once shrouded in shadows, I'd sit near his side and listen to his tales. When trout weren't biting, I'd listen to the same stories I'd heard a thousand times before, and after he'd finish, we'd sit in silence and look out across the still water. I knew the memory of his father cast longer shadows than the disappearing sun.

When scolding us kids, Dad was stern but spared the rod more than we deserved. Never losing his patience, he'd sit us down on the upright piano bench and speak in a direct tone but never harsh or cruel. Instead he was cautious, as if he was pulling a thorn from a bare foot, careful not to squeeze too hard or pick too deep.

Mom's approach to reprimanding us was simple—a hard slap to the side of the head or flicks to our ears with her fingertips, like she was thumping melons at a roadside produce stand. When pushed past her limits, she'd reach for one of Dad's leather belts.

Dad's battle with the bottle kept Momma praying on her knees well into the night. The shag carpet on her side of the bed was well worn from kneeling. Her own father's unquenchable thirst had given her a keen sense that life can wear a man down. She had witnessed her father's battle and recognized the same weakness in Dad.

"If a man is brittle, the bottle will break him," she said.

On nights when Pops came home after sitting too long on a barstool, his unfamiliar cold stare chilled us, as if some stranger resided in our little house—a stranger who stumbled on the floorboards and slurred my name when he called out for me.

"Zachariah! Zachariah!" he'd shout up the stairs. "Where are ya, boy? Come see your old man."

"I'm doin' homework, Pop," I'd reply.

He would pull Laura by the forearm onto his lap. "Hey, baby girl, come see your daddy." His breath was sour, and he laughed too loud. Laura looked over to Momma with frightened eyes, like she'd been called off to the principal's office.

My sisters and I welcomed an early bedtime on those nights, making the climb up the stairs to our rooms, happy to lock the doors behind us.

So Mom and we kids learned to step lightly when this *other* man stumbled through the back screen door. My sisters and I were rushed upstairs when his truck came down the drive.

Whatever battles waged on between Mom and Dad downstairs, I knew with certainty that Mom won them all handily.

Late one night Pop was leaning back in a wooden chair, his boots kicked up on the front porch railing. I listened as he confessed to his best bud, Saul Custer, "I only drink when I gotta quiet my head." Dad folded his arms across his chest, rocking the chair on its hind legs. "There's no harm in quieting the mind."

"Lloyd, you know if it gets out of hand there's places where you can go," Saul reminded him. "And they can help ya out."

Dad chuckled, saying, "Nah, I've got a handle on it."

Pop worked steadily on a tractor through the growing season, but every year after the combines left town, work dried up. He could've followed the harvesting season elsewhere, traveling on to California, but he chose to keep us grounded. He knew firsthand the pitfalls of uprooting a family. He refused to move Momma and us kids from place to place like vagabonds. If struggling to make ends meet for a few months each year was the sacrifice over living like gypsies, we would make do with less. So Dad looked for temporary work, selling cords of cedar firewood or working handyman jobs for a few months during the winter, when the sleeping fields were quilted in snow, and hopped straight back on the tractors in March.

Dad's best friend, Mr. Saul Custer, was a Negro man. I suppose Dad and Saul had known each other long before I was born.

During harvesting season Dad and Mr. Custer worked the combines side by side.

The Custers were the only Negro family in those parts. For a time Saul; his wife, Loretta; and their twin girls came over every Saturday night. My family had never stepped foot in the Custers' small house out past the gravel pits, but every weekend around sunset, Saul, in his metallic-blue Pontiac, drove up the drive with Loretta and the girls. Our two families broke bread each Saturday, with barbecued ribs and collard greens. We played ping-pong under the carport until the mosquitoes drove us inside.

Saul Custer had served his seven years in the military and, while on leave in New Orleans, met Loretta. He'd work as a mechanic in the army, and I suspect Mr. Custer knew more about a car's engine than any man I'd ever met. He and Dad spent hours back in the shed out behind the house, working on cars jacked up on cinder blocks. With the skill of a surgeon, Saul dismantled and rebuilt the innards of a combustion engine. It was easy to understand why Dad admired Mr. Custer. He was a mild-mannered, gracious man with big, strong, round shoulders and smiling chocolate eyes. His jovial laugh could be heard from as far away as Pop's work shed.

Late into the evenings, Saul and Pop paired up against Mom and Loretta over feisty games of dominoes. Laura, Kate, the twins, and I fell asleep on the floor in front of the TV while the foursome played until the wee hours of the morning.

"Lloyd, if you two are going to cheat, let's just put the dominoes away right this instant," Mom would scold the two laughing men.

Dad and Saul would grin at each other from across the table, like two delinquents who'd just stolen something from the five-and-dime.

Loretta didn't need to speak a single solitary word. She'd just set her stare on Mr. Custer, burning a hole clean through him until his back would straighten, and he'd gulp hard like he was swallowing a marble.

Besides Mom, Loretta was the prettiest lady I'd ever seen. She dressed like every day was Easter Sunday. Her skin was smooth and brown, like caramel syrup, and when she passed by, the air was scented with vanilla. She lined her sleepy dark eyes like a cat's, and her long lashes curled up like the legs of a black spider. Her teeth were pearl white, and when she smiled her cheeks ripened like two perfect plums. Loretta spoke softly and elegantly, like she knew better.

I knew Mom felt a real fondness for Mrs. Custer when she proclaimed that Loretta was "the salt of the earth." The pair would exchange recipes and gossip around the kitchen table.

"Loretta is good people," Mom announced, "and she makes a mighty fine piecrust."

In the autumn of 1957, after Saul had managed to save up a respectable sum from his seasons on the combines and Loretta had put away the money she'd earned sewing uniforms for the high school marching band, the Custers opened a small grocery store on Digby Street. Loretta worked behind the register, and Saul stocked the shelves. Every week Mom made the drive over to Custer's, where we shopped for our groceries. Saul let Laura and me choose any piece of candy we wanted from the metal racks below the register.

On Sunday at church, Mom boasted to the other ladies that Custer's Grocery stocked the freshest produce in Durango, but folks never patronized Saul and Loretta's little store. The aisles remained empty of pushcarts, and food spoiled on the shelves. Saul was forced to board up the windows and lock the front door after only nine months.

Sitting at the supper table one night, I heard Dad tell Mom, "It's a crying shame what happened to Saul and Loretta."

The summer sun was in full blaze as Pop worked alongside Saul to clear out the store's racks and disassemble the shelving and storage bins. I swept the wooden floors while the two men worked away in the sweltering August heat. Dad and Saul crated dry goods and loaded coolers up on the back of the pickup. Standing on two ladders, together they took down the electric sign that hung over the storefront and packed it away in tissue paper like a gift that needed returning.

After that summer Saul and Loretta didn't come around much, and our Saturday afternoons were quiet without the Custers' visits. The ping-pong table was folded and put in the back of the work shed. Dad told us kids, "Saul is a living testament to what befalls a colored man who dreams too big in these parts."

———

I was delivered into this world kicking and squalling while a late-winter blizzard raged outside. By midday it was black as night—or so Pop would recount his tall tale of the day of my birth. He reported, after a few unseasonably warm afternoons, folks had breathed a sigh of relief, hoping the long, cold winter was coming to a close. But on the morning of my birth, a violent sky rumbled.

I sat at Pop's feet as he told the story. "The black storm arrived over the mountains from Ouray, the kind of raging, angry sky that made a God-fearing man believe the Second Coming was at hand." He said. "Even your Momma agreed it was unlike any storm she'd ever seen."

Mom shook her head. "Child, you being birthed on such a night accounts for your nasty, trigger-fast temper."

"Flash floods and mudslides crippled much of Southwestern Colorado. Lightning cracked and splintered the sky into broken pieces." Pops said. "A wild wind rattled the window glass in its frames, and a hard, icy rain fell throughout the day. When the swollen Animas River breached its banks, its muddy waters ran down the center of Main Street." Dad continued, with animated bright eyes. "Your Momma's painful contractions forced us out into the storm to find passage to the hospital. Tree branches snapped, and a hard-driving rain kept falling in buckets."

"Okay, Lloyd, don't you think you're kind of stretchin' the blanket a bit." Mom chided.

"Babe, you weren't of a clear mind." Pop remarked. "I borrowed your cousin Dell's canoe, and paddled your momma right down Main Street into the front doors of the hospital. Winds tumbled the electrical poles like matchsticks, and the hospital's corridors went dark. After five hours of hard labor, your momma pushed one last time and you came into this world, spitting and squalling like an angry goose. When the doc slapped your bare ass, the nurses ran from the delivery room, covering their ears."

"You were my precious gift sent from God," Mom said.

"Boy, that's not exactly what she was saying on that particular evening. I swear, you were so fat, it took three nurses just to lift you, wash you up, and powder your ass with talcum."

Mom's account of my birth was quite a different story, but I preferred Pop's colorful retelling.

I was named after my father's father, Zachariah Aaron Nance. Everyone called me Zach for short.

Not a single feature or distinguishing characteristic set me apart from the other local boys kicking around town. I suppose my broad chest and strong jaw resembled the likes of the army recruitment posters in the storefront windows, but my mug would never be projected onto a movie screen or spread across the glossy pages of a magazine. My brown eyes were nothing special. They didn't carry a spark of light like Pop's glistening, smiling blues. Instead, mine were flat and dull, the color of two shallow mud puddles. I wasn't gifted with Mom and Kate's golden-blond manes. My dusty tangle of brown hair clearly possessed a rebellious mind of its own and was untamable by any brush or comb.

On Sunday mornings, dressed in my best, Mom would comment as I walked down the stairs, "Well, look at my handsome boy." But I reckon that's something all moms feel needs to be said, just like, "All my children are smart," or, "My young'uns don't ever lie."

As I grew, my body filled in where a working boy's tends to— my shoulders widened, and my arms and legs grew defined. I never had a problem finding girls who wanted to stroll around Durango on my arm, because it seemed local girls spent most of their waking hours just trying to be found. Laura said the girls liked my "type"—sturdy and strong, made for working and not for talking. But even as my body grew powerful and muscular, I learned at an early age to keep my eyes to the ground. I reckon as soon as I understood that I was a different sort, I learned to lay low like some snake. I'd slither away, avoiding detection. In an instant, if someone went looking in my eyes for anything more than the son of a poor farmer and a pious Christian woman, I knew to recoil. Bending my bones and contorting my frame into something miniscule and insignificant. Pushing my innards from their proper places into a twisted tangle. I learned to hide in the darkest places and disappear into the smallest of nothing.

Playing in baseball and football leagues kept my nose out of mischief in the school yard, but my quick temper got me into a heap of trouble on the streets. My temperament was easy to sour, like buttermilk left out in the blazing sun. Ever vigilant, Momma kept me in check, aware that the slightest tilt could set me off snapping like a river turtle.

During one of my tantrums, Mom would look hard at me. "You'd best choose your words very carefully, boy. The Holy Ghost is an earshot away, but your father's belt is even closer."

I grumbled back, shrugging my shoulders.

"Do you hear what I'm saying?" She'd take a hold of my chin, bringing my eyes to her direct gaze. "You may be growing taller than me, but I can still whip your hide. Do you hear what I'm saying to you?"

"Yes, ma'am."

So every night, palms pressed together, I prayed to the Lord that he would see fit to let me pitch a solid game from the mound, and requested that he douse my red-hot temper with cold holy water. I prayed with the knowing that he took a personal interest in my soul's salvation—on account of we'd already become acquainted in my room one evening.

———

Like the majestic San Juan Mountains and the churning rapids of the mighty Animas River snaking through the center of town, the Durango-Silverton Narrow Gauge train was a calling card for our quaint little city. Nearly every postcard stacked on the gift shop racks displayed a photograph of the old steam engine riding the rails along the steep cliffs of the San Juans.

The first railroad line had arrived in Durango in 1881, and by the following summer sticks of dynamite had cleared the rugged mountainside to lay tracks all the way up to the small mining camp of Silverton. The train hauled the mined ores, both gold and silver, from deep in the San Juan Mountains. A few passenger cars were added, and folks started riding the steam engine up the countryside to view God's handiwork from its small windows.

In the autumn of 1889, after much of Durango was nearly destroyed by fire, the Narrow Gauge delivered the lumber and supplies needed to rebuild our little town. Throughout the train's history, constant mudslides, flooding, and heavy snowpack hindered its progress.

When the last ore mines finally shut down in Silverton, the railroad closed down for over a decade. Wilderness reclaimed its path. The iron tracks rusted, and the wooden rail ties rotted out. It wasn't until after World War II that the train routes were reestablished. About the same time, Hollywood discovered our rustic Western town and its old, dusty steam engine train. The train's passenger cars and caboose were repainted and polished up and soon starred in a dozen or so Hollywood Westerns. Filming took place in and around town, and Durango and its historic train were featured on the big screen.

Hollywood came to town to film *Butch Cassidy and the Sundance Kid* and we loaded in the car to go watch the filming on old Baker's Bridge. For two months cars lined the streets around town, as locals followed the film crew, turning up to catch glimpses of the film's leading men, Robert Redford and Paul Newman.

Mom and her best friend, Betty Pilchard, got dressed to the nines and hung around the lobby of the Old Strater Hotel, waiting to catch a glimpse of Robert Redford. The pair never managed an introduction to Mr. Redford, but Mom swore she saw his right hand wave from the train's caboose as it departed for Silverton.

When folks lost interest in buying movie tickets to Westerns, Hollywood film crews packed up and left town, but tourists kept coming in carloads for the downhill skiing, the camping, and visits to local dude ranches. Tourists boarded the train every morning to ride the rails forty miles north to Silverton.

Like clockwork the whistle sounded each morning, and plumes of gray steam rose high above the tallest pines. The train's tracks hugged the banks of the Animas on one side and the steep, rugged cliffs of the San Juans on the other. After the scenic trip up the mountain pass, the old train would pull into the small station in Silverton. Hundreds of tourists disembarked, flooding into the muddy streets, cafés, and gift shops of the once-quiet mining town.

After a few hours of spending their tourist dollars and taking snapshots in front of the old saloon, they climbed back into the passenger cars with T-shirts and souvenir coffee mugs. The whistle would signal the train's pending departure, and the chugging old steam engine would start its journey down the mountain pass, back through town, and into the depot.

On one afternoon, waiting for the train's return into town, Toby and I hid in the oak thicket near the tracks. As the train passed by, filled with tourists snapping photographs with their cameras, we dropped our trousers down to our ankles and mooned the riders in the clear light of day. When Momma caught wind of our antics on the tracks, she chased me around the front yard, swinging a lawn hose.

"Boy, the next time you two plan on broadcasting your backsides to complete strangers, yours will be branded with my handprint."

———————

My first acquaintance with Toby Zane and his wicked left hook was on the first day of fourth grade. Puffing chests like two fighting cocks, Toby and I squared off at the bus stop. Laura held my schoolbag, and the other kids cleared a circle. It took all of nine seconds for Toby to lay me out flat on my back on the pavement.

After he had handed me the undisputable ass-kicking, I determined I'd best position myself on Toby's side of any schoolyard brawl. Sitting across from each other in the principal's office, Toby and I became best buds.

He was as mean as spit if his back was pushed against a wall, but he preferred telling Pollock jokes and spending hours ogling *Playboy* magazines in his pop's work shed.

Toby had pimply skin and one crazy eye that traveled its own wayward path. Just when you had him straight in your sight, his left eye went wandering off in some distant direction. I learned quickly to focus on the end of his nose when speaking directly. His two front teeth were casualties in a ruckus at the bowling alley. Afterward some poor man's dentist replaced his missing chompers with what looked like two crooked kernels of yellow corn. The metal zipper on Toby's frayed jeans seemed to remain open more the fastened. He played a mean shortstop on the field and could cast farther off the pier than I could by fifteen yards.

Toby's pop mowed the lawn in his long johns and I never once saw his momma out of her terry cloth bath robe and a head full of plastic pink curlers. His folks fought like two swinging wrecking balls, hell-bent on flattening everything in their destructive paths. He and his sister spent every waking hour trying to steer clear of their flying debris. Many nights he ate dinner at our supper table, and when he wasn't held up in his Pa's shed yanking it to a *Playboy* pinup, he attended church service with my family on Sunday mornings. That was until one particular Sunday, when it was determined that Toby was the delinquent who had taken a poop in the top tank of the toilet in our church's restroom. From the other side of the locked door, Brother Bledsoe heard the shuffling of the porcelain lid. After Toby exited, the deacon discovered the floating turd in the upper tank. Such an uproar ensued, I worried poor Toby wouldn't make it off church premises with his life.

The next day in the schoolyard, I asked, "What were you thinking, dummy? It's one thing to drop a deuce in the top tank at school or the bowling alley but that's the house of God." I squared his shoulders with mine. "Toby, that's the Lord's toilet."

He thought on it for a while and shrugged his shoulders. "I was just trying to be funny." He confessed. "It was just a silly prank. Can't they take a joke?"

I explained to Toby that Baptist folk aren't much for laughing.

He nodded his head and declared he'd convert and become a Catholic because their Jesus seemed more apt to forgive and the Catholic girls were easier.

After that Sunday, no matter how many times I pleaded, Momma forbid Toby from ever joining us again to church services. When I asked Mom how she could deny Toby access to the Lord's house, she said, "Until that boy learns to take a proper shit, he will have to wait on salvation."

Momma was not one to cuss so I knew never to ask her again.

The first tallywacker Laura ever set her eyes upon belonged to Mr. Toby Zane.

She confessed at the supper table one evening to the inadvertent pecker sighting.

"Momma, it was so gross." Laura twisted her mouth in disgust. "It looked like some dirty wild mushroom and a sack of purple walnuts."

Little Kate listened on intently to her older sister.

"Okay, that's quite enough." Mom silenced Laura, while Pop snickered from behind his newspaper.

The first few times I pointed out to Toby that his barn door was open wide, he'd scramble to secure his fly but by the sixth or seventh reminder, I just figured he preferred it unfastened.

Momma said, "Somethin' just ain't right with that child. I believe he delights in having his privates public." She shook her head. "And making matters worse, he apparently has an aversion to wearin' underpants. Next Sunday, I'm gonna ask the Sisters to say a prayer for that child."

Due to the repeated trouser snake spottings, I reckon, Toby's was the first exposed flaccid male member for most of the girls in our fourth grade class at Durango Elementary. But the principal's blistering scolding traveled in through one of Toby's unwashed ears and blew right on out the other side. By the next day, his manhood was again peeking through the open metal teeth of his britches.

CHAPTER 2

——◆——

Baptists are the sweetest, most cordial and kind-hearted
folk—until you try to sit in their usual Sunday pew.

UNKNOWN

PASTOR BARNETT SPOKE TO GOD.

Other than the singular exception of yours truly, I reckon our preacher knew the Almighty better than anyone in these parts.

The pastor chatted up the Lord Savior in his quiet hours, arriving each Sunday to his pulpit, ready to deliver a blistering sermon inspired by the Holy Ghost himself.

Pastor Barnett was a short, gritty, fat, red-faced man who smiled when he was angry and cried at his happiest. He combed his thinning gray hair up and over the bald spot on top of his bumpy, brown-spotted scalp. His ample belly hung off him like a sack of flour. From his ears grew wiry puffs of black hair, like two gerbils homesteading. The preacher's big, round, bloated head looked as if he'd held his breath far too long. The top white button on his collar strained under the tension of his thick neck, an unraveling thread through the center of the buttonhole seeming to weaken with each booming "halleluiah!"

As a kid, I feared that in the midst of one of his fire-and-brimstone sermons, his bloated head might just pop during church service—like some giant red balloon inflated well past its limit, it would finally succumb to all the pressure. From my vantage point in the second-row pew, I sat waiting, preparing to shield Mom and me from the impending explosion. I imagined poor Sister Rose Millard, who directed the choir from the church organ near the pastor's pulpit, splattered with blood and chunks of spotted scalp.

From his wooden pulpit, Pastor Barnett gazed out over his faithful congregation, evangelizing on heaven and hell, redemption, and salvation. I didn't understand a single Scripture I'd memorized from those three-by-five-inch cards in Sunday school class, but I believed every syllable to be true. The caped superheroes in the comic books stashed in a shoebox beneath my bed didn't hold a flicker to the powers of the carpenter from Nazareth.

Mom dragged us kids from our beds every Sunday morning.

"You children better get movin'!" Momma would holler up the stairs. "Hop in the tub, and don't forget to scrub them elbows. Zach, wash behind your ears—it's black as night back there!"

From beneath my covers, I commented low to myself, "That's foolish. No one never goes looking behind my ears."

But Momma's fine-tuned hearing could detect the slightest mumbling.

She called back up the stairs, "Young man, don't smart back to me! Your clean soul is the Lord's concern, and the filth behind your ears is mine."

I never knew how Momma could hear the faintest whisper, but I soon learned if I didn't want her to hear an opinion, I'd best to keep it to myself.

Standing shoulder to shoulder in front of the small basin, Laura and I fussed and fought, brushing our teeth and hair, while Katie roamed through the house, squalling and looking for her missing hair ribbon.

Resembling three perfect little Christian soldiers, we dressed in our church best and our polished shoes while Pops, lounging in his T-shirt and flannel pajamas, read his newspaper and paid no mind to the morning's chaos and commotion.

Frightened that Pops wouldn't be joining the rest of us through the pearly gates, I asked him how it could be that a man with such a silent faith could go to heaven but never step foot in a church. "Some folks need to be reminded of the Lord's will every Sunday," he responded, tapping his index finger on his forehead, "but I got it all stored and cataloged right in my noggin."

"Are you sure you'll go to heaven?" I asked him again, looking for more assurance.

"Absolutely, son. When the earth swallows up my carcass, the heavens will swipe up my soul."

And that was that.

On the drive to church, little Kate bawled, strapped in her car seat. Laura and I waged war in the rear, drawing an imaginary property line to stake our separate spaces on the backseat cushion.

"If you cross the line, I swear I'm gonna knock the tar out of ya," I warned with a balled-up fist.

"Zachariah, that's quite enough!" Mom hollered.

Itching for a fight, Laura inched her index finger across the border, invading my territory.

With Momma trying to maintain focus on the road, her right arm reached blindly into the backseat, searching for the nearest head of hair to yank. "I'm gonna whip you two to within an inch of your lives," she threatened, struggling to keep the old Plymouth in the right lane.

The sidewalks emptied and the streets cleared on Sunday mornings as all God-fearing citizens divided into various churches and cathedrals.

The Catholics and Lutherans constructed impressive stone-and-mortar steeples and wide, paved parking lots. The Catholics were even equipped with an indoor swimming pool and private elementary school.

Our little church was a modest sanctuary sitting in the middle of a grassy patch. A scrawny steeple was constructed with stick framing, and wood shingles covered the steep-pitched roof. The parking pad out back was shoveled gravel. On Sunday afternoons when church let out, the unpaved lot looked more like a crash-up derby, as the dozens of escaping cars kicked up dirt.

Inside the white doors, twelve rows of walnut pews faced the wooden pulpit. Bound hardback hymnals were slid into long, narrow nooks running along the backs of the pews. A life-size carved likeness of our blue-eyed Lord Savior was suspended from the vaulted ceiling in front of a stained-glass window, the trumpeting angels etched into the panes reflecting in the sunlight like jewels.

When my spirit was troubled, I'd slip into the sanctuary and take a seat in the front-row—just Jesus and me. He hung suspended on the old wooden cross, high above the pastor's vacant pulpit. Crimson-red paint bled from open wounds in his palms and spilled from the piercing crown of thorns atop his head. The blue of his eyes had faded pale, and a coating of dust gathered on his bare shoulders.

As a kid, I'd arrive to church each Sunday half expecting he'd be long gone—ascended into the heavens overnight, having taken all the good ones with him. But every week he was still there, hanging like one of Mom's macramé pot holders, dusty and fading in the sun.

Standing at the front door, Pastor Barnett would greet the congregation before service. On most Sundays his clip-on necktie was smudged with tiny, milky-brown dribble stains—his morning gravy dotted up and down the length of his tie. Velma, his wife, blotted out the breakfast drippings using her spit and lace hanky.

"Well, hello, Miss Laura. Don't you look purdy. Zachariah, you're looking mighty sharp this morning, and little Kate looks like an angel." The portly minister patted the top of my head and smiled at Mom as if she were his lunch. "A good morning to you, Sister Nance. Don't you look pretty as a picture."

Mom's eyes turned away, her cheeks blushing pink as she hurried us through the doors.

Despite the morning's quarreling, by the time she situated us on the narrow pew, we three delinquents looked like smiling cherubs sitting all in a row with our straight backs pressed against the wooden bench.

"If you children so much as move a muscle," Mom warned in a whisper from the corner of her mouth, "there's gonna be hell to pay at the house."

My sisters and I sat frozen until the closing prayer.

The pastor's hands gripped the edge of his pulpit. He preached until his knuckles were white and swollen. Pastor Barnett taught me of the glories of heaven and warned of the fiery plight of the sinner. He said that some folks' faith is as fragile as tissue paper and that they reach for it only when they're teary eyed and troubled. The pastor instructed us that our faith should be as strong as leather hide.

I was too young to consider whether Noah had truly sailed in a wooden ark or if Jonah had slumbered inside a whale's belly, but my faith was grounded someplace deeper than the quirky particulars of the Bible's fables. My faith was more than a promise of everlasting life, more earnest than a mother's constant prayers for her son to be born again. I believed in God's existence like I believed in the sun's warmth, not only because I felt it on my skin but because everything—the mountains, trees, fields, and flowers—all needed it to grow and flourish. My faith was strong in the knowing that God existed, not because I could see him but because I sensed his eyes watching me. As I hiked the valleys and woods, he followed my every step. As I went about my days, I knew with certainty he was there keeping watch, just like the old hoot owl sitting high up in the sycamore, whose wide, glowing gold eyes watched me in the night as I carried the trash out back to the bin.

As we were driving home one afternoon, I asked Momma how I could be certain God loved me.

"Baby, if God has his eye on the littlest sparrow, you can be certain his eye is watching over you." And she squeezed my shoulder, smiling like she knew a secret I'd also know someday. I believed her every word, because Momma didn't lie. "You're safe and sound, baby, in the righteous arms of the Holy Ghost."

It was near that same time when Jesus Christ himself came a-calling. Mom always said the pathway to heaven was narrow. I reckon she had no idea the trail crisscrossed right through the middle of my messy bedroom, but sure enough, Jesus was there hiding in the darkest corner of my closet. He stood as quiet as the dead, watching from a sliver of a crack in my closet door. Waiting until Momma had left my bedside, he stood cloaked in shadows until the coast was clear.

I was flushed with an awful burning fever, and Momma kept me home from school for nearly a week. She stayed at my bedside, keeping vigil throughout the night. She took to sleeping by my side on my narrow bed, covering us both with a crocheted afghan, her knees bent with mine. My head fit in the nape of her neck like the last piece of a puzzle.

Laura was at a sleepover at Stella's, Dad was away, and baby Kate slept soundly in her crib. I was eight or nine years old, the age when a sick boy ain't yet embarrassed to be held by his momma. I was hers, and she was completely mine. Night was kept at bay by the thinnest sliver of glass in my bedroom window.

Placing an ice-cold cloth across my forehead, Mom battled my temperature. When I stirred she pulled me closer, folding her arms around me like the petals of her prized roses. She stayed with me, humming a hymn in my ear.

Across the room, Jesus stood waiting, patiently listening for the sound of Mom's footsteps traveling down the stairs. The slightest slice of moonlight cut through my darkened room.

The rustle of my shirts on their wire hangers first caused me to take notice. Peeking over my shoulder to the dark side of the room, I pulled the crocheted throw over my head. Lying as still as the night, I peered through the yarn netting and watched the crack in the resting door. My cheeks flushed red hot from the fever.

In the corner the door to my closet started a slow progression open, sending me deeper under the covers. I lifted the blanket's edge and watched as the closet's black interior grew wider. I mouthed the word "Momma," but only air escaped from my parched lips. Stillness waited behind the door, but then came a shuffling in the shadows, like a flurry of black crows.

A figure emerged from the doorway. I swallowed hard, but a knot was lodged somewhere deep in my throat. The robed silhouette, arms opened wide, moved toward my bed. I held my breath, afraid to exhale. His bare feet made a path through the abandoned toys strewn around my bedroom floor. As he passed through the light of the half moon, I saw the crown of thorns that pierced his scalp wrapping around his head like rusty barbed wire.

From under the quilt, I felt his hand brush my right leg. My scream evaporated into a faint sigh. Dried blood was caked in his hair like mud on the soles of my sneakers. Jesus knelt down beside me, but I turned my eyes away to the wall. He laid his hand on me, running his fingers along my forehead, brushing aside my sweat-drenched hair. Not moving a single muscle, I lay still as the night while the Lord caressed me. His fingertips were as hard as Douglas fir as they dragged against my skin. I turned to steal a glimpse but was frightened by his flat, fixed eyes and frozen half smile. He tilted his head closer to mine and moved nearer. I quickly turned, but his breath was on my neck. He smelled of mothballs. I wanted to holler for Momma, but his voice was upon me. His whispers sent shivers racing down my spine. I fought to wake from the fevered dream, but Jesus was tempting me back to sleep, his singing low and hushed. My heavy eyes stayed transfixed on the bare plastered wall as his mouth lingered near. Resting my head deeper into the sweat-soaked pillow, I drifted to sleep with Jesus humming the sweetest hymn in my ear.

Come morning, my fever had broken, and sunlight streamed in from my open window. Downstairs, Momma was laughing about something on the phone with Sister Combs. His will had been done—I was healed by the power of the Lord Jesus Christ.

From that night on, I understood what Pastor Barnett already knew: that Jesus was as close as my bedside, as near as a prayer. He lingered in shadows, watching and waiting to catch me if I should stumble. I knew with absolute certainty that I held his favor. After that night, every Sunday I sat listening to Pastor Barnett, content in the knowledge that he and I were kindred spirits.

———◆———

If Pastor Barnett sat at the head of our holy supper table, then the Sisters of the First Assembly of God prepared our proverbial holy potluck. These unyielding women of faith were the backbone of our small community: God-fearing spinsters, retired schoolteachers, and Bible-quoting momma bears who protected their offspring from the evils of the godless world. They were lonely widows, silver-haired grandmas, and housewives who read Scripture at night in their quiet hours.

The Sisters of the First Assembly of God strolled through the park in packs or sauntered in pairs along the river walk, their arms intertwined. Delicate white-lace gloves graced their hands and practical black-leather purses dangled from their forearms.

The single distinguishing characteristic of the Sisters was their glorious, intricate piles of teased and sprayed hair. Fabulously ratted bouffants crowned their well-worked scalps. Masses of gray, blond, brunette, black, and bleached locks were sculpted into coiffured cotton candy.

These architectural marvels were constructed and maintained inside Gladys's Beauty Shop on Main Street. The bustling beauty salon was headquarters for these great ladies of faith. The Sisters traded local gossip like baseball cards as their tresses were tightly twisted onto tiny plastic curlers. The ladies who couldn't afford Gladys's price tags gathered in kitchens to perform home perms on one another's locks. At Gladys's, after applying a pungent liquid solution to their scalps, they sat under rows of big plastic hairdryers until their hair was crispy. These new permed ringlets were then teased into great mounds of sprayed hair. Several of the elderly Sisters preferred theirs tinted soft pink or pastel purple, like Katie's candy taffy.

The April afternoon Mom walked in through the back screen door after having her long, luxurious blond locks cut off, Laura and I saw the aching disappointment in Dad's eyes. Upon surveying her newly ratted hairdo, Pop managed a half smile. "You sure look pretty, babe."

She anxiously rubbed the sides of her bald neck, searching for locks no longer there. Seeing Dad's disheartened expression, Mom promised, "It will grow back, Lloyd. I will let it all grow back."

It never did.

After that afternoon Dad said Mom's hair spray receipts exceeded our gas bill, and if her do got any higher, it would be necessary to raise the ceiling rafters.

Over the passing years, Mom was elevated to an honored position among the powerful ladies of the First Assembly of God church. Her unflinching and steadfast faith became widely admired, and her sweet, quiet nature was a welcome trait among the circle of devout but strong-willed women.

~THE SISTERS~

If the Sisters of the First Assembly of God had a designated anointed leader, Nettie Bledsoe was their commander in chief. Nettie, a big woman, tipped the scales at well over three hundred pounds. She led the faithful flock of women in a host of community and charity efforts. Spearheading the church fund-raising, Nettie scheduled bake sales and camp meetings and orchestrated the ladies' busy social calendar.

Nettie sported two big, pendulous breasts and a bloated belly that rode low over her short, thick legs. As she shuffled about, her fleshy thighs appeared to wrestle beneath her polyester skirts. From her trunk-like legs sprouted two tiny feet, stuffed and laced into a pair of practical black-patent-leather shoes.

She was as bighearted as she was rotund, charitable to a fault, and a tireless worker for the church. Nettie smelled of cinnamon and baked pears. Her contagious joyful laughter entered the room well before she did, and when dealt a potent canasta hand, her snorting guffaws could be heard in the next county. On Sundays, Nettie's sidesplitting laughter would echo through the halls of the small church. Whether at a whispered off-color joke, at a misstep, or even at her own expense, she was eager to share a good laugh.

Sister Bledsoe's ample size was the ridiculed brunt of much joking by us schoolkids. Still, no matter how many mean-spirited jeers were directed at Sister Bledsoe during the week, come Sunday all was forgiven. Nettie would arrive to church hugging the necks and kissing the washed-clean faces of the same rotten brats who hollered at her as she waddled along Durango's sidewalks. Always carrying in her purse a bottle of Jergens lotion, she'd apply the cream to our chapped lips or sunburnt cheeks. Nettie believed all the world's ailments could be healed by Jergens. Cuts, callouses, corns, bruises, and belly-achin' could all be soothed with a smear of the creamy lotion.

Every Sunday Homer Bledsoe, Nettie's husband, pulled into their reserved church parking space nearest the front doors then circled the truck and opened the passenger door for his missus. Nettie took her time, shifting and repositioning her substantial frame in preparation for an exit from the vehicle. Finally maneuvering out of the pickup cab, she'd shuffle up to the church doors, handing out Tootsie Pops to every child from a plastic bag. After

Sunday school class, all of us kids came out running, our smiles stained the colors of the hard-candy suckers. I gazed in awe at this colossal laughing creature with massive blue, teased hair.

Homer Bledsoe was a thin rail of a man with an intricate sweep of hair over his bald scalp. Since he was a man of few words, Nettie did all the conversing for the Bledsoes. But what Homer lacked in oratory skills, he more than made up for with his prowess at the game of horseshoes. Homer was the master of the perfect pitch. After church service, the Sisters of the First Assembly of God gathered on the front steps, sipping iced tea, while the men folk loosened their ties, rolled up their sleeves, and pitched horseshoes in the shade of the trees.

Dad said a man's pitch spoke to his character and a fine toss was revered and celebrated in these parts. Homer's technique and form was the pinnacle to which all the men aspired. They gathered and watched as skinny old Brother Bledsoe perfected the science of the toss. His strategic, steady throws were the stuff of local legend. Tournaments were a serious matter—not honoring the game was frowned upon and determined to be a serious lack of integrity.

On several warm Sunday afternoons, the lady folk had to step in and squelch feuding opponents before punches were thrown and fists started flying.

While the Sisters clucked like busy chickens, their men stood silent as students, observing and studying each toss. They praised the perfect pitch and snickered at a miscalculated throw from a novice.

Sister Rose Millard was a meek, pious woman who directed the ladies' choir. She was mousy and bone thin, with stiff, sprayed mauve hair like a great tumbleweed perched atop her tiny shrunken skull. When a strong wind blew through, her starched bouffant bent and bowed in the direction of the gusts. Her pale, paper-thin skin was translucent like a tissue, and she smelled of Virginia Slims and medication. Her floral skirts were worn high on her waist, exposing skinny legs with tiny, mushy knees resembling two wads of chewed pink bubblegum.

Rose's silver-rimmed spectacles had dense goggle-like lenses that teetered on the edge of her slender rail of a nose. As Rose spoke she twitched and twisted, contorting her face as if in midseizure, in an attempt to keep her spectacles from traveling clean off the end of her nose. Sister Millard's magnified, shifting eyeballs and twitching facial contortions frightened young toddlers and spooked family pets.

Seated behind the electric organ, Rose worked the ivories with two bony, veined, and gnarled hands that looked to be reaching from a grave in a horror movie. She pumped and praised when leading the ladies' choir in song. Rose's mass of purple hair bobbed and bounced as she whipped her organ into a frenzied crescendo.

Momma said Sister Annie Combs was a half-baked pie—crusty around the edges but mushy in the center. Annie was a retired schoolteacher who'd never married. She was a fragile but feisty woman who had conveniently forgotten the names of her three nephews but easily recalled the names and pedigrees of her last fifteen cats. She buried each feline deep in her garden in a J. C. Penney shoe box.

Annie applied her makeup like she was painting the wide side of a barn. Glimmering eye shadow coated her wrinkled lids, and lipstick smudged the front of her yellow teeth. Like the artwork of a child with a red crayon, her lipstick traveled well outside the lines, smearing past the perimeter of her thin lips. The other

Sisters hadn't the heart to tell Annie, so we all just came to expect her arrival at church with a minefield of makeup, painted up like a born-again Christian clown.

When Annie wasn't tending to her cats, she sat on an old couch on the front lawn of her mobile home on Route 160. Most of the day, Annie sat, propped up and wearing a wide-brimmed sun hat, balls of yarn piled on her lap, knitting beanie caps for the neighbor children. Yellowing foam squeezed from the ripped seams of the dirty couch, and at night the upholstered innards served as the den for a family of wild raccoons.

As a matter of neighborly courtesy, it was customary for passing automobiles to toot their horn when traveling by the always waving Sister Combs.

One New Year's Eve, and after sipping too much cooking sherry, Annie stood in her yard at the stroke of midnight and commenced firing her shotgun wildly into the night air. The sheriff arrived to find Annie snoozing on the filthy couch with the family of coons slumbering at her side.

Pops sent me with the mower over to Annie's place once a month to tend to her lawn, and Mom included a cellophane-wrapped plate of her famous pot roast and blueberry cobbler.

Sister Betty Pilchard was Mom's best friend. A two-time widow who cruised the streets of Durango in a sweet metallic pearl-white Cadillac Seville with a sunroof and chrome-spoked hubcaps. A Southern belle beauty in her youth in Biloxi, Mississippi, over the decades Betty had transformed into an elegant silver-haired lady with fine-boned features and quiet social graces. Mrs. Pilchard carried herself like some great stage actress with a slow, syrupy Southern drawl, sporting fancy, intricate hats atop her head and her graceful neck wrapped in silk scarves bought at boutiques in

New York City. Sister Pilchard doused herself with sweet, expensive perfume from Paris, and every Sunday Betty adorned her blouse with a signature yellow rose clipped from her trellises. Tailored dresses and skirts perfectly fit her petite frame.

Mom quipped when Betty wasn't in earshot, "I swear that woman pecks at her plate like a persnickety bird. She needs a big helping of biscuits 'n' gravy."

Betty's most recently departed husband, Tucker, had owned a big dairy farm twenty miles south of town. When Mr. Pilchard died on the toilet at the Durango Diner of a sudden heart attack, a national dairy conglomerate out of Kansas flew into town and offered the widow Pilchard a big payday to sell the dairy. The lucrative deal left Betty set for life.

She purchased the biggest Victorian house on Thirteenth Avenue, with a white wraparound porch, detached guesthouse, and swimming pool. Betty drove her new shiny Cadillac right down the middle of Main Street. One afternoon she entrusted Toby and me to wash and wax it at her house. We spit polished the chrome bumpers and buffed the metallic paint.

"Laud mercy, you boys have worked wonders!" Betty gasped as she walked out onto her porch and admired her buffed Caddy glistening in the sunlight. "You boys can come by once a week and give her a good washin'."

So pleased, Mrs. Pilchard reached in her pocketbook and tipped us a ten-spot. Toby and I washed and waxed the Seville every week for almost two months until Sister Pilchard caught Toby taking a piss in her rose garden. Waving her flyswatter, she chased him down the drive, out past her mailbox, and clear out of sight.

None of the townsfolk knew exactly how much money Betty banked from the sale of the dairy, but she was living in high cotton. A colossal diamond ring sparkled on her finger, and two more glittering rocks bobbled from her ears. Mom counted over a dozen diamonds on the brooch pinned to Betty's fur stole. Her yapping, tiny poodle was dressed in finer clothing than most of us kids. The First Assembly of God deacons had her name inscribed on a stone plaque on the wall after Betty wrote a fat check to the church for a new shingle roof.

———

Katie was swinging.

I reckon she was always either spinning, splashing, squalling, or swinging. On this particular day, she was hanging by her knees, upside down, swinging like a monkey in a cage, all bare legs and ruffled white panties. Her face was completely covered, not a sign of her blond noggin, just two braided pigtails dangling from below the hem of her upturned polka-dot dress. With her arms stretched, she reached down to the passing ground, her short pink fingertips almost skimming the dirt.

"You know if you keep doing that, you're gonna throw up," I warned. "Your eyes are gonna pop right outta your head."

"Nuh-uh." She swung to and fro. "When I'm grow'd up I'm gonna be in the Olympics," Katie declared from beneath the inside-out skirt. "I'm gonna win a blue ribbon in the Olympics for gymnastics."

Laura, lying on her stomach on the lawn, was lost in a book. I chewed on a blade of grass on my back, and Katie swung like a trapeze artist.

"When you're grown up," Laura corrected her. "Not grow'd up."

The slipping sun painted the sky a pale lilac, the color of the dancing elephants along the elastic band of Katie's exposed underwear. She kept her pace, swaying back and forth, showing no signs of stopping. "I'm gonna be the best gymnast there ever was, and I'm going to the Olympics and win a blue ribbon."

"You won't do no such thing," I piped in.

"I am too!" Her scrawny little legs were bent clear over the monkey bars, and her tiny white ankles crossed at her bare feet.

"Katie, you don't win a blue ribbon in the Olympics." Laura looked up from her reading. "You win a gold medal."

"Well, then I'm gonna win a gold medal at the Olympics." She rocked her arms, propelling her swing even faster and higher.

Dad had welded together the pull-up bars and swing set for us in the side yard, from lengths of pipe he'd found by rummaging through the town dump.

"You know, if you really wanna go to the Olympics, you gotta practice every single day," I said, "and you can't live here with us no more."

"Nah." She swayed back and forth. "Ain't true."

"Uh-huh. You gotta move someplace where they make you practice every day. It's like a gymnastics prison camp, where they make you practice all day every day. No candy, no cookies, nuttin'."

"Nuh-uh, you're lying, Zach." Kate lifted her dress up, uncovering her red puffed face. "Laura, is that even true?"

"He ain't lyin'. If you really wanna go to the Olympics, most of those li'l girls go train in camps with other kids."

"See, I told ya. I hope you're ready to leave Mom and Pop forever."

"Shuddup, Zach. You're a turd." Undeterred, Katie kept up her swinging. "I'm going no matter what you say."

Laura went back to her book, and Katie went uncommonly quiet beneath her cotton dress. The slightest sniffle filtered from under her swinging skirt.

"Katie girl! For goodness sake!" Mom hollered from the back screen door. "Stop showing your bloomers to the whole wide world. That's no way for a little lady to behave."

Katie grabbed hold of the side bar, stopping her swinging. She flipped right side up and, with both feet safely back on the ground, took off bawling toward the house. "Momma! Momma! Zach and Laura said I gotta go to prison!"

Dizzy from the swinging and the blood rushing from her head, Katie ran a crooked path all the way back to the house and up the back porch steps.

"Momma, Zach said I gotta leave you and Pops if I wanna be in the Olympics." She ran into Mom's waiting arms, disappearing into her apron.

"Zachariah, stop telling your little sister she's going to prison!"

"Yes, ma'am."

"You kids come on to supper," Momma called. "And wash your hands, Zachariah. A garden could grow under them filthy fingernails."

Laura closed her book and looked over her shoulder in my direction. Cracking the first snicker, she covered her mouth to smother her own giggles. We lay in the summer grass, laughing under a watercolor sky.

——◆——

CHAPTER 3

SKIPPER JACKSON WAS A "SISSY"—it was a name folks called him behind his back.

He threw a hardball like a little girl and was too pretty for his own good. Endlessly polite, he covered his mouth when he giggled and batted his lashes when he stood at the head of the class to recite his favorite poetry. He arrived to school each morning in polished lace-up shoes. His shirts were starched and pressed, and his plaid slacks were hoisted by checkered suspenders with shiny brass buttons. His sandy hair had a razor-sharp straight part, and his rimmed glasses dangled from a silver chain around his neck. Skip spent his spare time sketching pictures in his binder notebook and reading by himself at a cafeteria table.

His pop was killed in an accident trucking produce from Denver to Colorado Springs, and his momma waitressed at the coffee shop inside the Woolworth's.

Most folks in Durango didn't take to Skipper's ways. I figured he didn't know any better on account of not having a dad of his own. At recess the boys hunkered low in circles to shoot marbles or played kickball in the field. Skipper steered clear, standing with the girls over at the swings. Us guys never knew what they were chirping about. They stood in clusters, whispering among themselves, and then broke out into frenzied giggles like happy chickens.

Bud Ellison was a big bull of a boy, tough as nails. Just a year older, in eighth grade, dark wiry scruff had already sprouted from his chin. Because he was bigger than most boys at the high school, we all opted to walk a wide path around big Bud Ellison.

One afternoon during recess, Bud strutted right up to Skip and leaned low into his face. "Jackson, you'd best start to man up," Bud warned, "or there's gonna be trouble." His rancid breath fogged the lenses of Skip's spectacles.

With one hard push from Bud, Skip stumbled backward and fell flat on his rear, his books and papers scattering on the playground.

The gaggle of girls led by little Lucy Cline made its way across the yard, and they placed themselves right in the middle of the scuffle. Lucy planted herself dead center between Bud and Skip. Wagging her finger, she yelled, "Bud Ellison, you're an asshole! Who do you think you are? Just leave him alone."

Little Lucy stood small before Bud, and he ignored her as if she were an annoying buzzing gnat.

"Skip's not hurting anyone," Lucy shouted. "You assholes, leave him alone."

"Zip it, Lucy," Bud replied. "You had best just keep walkin'."

Puffing her chest, Lucy snapped back, "You zip it, asshole!"

Little Lucy Cline was partial to the word *asshole.*

"Stop meddlin', Lucy." Bud towered over her. "This ain't none of your concern."

"I'm making it my concern."

Bud looked down at Lucy and drew a deep breath, losing his patience. "Lucy, you'd best stop your yappin'," he warned.

Skip dusted off his britches and scrambled to gather up his books.

"Bud, why don't you go and bully someone your own size?" Lucy crossed her arms, standing her ground. "Mrs. Baldwin is going to hear all about this, you asshole!"

"Lucy, I told you to step back. Didn't nobody ever teach you to mind your own business?" Bud grumbled. "What kind of man needs some girl fightin' his battles?"

Lucy didn't give an inch and pushed closer to Bud. Skipper stood quiet. Gripping his books in his arms, he kept his eyes turned to the ground.

Little Lucy said, "Come on Skip, let's go." She grabbed his hand and marched off with the other girls. As she passed, she eyed me and Toby. "You two should be the bigger men." An earshot away from us, she hollered back, "And Toby Zane, for the Lord's sake, put the lid on your pickle jar!"

I reckon Skip would have been better off if he'd just spoken up for himself instead of letting Lucy fight his war. We all knew full well the girls couldn't save Skipper for long if Bud Ellison wanted a piece of his hide—Bud would just wait it out until he got Skipper alone.

It was no sucker punch. Bud told Skipper straight up it was coming, right before taking the swing. He held his big thick fist in Skip's face, warning him he was gonna sock him in the jaw. Bud had cornered Skipper near the baseball concession stand on the way home from school. Toby and I were cutting across the baseball field when we walked up on them. Big Bud was taking off his jacket and rolling up his sleeves. Skipper was cornered like a hunted red fox, pleading for Bud to let him go.

"You faggot!" Bud's first punch landed right on Skip's face, shattering his glasses and cutting his left eyelid. The second blow to his gut knocked out Skipper's breath—he fell to the ground, gripping his stomach. An awful sound of wheezing for air came up from his throat. It wasn't like it could ever be a fair fight. Bud outweighed him by fifty pounds and towered a foot over Skip's bony frame.

"Pick him up! Get him up!" Bud yelled to Toby and me. "Pick his queer ass up off the ground."

I looked over to Toby and waited for a reaction.

"I said, pick him up!" Bud ordered.

Toby slowly knelt down, grabbing Skipper's right arm.

"This ain't our fight, Toby," I said.

Bud scoffed and narrowed a look at me. "Nance, I believe you're a fucking queer."

"I ain't no queer."

"Pick him up, faggot," Bud barked.

Toby called out. "Just do it!"

Roughnecks like big Bud threw plenty of hateful words around the schoolyard. Hard sunbaked clods of cutting curse words aimed at the weakest of us. Whenever he came out slinging mud and swinging his two thick fists, we all scattered, running for cover. The bruises faded, and cuts scabbed over, but *faggot* was mud you couldn't scrub off; no matter how hard you scoured, the word stuck to your skin like a foul tattoo.

I bent down and scooped a whimpering Skip off the dirt by his limp arm.

Before Toby and I had him standing upright, Bud took another hard swing to his stomach. Skipper cried out, twisting his torso away from Bud's fists, but another blow landed on his nose and sent blood splattering all over Toby's T-shirt.

Writhing in pain, Skip broke loose of our hold and fell to the dirt, folding like a gunny sack when he hit the ground. He rolled back and forth with his legs drawn tight to his chest, wrapping his arms around his head to protect his bleeding face.

Toby looked down at his bloodstained shirt and, without a thought, gave Skipper a hard kick to his backside. "Look, you fuckin' queer, you ruined my best T-shirt." Toby threw his backpack over his shoulder. "My momma is gonna tear my hide." He stomped off, calling out for me to follow—but I stayed behind.

Skipper coiled up, rolling in the dust. His clean white button-down shirt was covered in blood and dirt. Heaving, he struggled to catch a breath between cries and coughs.

Bud leaned over Skipper, who was sniffling and pleading for his momma.

"There's no room in Durango for faggots." Bud sneered and gave Skipper one more final hard kick with the tip of his boot.

Skip yelped like an injured dog. He moaned and curled back into a ball on the ground, recoiling like the garter snake I'd poked with a stick in Mom's garden.

Examining his cut knuckle, Bud spit on the ground near Skip's head. A stream of piss ran out from the leg of Skip's pants.

Bud wiped his mouth with his forearm. "I'm not sure about you, Nance. I'm startin' to think you're as queer as Jackson."

I held big Bud's stare. "Ain't true." I hawked up some snot from the back of my throat and spit, hitting Skipper balled up in the dirt.

Bud smirked and sauntered out across the ball field and over to the parking lot.

I waited until Bud disappeared. "You all right? Skip?" I kneeled at his side. "You gonna be OK?"

He rocked on the ground, answering with only a muffled cry.

A passing teacher walked along the sidewalk, and I ducked low behind the concession stand. I whispered again, "Are ya OK, Skip?"

Blood and saliva spilled from his mouth.

"I want my momma," he cried, lying in a puddle of his own piss. "I want my momma."

He snuck a peek from between his fingers, looking for any trace of Big Bud. His bloody wide-eyed gaze resembled the six-point buck Toby had tagged during hunting season. It wasn't a clean shot, so we'd tracked the bleeding deer a mile back into the forest. By the time we'd found him, he'd bled out and lay in the tall grass, helpless and frightened, breathing his last shallow breaths. Toby put him down with one shot to the temple. The same frightened, pitiful look flooded over Skip's desperate eyes.

The Adams twins, carrying their pom-poms and schoolbooks, came out laughing from the gymnasium doors, heading in our direction across the field.

I scrambled, grabbing my backpack. "I gotta get out of here. Skip, I gotta go." I took off in a full sprint toward the parking lot.

I left him there and never turned back. I never knew who found Skip or how he made his way home.

His wooden desk sat empty the following Monday and all the Mondays after that. Skip never returned to Durango Middle School.

Toby and I sat nervously, fidgeting at our desks, waiting to hear our names called out over the loudspeaker, beckoning us to the principal's office. We looked at each other from across the classroom like two felons awaiting guilty verdicts to be handed down. The days plodded along until the final bell sounded. Outside the gym, big Bud Ellison pulled the two of us into the locker room. With his hairy knuckles rolled into a thick knot, he warned us to keep our mouths shut.

Toby overheard a teacher telling a couple of girls in class that Skipper's momma enrolled him in the private school in Cortez. Toby and I exhaled, knowing we'd dodged a bullet.

The next week at the pep rally, Little Lucy Cline marched up to Toby and me.

"You two assholes should be ashamed!" She distorted her face in utter contempt. "Skip told me everything! You two make me sick. Do you know he can't hear from his left ear? Did you know that?" She stuck her tiny pointed finger into my chest. "And did you know he's got busted ribs and five stitches over his left eye? Huh?"

"Lucy, we had nothing to do with that." Toby defended himself. "Bud was picking for a fight, and we didn't even know it was going down."

"You're both pathetic! Both of you!"

"Lucy, are you going to say anything to anyone?" I asked.

She shook her head in disgust. "He's a bigger man than you two will ever be!" Walking off, she added in a huff, "I'll never understand why you boys are so rotten."

"It wasn't our fight, Lucy," I called out to her.

She turned around, stomped back over, and stared me down. "You're assholes! You're both going to get yours one day. Just you wait!"

I asked again, "Are you going to tell anyone?"

Little Lucy hawked up some saliva and spit it at my feet. She took a long, hard look at me, like she'd figured out I was smaller than the smallest creature. "I sure should tell, Zachariah Nance, but Skip says it's best just to let it go."

Big Bud Ellison had no right doing what he'd done out in the baseball field that day. He was a hateful waste of flesh and bone. But Momma said, "Deliberate cruelty is the wicked work of the weak. It takes strength to be kind." If God was keeping score that day on the ball field, I was no better than big Bud Ellison. I knew deep in my gut that Jesus didn't give one speck about my apology. He and I both knew I was just covering my bases.

———◆———

Kate was suspended off the ground in a tractor tire tied with three ropes to a sturdy branch. Mom tended to her garden, and Laura was lying on her back on the lawn.

Momma worked the dark soil on her hands and knees. Only the crest of her blond bouffant peeked above the thick, unruly tomato vines.

Winding the ropes, I coiled Kate's tire swing until the braiding was stiff and taut. When I released the tire, it sent her spinning deliriously like a top.

"Zach, you know anything about the dustup with the Jackson boy?" Mom asked, bent low in a row of her treasured tomato bushes.

"Nope. Nothing." I stuck my hands deep into my pockets.

"Nothing at all?"

"No, ma'am."

"Well, you'd best keep your nose out of trouble. You hear?" She looked up and held my sight with a stern eye.

"Yes, ma'am."

"I hear his momma pulled him from school," Laura said.

"It's probably best," I added. "'Cause Skipper never did fit in."

Momma continued with her gardening.

I paced up and down rows of radishes. "They say Skip is light in the loafers," I said. "He only hung round with the girls."

"Skipper's a nice enough boy," Laura called out, "despite him being a queer and all."

From the base of a tomato stalk, Momma snapped, "Hush up, missy. There's a bar of soap with your mouth's name on it." She turned back to breaking baked mud clods in her palms, always careful not to disturb the ripening fruit.

It was a mean July sun on a mid-April afternoon. Mom wiped sweat from her brow with the back of her forearm. "It's a sin against nature, but a boy who struggles with such perversions has only to get it right with God, and all is forgiven."

"Skip was just asking for trouble," I responded, kicking the ground with my sneaker. "The way he sauntered through town wasn't right."

"I'm not sure how that's any of your concern. You tend to your own business, and leave Skipper to tend to his. Every sinner can repent and be washed in the blood of the lamb. God's judgment is no harsher on the Jackson boy than on a dishonest whippersnapper who can lie to his mom without so much as a wince." Mom caught my telling eye. "Sin is sin." She said. "It's an easy thing to have compassion in your heart for a struggling soul. God's mercy is great, but I won't abide someone who lies with ease. Do you understand?"

"Yes, ma'am."

"Then go on inside, and get to your schoolwork."

Skip weighed heavy on my mind. Night after sleepless night, on bended knee, I asked for forgiveness. I prayed wasted prayers, knowing with absolute certainty that Jesus had turned his ear from me. All his favor was spent, wasted out on the schoolyard. My futile pleas for mercy dissipated like black smoke in the dark.

I dreamed for a string of nights that an angry God waited just outside my window. Across the way, somewhere out in the Ellison cornfield, he crouched low in the dark rows of stalks, howling at a lonesome pale moon. His thick, filthy fingers scratched at the dry earth with long, yellowing nails. God was biding his time. While I slept a troubled sleep, he waited, hunched over with a bent back and burning with a righteous fury buried deep in his belly like a rancid poison. He lay in wait, readying to unleash his wrath for my sins, preparing to topple our little house down to the ground.

CHAPTER 4

———————◆———————

THE MORNING OF SOPHIE DRAKE's big birthday party couldn't have arrived soon enough for Kate. I came tromping down the stairs to find her sitting at the kitchen table, dressed in her party best, with a head of tight blond ringlets. Itching to get started with the day's festivities, Katie hadn't slept a wink.

"What the heck are you doing up so early?" I asked, focusing my eyes. "And what happened to your hair? You look like Betty Pilchard's poodle."

Concentrating on buttering her toast, she didn't look up.

"I don't wanna be late." She smeared grape jelly on her bread. "Pop's taking me to Sophie's."

"It's six a.m., dummy."

"Zachariah!" Mom sounded off from up the stairs. "Be nice to your sister."

"Yes, ma'am."

Laughing at me, Katie stuck out her pink tongue in my direction from across the table.

"So, how old is Miss Sophie gonna be?" I asked.

"Seven." Katie shoveled Frosted Flakes into her mouth, milk dribbling onto her chin and back into the bowl.

Opening the fridge, I surveyed my options and took a swig of orange juice from its plastic container.

Katie hollered. "Zach's drinking orange juice straight from the jug!"

"Zach!" Mom yelled down the banister. "Get yourself a glass, and don't drink from the container."

I pulled a chair up to the table and poured myself a bowl of Kellogg's. "So what all's happening at Miss Sophie Drake's big shindig this afternoon?"

Katie wrinkled her nose, deciding if she would answer. Instead she took a big bite of toast and opened her mouth wide as she chewed, exposing its contents to me.

"Ugghhh. You're a disgusting little brat."

"Zach, enough already!" Mom came walking down the stairs. "Aren't you supposed to be outside helping your father?"

"Yessum."

"Well, then finish up your breakfast, and head out."

Katie giggled into her bowl of flakes.

"Young lady, I know what you're up to, and you're workin' my last nerve. If you want to go to Sophie's party, you'd best start behaving."

"Yes, Momma."

"Now, stop your lollygagging, and go clean your room."

Katie hopped from her chair and tore up the stairs.

"Hey, squirt!" I called to her. "Have fun at Miss Sophie's party."

Dad was out back in the work shed, knee-deep in rakes, shovels, and tools. We fidgeted with his mower's spark plugs until it easily started on the first pull of the rope. Arranging all his hammers, wrenches, and screwdrivers on designated hooks on a big board positioned on the back wall, I worked alongside him all morning until I felt the itch to go trout fishing on the reservoir.

"You wanna drive up with me to Echo Basin to deliver your little sister to the Drake place?" He asked.

"Naw, I was hoping to see if the trout are biting."

"Skedaddle then. Get on out of here."

By lunchtime my fishing reel rested in my hand as I kicked back on the rickety wooden dock that stilted its way out over the water of Vallecito Reservoir.

———

"Come on, little lady. If you wanna get to this party before the Second Coming of Christ, we gotta get moving." Dad lifted Kate onto the seat of the truck and placed Sophie's wrapped birthday gift and a tin of sugar cookies on her lap.

Mom leaned out the back door. "Kate, don't forget to put on your sweater. The afternoons are gettin' chilly." Mom disappeared behind the closing door but popped her head back out. "Remember your manners, missy! Say 'thank you' and 'no, thank you.'"

The bumpy road out to Echo Basin Valley was a roller-coaster ride for my sisters and me. We pleaded with Pop to take us down the winding mountain pass. After each bump in the road, the tires of the old pickup left the pavement. We lost our stomachs as the rusted springs of the vinyl seat cushions bounced and squeaked.

Sophie's house sat at the bottom of the steep and narrow Echo Basin Valley, where sunlight struggled to find every nook and cranny. At winter's end the Drakes were always the last family to dig their way out of the snowpack.

Dad and Katie started off down through the winding pass.

"Faster, Daddy, faster!" she squealed as the truck's tires lifted and landed back down on the blacktop. The next bump took her even higher, followed by another and then another. She held tight to the wrapped gift and cookies with one hand, gripping the door panel with the other. Her small knuckles turned white.

A cold wind whistled through the truck's open windows, blowing Katie's straw-gold ringlets into her eyes and into her laughing mouth. Dad fought fourth gear and accelerated down the mountain pass, to Kate's delight. She bounced and giggled as she lifted and landed back on the seat.

I suppose in the tug-of-war between fate and luck, sometimes the horseshoe tips wrong side up, spilling the last drops onto the ground. Empty and out of luck, the awful inevitable comes a-calling.

Dad reached over to squeeze Katie's knee, and the pickup slowly drifted into the oncoming lane. By the time he saw old Ben Cramer's tractor, it was too late. Dad turned the steering wheel sharply, avoiding Ben's rig. The truck tires caught in the loose gravel on the road's edge, pulling the pickup off the pavement. The truck careened down the steep embankment and into the ravine. Katie's screams echoed throughout the hillside.

The runaway truck struck a boulder, flipping and shearing the cab. It rolled twice then cut through the pines, tumbling farther down through the creosote and scrub brush. The truck landed upright, finally skidding to a stop in a dry creek bed. The screaming gears and wildly spinning tires were followed by an eerie momentary silence. A single plume of gray smoke rose into the air above the pines.

Dad fell forward, his chest slumped on the steering wheel, sounding the horn through the trees. An open gash on his forehead streamed crimson red to his chin and onto his flannel shirt. He was motionless but for his trembling hands, which quaked uncontrollably in his lap. He lay unconscious for a moment before slowly lifting his head and trying to focus his eyes.

Pinned between the collapsed steering column and the crushed door panel, he twisted, trying to free himself.

Old Ben Cramer frantically made his way down the embankment and through the brittle brush to the remains of the mangled truck. "Lloyd!" he yelled out. "Lloyd, are you OK, son?"

Pieces of torn metal were strewn about the trees. The truck's axle, ripped from its frame, was now suspended from low-hanging branches. The wildly spinning back tires came to a gradual halt. Shattered glass was scattered like Sister Prichard's diamonds on the forest floor, and the sweet stinging smell of burnt asphalt and spilling fuel lingered in the woods.

The bones in my dad's left hand were crushed, his ribs fractured, and his right lung collapsed. Bloody and broken and crazed like a madman, Dad found his way out of the twisted metal. Stumbling through the trees, he howled, "Katie! Katie girl!" like a wild rabid dog. Panicked, he scoured the wreckage, climbing in and around the truck's mangled carcass, and pulled at the forest's thick underbrush, searching and screaming her name.

It was old Ben Cramer who first came upon Katie. She had been thrown nearly thirty feet from the pickup's resting place. Her lifeless body came to rest on a cradle of creosol branches, so much breathtaking loss born on a brilliant sun-drenched afternoon.

"Here! Over here!" Ben yelled out. "Sweet Jesus, she's here, Lloyd. Katie's here!"

Dad struggled through the thick brush to the side of his youngest. He pulled her into his broken chest, and like a river of sorrow that cuts a path with torrents of muddy water, rock, and bone, his cries ripped through the mountainside.

Old Ben Cramer struggled up the embankment and waved down a passing flatbed. Several cars stopped to help. Strangers carefully coaxed Dad, who sobbed, inconsolable as he carried

Katie up the steep incline. With the others guiding him through the trees and thick underbrush, Dad found his way back on the road, barking at anyone's attempt to take Katie from his arms. The gathered strangers hoisted Dad onto the flatbed and covered him and Katie in blankets. The truck sped off, heading thirty miles back into town. Dad cradled little Katie's broken body in his arms all the way to the hospital.

I've tried to imagine his long ride on the back of the flatbed, through the mountain pass and on to the hospital. After all these years, I still wonder why God abandons a man when life gets bent and bruised beyond recognition. I wonder what breaks in those brittle moments, what he surrenders and what still remains. Why God turns his back remains a mystery to me. Maybe there are precarious bends in the road even God's mercy can't foresee. I suppose none of us can say how we'd cope if life were to make a sudden blind turn. How could we ever know or begin to understand until stunning loss whispers the answer in our ears?

———◆———

CHAPTER 5

DRESSED IN HIS ONLY SUIT and tie, Dad held his bandaged, broken hand tight to his chest. As Pastor Barnett delivered the eulogy, I watched Pop from the corner of my eye. He looked like a man who hadn't seen sleep in days, the kind of tired that sits heavy on your shoulders, weariness that settles in the bones. Wiping the stinging regret from his eyes, he never turned his attention away from the small white casket. Laura and I sat as still as stones. Mom folded her delicate hand on top of mine and wept silently.

The pastor read a verse from Corinthians and led the congregation into a hymn.

> Blessed assurance, Jesus is mine;
> Oh, what a foretaste of glory divine!
> Heir of salvation, purchased of God,
> Born of His Spirit, washed in His blood.

The Sisters of the First Assembly of God stood directly behind Mom like a great wall of teased hair, polyester, and talcum powder. Their black purses dangled from their forearms as they blotted their weepy eyes with white tissues. Shoulder to shoulder they stood watch over one of their own.

Angels, descending, bring from above
Echoes of mercy, whispers of love.

Sister Baldwin rested a gloved hand on Mom's shoulder, raising her other up to the heavens in prayer, while Sister Combs gripped Mom's hand and bowed her head in silent prayer.

This is my story, this is my song,
Praising my Savior all the day long.

Pastor Barnett closed his Bible slowly and deliberately, like a doctor who'd just delivered a dire diagnosis. He placed himself between Katie's casket and our four small chairs. "Dear Lord, I ask you to take the Nance family into your arms." He raised his Bible over our heads. "Keep them safe, dear Lord. Guide them to the higher rock."

The Sisters joined him, crying out, "hallelujah."

With the congregation's heads bowed and eyes closed, I cocked my head to spy on Dad again. His boots had never stepped foot on the floorboards of the First Assembly of God church and I worried how he was handling all this ruckus. He sat still, with his tall frame propped up on a tiny aluminum chair. He stared at Katie's coffin, which was blanketed in Mrs. Ellison's white roses. His eyes were as red and hollow as the dark abandoned mines bleeding mineral-stained crimson water.

Momma was unhinged. She sat at my side, weak and unsteady, gripping the side of the folding chair with one hand, as if she feared she might lose balance. Her swollen, pale eyes darted nervously back and forth as she fidgeted with the pearl buttons on her silk blouse like they were a string of worry beads. I leaned against her and rested my head on her shoulder. Reaching over, she touched the side of my face. Her palm was cold and damp on my skin. The rapid pace of her shallow breathing was more frightening than the sight of Katie's casket teetering over the black hole in the earth.

Laura nudged my side with her elbow, nodding in the direction of a sycamore. Standing back from the church folk gathered in the cemetery were the Custers—Saul, Loretta, and the girls. They stood quiet and solemn, paying their respects. Loretta wore an emerald-green dress with gold buttons. She smiled at me, signaling with her fingers the quickest wave. Mr. Saul stood under the lonely tree. Inconsolable, his face was buried in the palms of his hands.

After the service was closed with a final prayer, the church ladies swept into action. Sister Bledsoe opened her big fleshy arms and pulled Laura and me into her smothering, heavy bosom. The sweet fragrance of her White Shoulders perfume wafted in my face, stinging my eyes and nose.

"Come on, young'uns," she whispered. "Come with Auntie. Let's get some rhubarb pie."

She squeezed us tight, burying us in her pendulous breasts as she guided us to her station wagon.

Sister Ellison and Sister Calvert flanked my grieving mother, slowly leading her from the grave into a waiting Pontiac. I watched the two ladies as they shuffled about, nervously attending to Mom.

"Come along, Alice Faye." Sister Ellison led Mom to the car. "We are right here at your side if you need a shoulder."

Sister Gladden opened the rear car door and carefully placed Mom in the backseat. "Hon, if you need anything, anything at all," she whispered, "I'm right here."

The two sisters slid in on either side of Mom like a pair of matching bookends.

The other ladies gathered up the folding chairs and sprays of graveside flowers. With their arms full, the Sisters of the First

Assembly of God loaded their cars while their men smoked un-filtered cigarettes in the parking lot and spoke of the changing weather.

As the slow, gradual procession of cars pulled away from the cemetery, I saw Saul Custer standing off in the shade of a cotton-wood with his arm stretched around my dad's shoulder. An early autumn breeze blew the heavy branches of the giant cottonwood, sending shimmering green and gold leaves to the ground like summer snow.

The procession continued on to the veterans' hall, where more sisters of the congregation hurried about, preparing a buffet. A feast of pot roast, fried chicken, skillets of cornbread, and stacks of Tupperware full of sweet and mashed potatoes waited for the grieving. Platters of grilled okra, fried green tomatoes, and corn on the cob passed from hand to hand. Tins of cookies, cakes, and fresh-baked pies followed shortly after.

When life left you empty, it was the singular goal of the Sisters of the First Assembly of God to fill those spaces with fried food.

One after the next, a line of mourners approached Momma and spoke in soft, hushed tones, like any jarring sound would break her into a million pieces.

It was clear the ladies had charted the day's events and deter-mined Sister Combs would keep a close watch over me throughout the day. Like some mother hen pecking at the ground behind her chicks, Annie stayed right at my side. Her compassionate smile was lined in pink lipstick that traveled from above her top lip, across her front teeth, and on below the corner of her mouth. Try as I might, there was no escaping Annie's white-gloved grip. I took any oppor-tunity to give her the slip, but relentlessly she'd only search me out again. Above the crowd I spotted the crest of her teased bouffant heading in my direction. Her voice called out, "Zachariah! Honey,

Zachariah, I can see you!" Hiding in the gathered crowd, I ducked and weaved.

I was nearly thirteen years old and didn't take kindly to Sister Combs, or anyone, pulling me about by the collar, but I understood the sisters were only looking out for my family and me.

From across the veterans' hall, I chuckled when I saw Laura's care was assigned to bloated Sister Nettie Bledsoe. Sis grimaced, rolling her eyes, as fat ol' Nettie smeared Jergens on her cheeks and then pulled Laura by the forearm from one congregation member to the next, showing her off like one of Nettie's prized blue-ribbon hogs.

It was that same Sunday afternoon when I first spotted A. J. McCord and his two brothers. They stood off from the gathered mourners. A. J. leaned against a tree with his thick thumbs hooked in his Levi's belt loops. His two big barrel arms and broad chest pulled at the seams of his unwashed button-down. Looking in my direction, he spit on the ground and wiped his mouth off with the sleeve of his shirt.

The McCords were new to Durango. Rumor had spread that the locals from another small town in Southern Utah had already run them out before they'd settled on Durango. The three strapping, potato-fed boys and their disgruntled father had recently moved into the Doyles' old place. Mr. McCord had relocated his sons from their home in Boise and had opened a hardware store on Main Street.

A year earlier Mrs. McCord, the boys' mother, had left Idaho with a traveling man without saying as much as good-bye. She'd grown weary of the constant strife of living in a house with three wild boys and an unkind man. On a frostbitten morning, she woke before sunrise and heated the cast-iron skillet. She baked a week's worth of buttermilk biscuits and gravy, boiled two dozen potatoes, folded her apron, and met her traveling man at the end of the driveway. The two sped away in his Mercury.

The public shame of his wife's abandonment drove Mr. McCord out of Boise with his three unwashed juvenile delinquents. After their brief stint in Utah, they settled on Durango for a fresh start.

With the grand opening of his Main Street hardware store, and hoping to garner some favor with the locals, Mr. McCord decided it wise to strong-arm his three resistant, unruly boys into the Methodist church services. But the restless hooligans wasted no time disrupting the peace and quiet of Durango by busting up anything that crossed their path, such as shooting out Sister Combs's front windowpane with a pellet gun and stealing green apples from the Gladdens' orchard.

After a few street brawls and a midnight joyride in a stolen car, Mr. McCord put his unruly boys to work behind the counter of the hardware store. There he hoped to keep a tight rein around their thick necks.

A. J. loitered with his two older brothers under a tree in front of the veterans' hall. The three good-looking but unkempt boys devoured fried chicken and corn on the cob like it was their first-ever home-cooked meal.

After gnawing a chicken leg clean down to the bone, A. J. wiped his greasy face with his hand, just in time for his dad to return with more full plates from the buffet line. It seemed the occasion of Kate's funeral offered the McCord men the opportunity to fill their bellies with free home cookin'.

Sister Pilchard whispered to Sister Ellison, "I don't think they're even Baptists." Shaking her head disapprovingly, she watched on while the three boys devoured the last slices of her pecan pie. "Disgraceful."

The two older brothers were the more handsome and took the opportunity of the somber setting to chat up the passing young ladies gathered in the park.

As Sister Combs pulled me around by my jacket sleeve, I met A. J.'s stare. He'd been watching me from across the way, and when our eyes met, he slightly dipped his head in my direction.

"Come along with Auntie Combs. Let's go get some sweet tea." She yanked my sleeve. "Lawdy, this sun is gonna cook my goose."

The brazen boldness in A. J.'s stare sent heat down my chest and through the soles of my polished leather shoes. Meaning to be off-putting, he leaned against the tree in a cocky wide stance, but he didn't scare me, not one bit. His dark eyes felt dangerous as a live wire. Still, I wasn't frightened—his glance gave too much away.

Later, after I moved to LA, I understood the recognition in his eyes. The faces of the men who stood in the shadows in the bars all shared the same familiar gaze. I suppose such deliberate glances and unspoken yearning become necessities when there's so much to lose.

I returned a nod to A. J.

When Sister Combs tugged at my sleeve, I grinned in his direction and shrugged my shoulders. But A. J. turned away, laughing at something one of his brothers said.

I lost sight of A. J. McCord in the crowd as Sister Combs pulled me deeper into the gathering of mourning family and friends.

CHAPTER 6

———◆———

THE WINTER OF 1962 WAS the coldest on record in these parts. It arrived through a broken windowpane in Katie's vacant upstairs bedroom. Freezing winds howled outside the shutters, sneaking in between the cracks of the loose floorboards. The yellow dog abandoned his home on the front porch, finding warmth in the crawl space under the work shed. The first week of September, temperatures suddenly plummeted and marked winter's early return, blistery and uninvited. Autumn's colors were swept from branches, and trees stood naked and lonesome in the frozen fields.

Winter piled on top of us like layers of heavy, icy-cold blankets, each storm colder than the one before. The local news warned Durango might not thaw until well into April.

After the funeral, after our drive home in a solemn and silent car, Mom disappeared up in her room. She remained behind the locked door for three days straight, her shades pulled down and linen curtains drawn tight. Mom returned to the marked Scriptures in her own mother's old Bible, pages as soft as tissue, bent at the corners years before her own birth and creased at some remembered passage. Every Scripture soothed her like a healing balm applied by her mom's own fingertips onto a troublesome aching pain.

I paced back and forth in front of Momma's closed door, suspicious of the silence behind the wood panel. I kept an ear pressed, listening for any signs of life, and prayed to heaven Momma would find a healing Jesus hiding in her closet.

After a few days, Laura finally worked up the nerve to knock. "Momma? Momma?" She spoke through the crack in the door jamb. "I got an A on my geometry test."

When only long silence answered from the other side, Laura turned to leave.

"That's great, baby girl," Mom's faint voice whispered from behind the door. "I'll be down in just a bit."

Dad fumbled in the kitchen, heating up platters of baked lasagna, meatloaf, or beef stew gifted from concerned neighbors. He carried the prepared trays up to Momma's room.

On the fourth day, Mom finally reappeared, down the stairs into the kitchen, wearing someone else's forced smile, pained and ill fitting, like she was walking in a pair of too-snug shoes.

"Good morning. How 'bout flapjacks and sausage?" she greeted Laura and me, trying hard to somehow pick up from where we'd left off before the accident.

We all struggled to find familiar footing, but it's a difficult thing—a soul being snatched up in broad daylight. One morning little Katie was running through the house, and by supper she was long gone. Her little spirit was lifted from the pass at Echo Basin, carried off above the tallest treetops. Reminders of her were scattered all about the house. A pair of little yellow sneakers rested on the back stoop. Strands of hair ribbons she'd hidden inside the piano bench remained undisturbed under sheet music. Traces of her small fingers and toes imprinted her pink bedroom. Her favorite baby doll watched from the highest shelf on the wall, waiting for her return.

Momma's reemergence from her room seemed to signal Dad's exit. He picked up in the night and didn't return for three days. During those weeks Laura and I walked through quiet rooms. We were orphans to a mother locked behind a door and a father chained to a barstool. When he finally stumbled in, red and weary eyed, smelling of smoke and sweat, his words slurred, as if his mouth were full of cotton.

The rush of condolences from family and friends, and the steady arrival of neighbors bearing plastic Tupperware bowls of food, dwindled to an occasional call or postmarked sympathy card.

Laura was thumbing through a magazine on the front porch swing, and I was loafing in the yard when Dad drove up the gravel drive. Laura looked up and walked to the porch's edge to greet him. I waited to see which man had come home to us. The mutt's tail wagged wildly, and its long, loose pink tongue licked Pop's hand as he came up the porch steps.

"Hi, Daddy." Laura hugged his waist and laid her head against his flannel shirt.

"Have you kids caught up with your schoolwork? You've missed quite a few classes over the last few weeks."

"Yes, sir," Laura replied.

"Where's your momma?" He kissed Laura's cheek.

"She's inside, Dad. Upstairs."

"Zach, you keeping up with your homework?"

"Yes, sir."

"Good. I'll want to see your report cards." Dad disappeared inside the house.

"Alice!" he hollered.

Laura and I held our breath, awaiting the ruckus to commence upstairs.

"Daddy looks good." She smiled.

"He smells foul," I replied.

It took only the time for him to make the trip up the stairs before angry voices filtered through the open windows above us.

"Lloyd, you're drunk."

"Alice, for God's sake. Don't start in."

"I told you, don't come around after you've been drinking. I won't have it."

"Get off my back. Let me just have this. Don't you think I've earned the right to have a drink?"

"The right to get drunk? The right to stay out all night and not have the common decency to call and let me know you're safe? Just to let me know you're still alive? I've been fretting all night."

"Alice, I gotta have time to work through this in my own way."

"Lloyd, I smell it on your breath. If this is what I can expect, just don't come home. I don't want the kids to witness this spectacle. And after all that's happened, it's foolishness to be drunk out on the road. Do you hear me? It's plain foolishness." Momma unraveled like a pulled loose thread. "You're gonna land in a jail cell or worse."

"Alice, I wasn't drunk out on Echo Basin Pass." Dad's voice broke. "Just say it, Alice Faye. You think I killed her. You think it was all my fault."

"I've said no such thing. I've never even suggested it. It was an awful accident. I'm begging, you need to sober up. Can I put some coffee on?"

"I don't want no damn coffee," Dad barked. "I see how you look at me. I can see it in your eyes. You can't even stomach to look at me."

"Stop it, Lloyd!" Mom tried to silence him.

"You can't even look at me, babe."

"I'm begging you. The kids are already in pieces. Don't let them see you like this. I couldn't bear it if you start up with the drinking again. You promised me, Lloyd. Remember the promise you made to Daddy?"

Laura was overcome with emotion. Dropping her book, she ran off the porch and out across the pasture. I watched her disappear into the woods.

I sat quiet, listening to the voices from their small second-floor window.

Dad's tone turned soft. "Baby, come here."

"You're drunk, Lloyd."

"Babe, come over here. Lie down here beside me."

"You're drunk," she repeated.

"Please, baby."

Only the faintest whispers filtered through the linen curtains. I heard Mom weeping, and Dad's murmurs sounded like a song. Was he singing? I strained to decipher his voice, but their window went quiet.

Later that night Laura slowly turned the knob to my room. She walked in on tippy toes. Sneaking across the floor. Pulling back my covers, she climbed into my bed.

"There's no sleeping tonight," she said, settling deeper into the blankets. Her long wild strands of hair spilled about her pillow. "Pops will come around and see the error of his wicked ways."

"You think so?" I whispered, relieved because Laura was more right than wrong on most matters.

"I'm sure of it."

We shared a sleepy conversation while Laura rested near my side. We stared up at the ceiling while Laura quoted Scripture like Sister Baldwin in Sunday class. My sis spoke on matters with an easy assurance. Her comforting, confident tone calmed me.

She yawned, stretching her arms. "Well, I'm going on back to bed."

"No, stay here with me for a bit longer, just for a short spell." I asked. "Will you?"

She shook her head.

The house was quiet. The two of us lay listening to our own breathing.

"You know," she said, "if two or more folk come together and ask Jesus for healing, it will be done. And if you stay real still and not breathe a word, we'll hear the voice of God with his answer."

With our heads bowed, I snuck a peek over at Laura. Her hands clasped together, eyes squeezed tight, and her small lips mouthed a silent prayer. I sat listening for the longest time, but the only conversing was the deafening sizzle of cicadas bickering among themselves through the open window.

When Laura's prayer concluded, she looked over at me, grinning with a satisfied expression. "Could you hear him?" She searched my eyes for confirmation.

"Yes. I heard his every word."

"Me too." She beamed. "His will be done," Laura declared and climbed from my bed, assured our dire predicament had run its course.

After that night we couldn't forecast Dad's reappearance. Holding our breath in the evenings, we waited for the sound of his pickup. For a string of lost weekends, he was a no-show. In the wee hours of the night, his return woke the sleeping house. All at once downstairs clamored and rattled, like the afternoon when a crazy black crow flew in through an open window and flailed through the rooms, hit walls, and broke Momma's delicate china.

"Alice Faye! Alice Faye!" Dad hollered. "Where is everyone?"

Momma rushed down the stairs, shushing him. "Lloyd, you'll wake the kids."

"Where are my babies?"

"Shhh, Lloyd. It's two a.m."

"You're not gonna keep me from my babies!" he yelled.

"That's nonsense. Now hush up before you wake the house."

Some nights Dad climbed the stairs and promptly fell fast asleep in his bed, dozing it off, and the three of us sighed a collective breath of relief. But on those evenings when he was scratching for trouble, he stumbled through the rooms downstairs, cursing to himself. Momma sent us off to our rooms, and we all steered clear until the booze lulled him to sleep.

Only the church ladies knew the depths of Mom's sorrow. She mourned in silence. While we never knew the tears shed in her quiet hours, Laura and I felt her desperate grief in different ways. The casual hugs before we headed off to school were now tighter, longer embraces.

Her arms wrapped around my neck, squeezing, she said, "Now run along, and be safe. Remember to watch when you're crossing the street."

"Momma, you're chokin' me."

"Get going. And remember to listen to the bus driver."

A few mornings I didn't know if she'd ever let go. Her locked arms held a moment longer, squeezing a little harder. Standing on the porch, waving good-bye as we set off walking down County Road 250, Mom watched until we disappeared up the steps into the dusty yellow school bus. From my window I saw her still waving in the distance as we pulled away.

I worried about her while Laura and I were at school, about how she spent those hours alone. I was always afraid we'd come home and find her in pieces on the floor. We never knew when a heavy spirit would move, but in a moment Momma's bright eyes would cloud over gray. Suddenly she'd look around the room as if she were lost in her own place—stand up from the table in the middle of supper and make the long, slow climb up the stairs, disappearing to her waiting room. Her feet trudged up the wooden treads like she was carrying a heavy sack of stones.

Before the accident my sisters and I lay on Momma's bed, with the windows open wide and sunlight streaming in. The cool cross breeze and scent of her sweet perfume filled her room. We three kids lay on our stomachs on the floral bedspread, elbows bent, with our chins propped up in our small hands, watching Mom curl and tease her hair. She applied her makeup and lipstick in the mirror like painting a portrait.

Now Mom's bedroom was her own private sanctuary, off limits, filled with shadows, smelling of dust. When she latched the door behind her, I worried I'd lose her forever to the other side of the locked wood panel.

Laura asked Dad if Momma would ever return to us. He answered, "She will come round. It will take some time, but she'll come back to us. Some folks can be in high cotton one day and down deep in the weeds the next. You just gotta hold on tight until harvesting season comes round again."

So Laura and I waited. We watched on the horizon for any sign. Sure enough, by the time the giant green combines rolled back into town and swept through the fields that surrounded the house, Momma's door was unlocked and swung wide open. The morning sun shone through her windows, and I recognized her sweet smile at breakfast.

After her return to us, it was only on holidays—Halloween, Thanksgiving, or Christmas; any day involving joy and family and children—that her grief reappeared. The light left her face, and an ominous sense of foreboding filled the rooms.

"Losing is a hard thing," Mom confessed. "Letting go of something you know by heart...There's nothing harder." She went digging at the bottom of her purse for a wadded-up tissue to wipe her eyes.

I understood. With each passing day the rooms remembered Katie a little less. The lawn forgot her spinning somersaults. I struggled to recall the sound of her giggles and the reflection of her green eyes. I let go of my youngest sister piece by piece, like pulling petals from one of Momma's roses.

Dad said, "Yearning for something that's long gone and never coming back is a foolish man's game. The most you can hope for are days to keep moving and wounds to callous over."

Mom found refuge in reading Scripture, clinging to her faith, sewing her quilts, or tending to the garden. She threaded hope like a needle, stitching piece by piece, trying to keep us together. With Pop's disappearing act, Mom struggled to maintain normalcy. She required our chores to be completed before the television was turned on. She demanded the following day's school clothes be laid out on top of our dressers each night before bed. After supper, when the day was done, she expected it to be closed with a prayer of gratitude.

Whether Dad's return was in the dead of night or early morning hours, Mom didn't let it disrupt our routine. Whatever angry words and threats spilled between them, she insulated Laura and me from the impending storm.

Late one night Laura and I woke to the sound of thunder. Dad arrived home sloshed and belligerent, blowing through the house like a hot wicked wind. I heard the sound of Momma's cries, and Dad was spewing anger and excuses. They argued deep into the night.

Opening my bedroom door the slightest crack, I saw Laura already standing in her doorway and listening to the battle being waged downstairs. From her end of the hall, she looked at me with wet, weary eyes, mouthed a good night, and closed her door.

Moving as quietly as a church mouse across the floorboards, I sneaked to the staircase landing. On bended knee I listened to the commotion.

"Lloyd, we have two kids upstairs sleeping." Mom pleaded. "They're alive, Lloyd. Those two didn't die on the pass."

"I know that, Alice. For God's sake."

"Do you, Lloyd? Do you really? 'Cause you're hurtin' those kids. And now all this talk about you and other women."

"That's all foolish talk," Dad barked.

"Is it, Lloyd? You running around from bar to bar in all hours of the night only stokes the fire. For God's sake, I can't show my face in town. Be careful you don't start something you can't ever turn back."

"Don't accuse me of nothing!" Dad's voice raised to a shout.

"Keep it down," Mom insisted. "You'll wake them."

"It's my house, goddamn it. Don't tell me nothing."

"Lloyd, there's no talking to you when you're like this."

"I won't be talked to like this in my own goddamn house. I just won't allow it," Dad cursed. For the first time in my memory, his restraint failed him.

"I can't make you stay, Lloyd. I can't force you to be here with us, but I can sure as hell stop you from making our lives a living hell while you're making your plans to leave." Mom's voice weakened.

"Alice…"

"No. I just can't do it, Lloyd. I've got children to raise. I'm trying to make this place some kind of a home."

"Alice."

"Katie's gone, Lloyd. It rips my heart out every mornin'. When it's just me and this house is empty, I go up those stairs."

"No, babe, don't do this."

"I sit up there in her room. I can still smell my sweet baby. I'm dying every day, and you're too busy drinking and carrying on to see what you're losing right in front of you. Go up those stairs, and look at our two kids." Mom's voice grew weary.

"Baby, I'm sorry. Let me make it better."

"No, Lloyd. I can't."

I heard their muffled cries in the kitchen.

With Dad's apology the wildfire was out for the night. Our small house was again quiet but for the running kitchen faucet and the shuffling of Mom clearing plates from the supper table.

I leaned uptight against the darkest wall, listening to the sounds of our resting house. A cease-fire had been called, and both parties retreated to their own corners. Mom's radio played low in the kitchen. Outside, the dog barked at a pair of headlights from a rental car carrying some lost tourists who'd taken a wrong turn on County Road 250. Using our gravel drive to turn themselves around, the trespassers were greeted by the yellow shepherd snapping at their tires.

I sat on the top step of our staircase. From my perch in the shadows, I spied Dad sitting alone in the front room. An amber light filtered from the lamp in the foyer.

He was, at once, older. His taut, strong jaw was now creased and slacked. Heavy folds in his lids drooped low over his blue eyes. He sat alone, watching a blank television screen. All around him hung black-and-white photographs of us on papered walls, and I wondered if he saw them. A thin trail of smoke from his burning cigarette in the ashtray rose into the shadows of the ceiling and dissipated.

Watching him, I thought, He's not so mean. Maybe more tired than threatening, more drunk than angry.

I crept closer, descending two more treads. Through the railing I watched him slowly rock in his favorite chair. He pinched the bridge of his nose, squeezing his eyes shut tight. His weak chin dropped low, and his mouth hung agape, like the homeless man who panhandled outside the grocery store. A thinner, more fragile man than the father who roughhoused with me. Life seemed to be whittling Dad down to a stick of a man, withered by time and loss.

The last embers in the fireplace cracked and popped, startling Pops back from where his thoughts had traveled.

His slow rocking came to a gradual halt. He rested there, still as the dead. Reaching for Mom's teasing comb that was lying on the table near her Bible, he pulled a single strand of her hair from its bristles. Dad wrapped the strand around his calloused fingers. Unmindful of anyone watching, he passed the honey-blond strand across his face, searching for her still-lingering scent.

Momma's music went quiet. The lights went dark, and I silently backed into my room and closed the door behind me. Climbing in bed and pulling the blankets over my head, I waited to hear their feet ascending the stairs to their room. I listened for the sound of their door closing.

I knew Mom would find some way to believe him. No matter the destruction and damage he'd inflicted, she would find a path to forgiveness. It was a familiar, well-worn trail she had walked before.

Watching him there, alone in the dark, I knew that I too would find some pathway back to loving him.

—◆—

The ear-numbing falsetto of Sister Millard led the congregation in song. Each Sunday scrawny Rose Millard stood near the pulpit and conducted us through the selected hymns of the morning's service. Her off-tune serenade soared to deafening heights.

Ascending into the rafters of our tiny sanctuary, her squealing rang out above the voices of the ladies' choir. No matter the swelling volume of the rejoicing congregation, it was Rose, like some squawking, dying goose, whose wayward octaves rang supreme. When the spirit moved her, an off-pitch wail rose from deep in her gut, lifting to an ear-splitting crescendo. Pastor Barnett grimaced over her shoulder, and the elderly folk scrambled to adjust their hearing aids accordingly. However, Sister Millard sang with such conviction and fervor that most folk overlooked her sour delivery.

One Sunday, Momma said Rose's impassioned solo of "How Great Thou Art" brought tears to her eyes but hemorrhaging blood to her ears.

"That poor woman can't carry a tune in a bucket," Mom declared.

The stray dogs who loitered on the front church stoop waiting for any potluck scraps howled along with Sister Millard outside the window.

On this particular Sunday, the tithing plate had passed down the rows of pews, and the pastor closed service with a solemn prayer. His final amen was Rose's cue to break into a rousing rendition of "I Saw the Light," but the commencement of Sister Millard's singing was the congregation's cue to push out hurriedly toward the exits. Like Moses's exodus from Israel, folks emptied the sanctuary, fleeing through the front doors to freedom. With everyone outside, Rose was left serenading a vacant hall.

The congregation walked into a full blazing sun. Gathering in the churchyard, we all sipped cold lemonade and munched on Sister Pilchard's fresh-baked chocolate-chip oatmeal cookies.

Laura sat in the middle of her circle of friends on a mound of grass, squealing with delight as each girl rated her favorite Hollywood heartthrob from the pages of *Teen Beat* magazine. The swooning girls debated their dream dates while a bunch of restless boys swung from trees and buzzed around them like pestering horseflies.

I tossed a few rounds of horseshoes with Mr. Walker and Mr. Murdy. The late afternoon sun cast a long shadow of the steeple across the church lawn, like a giant rocket ship on the summer grass.

I spotted A. J. McCord, who was standing off from the churchyard and loitering in the edge of the trees, away from the congregation.

"Hey, over here!" he called out, waving his arms. He wore an unwashed wrinkled T-shirt and ragged jeans that were frayed at the hems. His baseball cap bill was soiled black with sweat, mud, and motor oil. From a distance A. J.'s face looked to be in need of a scrub with bar soap, but when I approached I saw it was a scarce crop of black hairs sprouting from below his lip and chin—a boy's poor attempt at a man's goatee.

"Name's A. J." He extended his hand.

"Zach," I said. "Zach Nance." His big, thick fingers were calloused.

"My given name is Allen McCord, but friends call me A. J. for short."

"I'm Zachariah when Mom is swingin' a belt but Zach the remainder of the day. Are you liking Durango?"

"It's fine enough, I suppose. Sorry 'bout your sis. That's some really fucked up shit."

With all the well-intentioned sympathies from concerned family, friends, and neighbors, I thought A. J. McCord's plain, spoken clarity had finally summarized it best.

"Yup," I replied. "It's really fucked up. How come I never see you in school? You going to Cortez High?"

"Naw. Goin' for my GED. I pretty much just work the register at Dad's store. I've seen you come in." Committed to memory, A. J. recalled my exact shopping list from the week earlier: "Four-pound fishing line weight, size fourteen treble hooks, penny nails, a can of bug spray, and a twenty-five-pound bag of mulch."

"Yup." I laughed. Suddenly I felt stiff and awkward in my Sunday best, like some starched choirboy next to A. J., with his big bare arms and unruly curls sneaking from under his ball cap. His Levi's fit two sizes too big and slipped well past his waist, exposing the elastic white band of his boxer shorts.

"You really buy into this Holy Roller shit?" He motioned in the direction of the little white church.

"Naw" I shook my head unconvincingly. "Something I gotta do to keep my mom from bellyaching."

"I hear ya. So, four-pound is your fishing line of choice? You fishing for trout?"

"Yup. Or catfish if they're biting."

"Next time you're heading out, invite me along. I haven't had the chance to scout the best holes to dip my line." He raised the corner of his brow.

"You bet. Vallecito is jumping if you're out early enough or catch them at sundown."

"It's a deal, then. See you round, Zach Nance." With that he turned and worked his way back in the oak thicket like some wild mountain man.

"Come on by the store," A. J. called out before disappearing deep into the forest. "I can sneak out a few cold six-packs and all the spools of fishing line you'd ever need. My old man won't never be the wiser."

With the congregation starting to disperse, I searched for Mom's face in the thinning crowd, walking the churchyard and playground. The hall was empty. I poked my head inside each vacant classroom.

Just behind the pastor's pulpit, strains of soft whispers came from the choir room. I followed the hushed voices, and through a sliver in the door I spied Momma and several ladies in a cluster. Rows of purple satin choir robes hung along the four walls of the small windowless room. In the center, Mom stood alongside Sister Bledsoe, Sister Combs, Sister Pilchard, and a handful of other ladies. In a tight cloister, the women whispered among themselves. I struggled for any hint of the conversation.

In their white-lace gloves and polyester pencil skirts, the sisters moved about, quietly shuffling and murmuring. Gathering in a loose circle around Momma, they spoke in hushed tones, the whispers comforting her. Nettie Bledsoe gently patted Mom's back while Betty hugged her neck. With concerned eyes and compassionate smiles of assurance, the ladies tended to her.

"I need your prayers," Mom's faint voice requested of the sisters. "I need y'all to say a word for Lloyd and for the children."

Flattening my back against the wall, I held my ear to the crack in the door, straining to hear.

"The Lord's listening, Alice," Nettie Bledsoe replied. "He will hear your prayers, honey."

The circle of sisters enveloped Mom, each one placing her white gloves on a shoulder, on her hair, to her temples, upon her closed eyes. Squeezing both of Mom's hands, with heads bowed, silently they began to pray.

The ladies of the First Assembly of God prayed for their breaking sister and her broken man. The small square room was all at once filled with quiet voices reciting Scriptures and singing hymns.

Annie Combs raised her Bible high in the air over Mom's head, crying, "Shepherd her, dear Lord. Guide her on the path of righteousness."

Sister Ellison mumbled, speaking in some unrecognizable tongue. I pushed my back closer against the wall. Momma's soft cries became more somber, quickly swelling into an inconsolable wail. The quiet prayers of the Sisters rose to an aching frenzy.

"Be with her, sweet Jesus," Betty Pilchard cried out. "Merciful Lord, take her in your arms."

Covering my ears, frightened by the mournful sounds, I turned away. Not since the sheriff's car drove up to the house had I seen Mom in such a distraught state. When the uniformed man had broken the news we'd lost Katie on Echo Basin, he'd spoken in a hushed tone. Laura and I had waited behind the screen door.

Overcome with grief, Momma had collapsed to the ground at the sheriff's boots, releasing an anguishing yowl, the likes of which I'd never heard. Laura darted out the door to her side. I stayed behind the screen, scared by the sight of Momma so wrecked.

Sister Combs's voice lifted above the women's prayers: "Lord, wrap her in your arms! Lift her up! Watch o'er her babies. Hold them, dear Lord."

In the center of the prayer circle, Mom rocked back and forth, sobbing. Big ol' Sister Bledsoe blotted Mom's tear-stained face with a white tissue.

Nettie consoled her. "We're here, Alice Faye, right here with you."

I watched through the sliver in the door as Mom slowly slipped to her knees. Her legs bent like they were buckling under a heavy weight, burdens too heavy for her small shoulders. I wanted to jump into action, but instead I gripped my fists. As her fragile frame went limp into the waiting arms of big Nettie and Annie, together they broke her fall. Placing their forearms beneath Mom's listless arms and lifting her up, the sisters continued with their chants and prayers, unshaken and undeterred.

"Sweet Jesus, watch over her." Betty lifted her right hand in prayer.

"Have mercy, dear Lord," Nettie cried. "Wash her in your blood."

I turned, hiding my face in the palms of my hands, praying my own clumsy prayer, begging God to lift Mom and give her the strength required. I prayed that the faithful Sisters of the First Assembly of God had some direct line to the heavens. I didn't give a damn about Dad's soul—I asked for Mom, Laura, and me. I prayed he'd gift me the strength to protect them. I swore right there I'd man up and get myself on the straight and narrow, if only he'd navigate us through the storm, guide us in the right direction. I prayed he'd move us forward like a spinning wheel on a track, arriving somewhere better than this place.

Sliding along the wall, I backed out into the sanctuary and tore past the pulpit, down the center aisle, between the empty pews, and through the front doors. Running like a bat out of hell, I hid my face from the gathered congregation and sprinted down the road toward home.

CHAPTER 7

———————

Boys like me grow up crooked. Twisted and bent like gnarly white oaks reaching to find any sunlight peeking under the canopy of the taller pines. We stretch up toward the slightest breach of light slipping through boughs of the larger trees. Quietly and deliberately we watch other boys on the street corners. We study them in class, observe them playing on the field, and mimic them like the mockingbird who learns to attract by singing another bird's song.

My string of daily disguises and deceptions turned into a couple of lost years while I practiced becoming more like the other boys…always with the knowing I was the odd man out.

On my sixteenth birthday, I bought myself my first truck for $650. The jalopy was as unreliable as Toby's left eye until Mr. Custer and I rebuilt its engine. That same summer I lost my virginity on a blanket in the bed of my pickup to a willing girl from Mancos High. We wrestled around until the deed was done. Afterward, sharing a cigarette, disheveled and breathless, the young lady confided I was the best she'd ever had. Later Toby reported the accommodating gal bestowed the same accolade on his performance in the back of his Camaro.

I lifted religiously in the gym and watched my body become strong and fit like the other guys'. On Saturday nights I sat in the

Boyd's pasture and tipped back beers with these same local boys. Sunday mornings I stumbled through church service with blood-shot eyes and a thumping head, slumping low in the back pew to escape Pastor Barnett's fire, Mom's disappointment, and God's judgment.

I swung a mean bat for the La Plata County baseball league and played wide receiver for the varsity team. I dated the prettiest local girls, and when a rumor spread I'd knocked up Susie Marston, requiring her to sneak off to an abortion clinic in Grand Junction, I never denied the lie.

But boys like me are bound to get tripped up. We're shrouded in shame and yearning. We go looking for comfort where we ought not, always in the shadows and longing for recognition in the telling eyes of other boys like me.

During those years when youth was squandered and spent like paper money, I grew into a young man who didn't recognize his own face in the mirror. When I shaved in the morning, an impostor inhabited my reflection—he resembled no one I knew. His gaze matched mine with dull, flat eyes that held no light.

I kept the hard promises I'd made for those I cherished. Mom and Laura were my sole concerns. I reckoned they'd grieved enough loss and disappointment without needing an unrepentant prodigal son to walk through the door.

I took to drinking by myself to drown out the stranger in the mirror's reflection. The toll for my deception was mine and mine alone—it was enough knowing Mom and Laura were safe and sound.

While I searched out places to hide in public, stealth and undetected, Laura went looking for God. She found him on a sunny afternoon submerged in the muddy waters of Vallecito Reservoir. At the First Assembly of God camp revival, on a Saturday, Laura accepted Jesus Christ as her Savior.

Huge white-canvas tents stretched from limb to limb in a grove of oak trees. Rows of folding chairs and sawdust from the lumber mill covered the forest floor. Pastors from all over the county came for a weekend of nonstop hell dousing.

One after the next, visiting ministers wailed fire and brimstone at the shaken congregation with angry, prophetic warnings. They preached about the great battle of Armageddon, the following years of tribulation, and the horrific plagues of disease and locusts leading to the Second Coming of Christ.

Between the fiery sermons, the shell-shocked congregation gathered their wits and collectively exhaled. Neighbors and friends conversed over glasses of sweet tea and slices of peach pie. Young children in their Sunday best ran through the trees, playing hide-and-seek, while the old men stood in silent clusters, smoking cigarettes and chewing tobacco. The ladies of the First Assembly of God fanned their powdered faces and swatted flies with tightly folded pages torn from hymnals.

When it was his turn up at bat, Preacher Barnett positioned himself at the plywood pulpit. Our pastor seemed oddly uptight. He began his morning sermon with only the slightest spark, barely bright enough to keep us upright and awake on the makeshift pews. Homer Bledsoe's hungry gut growled with more conviction. As the preacher continued, he found his firm footing. His voice gathered strength as he spoke, stoking a fire with a few rousing hallelujahs. By the time our pastor was quoting Corinthians, a full-blown holy blaze was burning, his arms stretched to the heavens. Spit formed white puddles in the corners of his heaving mouth. The blistering sermon curled the ladies' toes in their sensible pumps. Mom gripped her Bible while Sister Ellison rocked back and forth like the Holy Ghost was moving in her soul. Annie Combs sobbed uncontrollably. Her teal eye shadow and black liner formed rushing rivers down her rouged cheeks, spilling off her quivering chin and onto her ivory silk blouse. By his closing prayer, Pastor Barnett had run the devil out past the La Plata County line. The congregation wandered through the forest, numb and anointed with sufficient guilt that salvation was soon at hand. The saved walked side by side with the struggling. They carried open Bibles, sharing Scriptures and witnessing for the Lord.

Toby and I played cards on a tree stump, devising our scheme to scare the shit out of some uppity girls visiting from a church in Grand Junction. The stuck-up chicks weren't giving us the time of day, so our aim was to give them a scare to remember. With a long, slimy dead snake Toby and I had discovered down by the creek, we conspired over a game of cards.

Brother Bledsoe strolled up and placed his hand on Toby's shoulder. "It's mighty good seeing you back with us on such a fine afternoon, Mr. Zane. I trust you have learned how to correctly use indoor plumbing since our last acquaintance?"

"Yes, sir." Toby replied.

"That's good to hear." Homer eyed the limp snake. "Remember, God's watchin' you boys. You may be able to hide your shenanigans from your mommas, but he's always watchin'."

"Yes, sir," we replied in unison.

"Alrighty, you boys have a blessed day." He cleared his throat. "And Mr. Zane, your cucumber has left the salad." He gestured to Toby's open fly

After service, as the setting sun began its descent behind the pines, the congregation silently made its way down the path to the shores of the reservoir. Knee-deep in the chilly water, Laura stood waiting, with her giggling best friend, Stella, at her side. The two shivered, laughing nervously as the church members moved down to the water's edge. Laura wore a powder-blue linen dress Mom had bought at J. C. Penney. Her long chestnut hair was pulled back from her face with a single white ribbon.

My sis had blossomed into a lovely young woman while I wasn't watching. Time moves at such a hurried pace, allowing only the briefest moments for admiring its most beautiful accomplishments. Standing in the reflecting water, my older sister was a stunner. Both she and Stella smiled as the congregation approached, but I recognized Laura was frightened as she twisted a long strand of her hair around her fingers.

She waved wildly when she first spotted me across the water, and I was filled with such pride I wanted to yell out to her in front of the whole congregation gathered at the water's edge.

As the choir led us into "Just a Closer Walk with Thee," Laura was baptized in the shallow waters of Vallecito. Pinching her nose with both hands, she lay back into the waiting arms of Pastor Barnett and his brawny son, Ricky. While the pastor prayed, the two slowly dipped Laura into the cold, murky water. She reemerged sobbing. The Sisters of the First Assembly of God stretched their white-gloved hands into the fading sky, rejoicing in the baptism of my sister.

Sister Bledsoe howled, "Thank you, sweet Jesus, thank you," waving her lilac-colored hankie in the air.

With his wet sleeves rolled up to his elbows, and wearing a smile of self-satisfaction, Pastor Barnett shouted, "Are you saved, Sister Nance? Do you feel the power of the Lord Jesus Christ?"

Laura wiped her eyes, crying to the heavens, "I'm saved! I am saved!" Searching the faces of the congregation, she hollered, "Mama, I'm saved."

I stood at a distance, watching from the cover of a cottonwood. There was no wiping the beaming smile from my face, relief that life still gifted us moments when shivers raced down my spine and the fine brown hairs on my forearms stood upright.

Laura walked from the water as my Mom and the praising congregation met her. They encircled her, welcoming her into the fold.

Brimming with pride, Mom pulled a soaked Laura into her chest. "Praise the Lord!" Mom shouted, overcome with joy.

The two took turns between spells of crying and laughter, arms stretched around each other's waist. I was grateful to God, knowing for a shining moment they were happy.

I spied Ricky Barnett walking from the lake. His brown corduroys were soaked, and water sloshed from inside his heavy boots. He pulled his wet shirt over his head, exposing a broad, defined chest. A thin trail of black hairs traveled down the center of his wet abdomen. My pulse quickened, and I knew I'd best turn, but I kept my eyes fixed. He pulled off his boots and soaked socks. Grabbing a dry T-shirt from his knapsack, he caught my telling stare from across the shore. I turned my head, diverting my eyes.

I was a month away from turning seventeen and wound so tight even a passing celebratory slap on my shoulder from hunky Will Phillips after I pitched a winning game felt as intimate as a stolen embrace. An off-color joke whispered in my ear at the gym by brawny Bo Atkinson was as near to a breathy kiss along my neck as anything I could conjure up.

Making my way through the jubilant congregation down to Laura, I hugged her waist, lifting her feet off the ground. She beamed, and a joyous laughter erupted between us.

She whispered in my ear, "It's your turn, Zach. I really want this for you. Jesus loves you. I want you to be this happy."

I squeezed her even tighter, and she buried her face in my flannel shirt. She was freezing cold, and I tried to warm her body by rubbing my hands up along her forearms.

Before the canvas tents were pulled from the tree branches, before the aluminum folding chairs were loaded onto trucks and the pulpit reduced to scrap lumber, Laura and I understood everything was different. Without a single word passing between us, both of us knew a part of her was lost to me.

Laura was my sole confidante, my ally, but we both sensed she was now traveling on a different path, our roads separate. Her trail was heading true north, and God walked near her side. My direction was less clear, and I'd be walking those miles alone.

No matter how much love we shared, the growing divide would soon be too vast to bridge. Her devout faith allowed little space for a man like me, a man whose desires would've called for a stoning by the same congregation that now embraced her. Doctrines and Scriptures and folklore erected a barbwire fence that divided us. Even before I fully understood my sin, Scriptures condemned my sort to a forsaken path.

I had spent my childhood working diligently to be a good boy—kind and responsible, respectful and loyal—but it wasn't enough. It would never be enough.

Pastor Barnett reminded us every Sunday that heaven's gates were not opened by good deeds alone. Salvation was sought and found, he repeated, only through the acceptance of Jesus Christ as our Lord and Savior. Abiding by his Scriptures was the narrow, precarious path leading to redemption. But good deeds were all I had to give. My best intentions weren't ever going to be good enough.

My desire was nothing new. This fire had burned inside men like me long before the first Scripture was inked on any ancient papyrus scroll. My fiery fate had been cast long before any carpenter was crucified.

———

For a time Laura's new passion pulsed throughout our small house as she radiated a light. Strolling light-footed from room to room, she walked like she had someplace to go. Untroubled, she laughed with ease again. This zeal seemed to follow her everywhere she went. I heard her humming hymns while washing dishes or separating laundry. With her new passion, Laura was bound and determined to make a brighter life for herself and us. She and Stella painted her bedroom the color of the sky, and they planted daffodils in the flower boxes on the front windows.

Laura brought home a pair of new yellow sneakers for Mom and included her in a new fitness regime. At sundown, after dinner, they walked the length of County Road 250 and back. I arrived home one evening from work to find Laura and Mom dancing, thrusting, and kicking with Jack LaLanne on the TV. Momma wore a neon-green headband wrapped around her forehead, sweating like a whore in church.

I watched on while Mom struggled to keep pace with Laura and Jack's thrusts and kicks. "Momma, I'm pretty sure this amounts to a sin in the Bible."

Momma gasped for air. "Hush up your mouth, Zachariah. Go eat your dinner. It's still warm in the oven."

Fortunately, only a few weeks later, Mom retired her neon headband and sneakers when she threw out her hip.

After that sunny afternoon at the reservoir, Dad's random comings and goings didn't play on our minds. When he returned home, we walked around him like he was a stranger in a room where everyone else knew one another. I reckon Dad sensed we were trying to make our way despite him. He was the damaged step on the front porch we stepped over to go inside.

While Laura attended college classes at Fort Lewis, she worked the register at the Safeway grocery store a few days a week. After work she tended to her roses along the fence line and tried to teach Mom how to operate the new sewing machine I bought her for her birthday. The two sat together at the kitchen table, studying the machine's instruction manual.

Mom threw up her hands in utter frustration. "This is foolishness. It just has too many dad-gum buttons and too many levers." Within a week the new sewing machine had found a home inside the closet, and Momma's old machine was returned to the small desk in the front room.

Laura's joy reenergized Mom as well. Pulling out sheet music from under the bench, she played her upright piano for the first time in three years. Mom put on her new sneakers and walked out into the sunlight more often, weeding her vegetable garden and planting petunias around the mailbox. One afternoon I drove up the driveway to find her throwing a tennis ball across the yard for the yellow mutt.

The three of us watched *The Carol Burnett Show*, eating off TV trays. And almost every night, we surrounded the set and guessed the puzzles on *Concentration*.

Returning home after a day's work, I found myself looking forward to rounding the bend on County Road 250 and seeing our little house.

Laura's new light certainly hadn't gone unnoticed by the local boys. There was something different about her face. Her wide almond eyes reflected the sun, and she always laughed when she smiled.

On several nights restless boys threw smooth stones at her window, softly calling for Laura from the street, beckoning her to come out for a midnight stroll. But Laura ignored their calls. Lying in her bed, she smothered their voices with a pillow planted atop her head. When one rock, thrown too hard by the Goodman boy, shattered her windowpane, every lamp in the house was switched on. Mom lit the place up like a lighthouse and came out on the porch brandishing a broom like a slugger's bat.

The telephone in the kitchen was ringing off the wall. Guys came sniffing around the house like dogs hunting for a coon. Because of the traffic of suitors, I was assigned the task of manning the front door, running off guys from the porch. Mom managed Laura's incoming telephone calls like a personal secretary.

"No, Laura's out for the evening," Momma announced. "Can I take a message?"

"Ma'am, do you know when she's comin' home?" a nervous voice questioned from the other end of the line.

"I certainly do not. And it's none of your concern nohow," Mom chided.

"Can I leave my name and number?" asked the potential suitor.

"Is this Geoffrey Paul?"

"Yes, ma'am."

"If this is the same Mr. Paul who loiters in the park, puffing on illegal substances, then you are barking up the wrong tree, son. If you think for one minute that I'm gonna place the care of my precious daughter with some long-haired hippie who smokes the marijuana, you are sadly mistaken. Now, say good-bye, Mr. Paul."

"Good-bye, Mrs. Nance."

Charlie Mull had set his sights on Laura well before she granted him a first date. He'd been hinting around town for months of his intentions. His mother, Beatrice, played canasta with Mom on Tuesday nights. In between canasta rounds, Beatrice quizzed Mom about Laura's status.

The Mulls were devout Lutherans, and Mom wanted nothing to do with the likes of their sort, let alone contemplating one as a prospective son-in-law. Still, she came home from a night of canasta and reported the depths of Charlie's affections. Laura sat at the table and listened to the gossip, smiling but not saying so much as a peep.

It was just like Laura to never show her cards. She held them close to her chest. We never knew if she was drawing dead or holding aces. Ever since the accident on the pass, Laura had taken on a more serious, reflective approach to matters—and any potential suitor knew this within minutes in her company. The other girls batted their lashes and giggled to attract the local boys, but my sis didn't play that game.

Laura's smoky eyes, long dark hair, and high school cheerleader physique attracted the most popular boys. A few eager guys traveled as far as Farmington and Grand Junction to catch a glimpse of the pretty varsity cheerleader. But when strutting boys came calling, Laura didn't even acknowledge them. She didn't stand for such nonsense.

I recognized Charlie Mull's mug from the summer Cortez baseball league the first time she brought him home to meet Mom. He had been the home-base umpire for a few seasons. Charlie never said much but was fair on the field and didn't take any guff from troublemakers on visiting teams.

An ordinary-looking fellow, mild mannered and docile, Charlie had small hazel eyes and prematurely thinning hair. His stocky frame resembled a middle-aged man's physique more than that of a twenty-four-year-old. He was shaped like a bowling pin, and a belt cinched his waist like a noose around a sack of flour.

He had graduated with an accounting degree from Fort Lewis. Working at the First National Bank branch in Cortez, he quickly made his way up to branch manager. Charlie was a devout Lutheran, and because there was an impressive list of more attractive Baptist suitors, I didn't believe he'd ever hold Laura's interest.

She was three months shy of turning eighteen when Charlie finally asked her out, and Laura reluctantly agreed. After their first date, downtown at the Palace Station Café, I could see Charlie Mull's odds were greatly improving.

One evening Laura arrived through the back door after a date with Charlie, beaming with a dreamy, love-struck grin.

Mom leaned over to me, her coffee mug covering her mouth, and whispered, "We've lost her."

"Charlie Mull?" I asked. "Never."

"Yup." She shook her head. "We sure have. We've lost her." She smiled at me from across the table with an air of someone who knew a secret. "Zach, it's gonna be just you and me fairly soon."

For Laura's birthday Charlie gave her two little singing parakeets. The tiny pair, dressed in bright plumes of blue and green, were crested in long red and white feathers.

From their wire cage sitting on the foyer credenza, the birds chirped at the yellow dog through the open window. The old mutt spent his days resting on the porch, listening to the brightly feathered creatures sing their sweet songs.

Charlie Mull made Laura laugh right out loud. He was a dead ringer when imitating local characters around town. He mocked the absurdity of small-town life. After a few beers, Charlie could imitate Lucy Cline working behind the counter at the post office and mimic Sister Combs seated on her couch as she waved at passing cars.

Charlie took Laura to Denver and Phoenix to see the traveling Broadway shows. She came home singing show tunes from *Hello, Dolly!* and *Oklahoma!* Charlie provided Laura with a glimpse of a bigger life. He complimented her intellect, not just her pretty al-mond eyes or slender figure. She appreciated Charlie's matter-of-fact, plainspoken manner. He was steady, with an easy disposition.

I suppose it was Charlie's ambition that most attracted Laura—his ambition at the bank, his ambition to be more than the circumstances he was born into, and, most important, his ambition to get the hell out of Durango.

This ambition was a driving force propelling Charlie forward. Relocating to a more metropolitan city was part of his bigger plan. His position at First National Bank was the first of many stepping-stones that could lead him out of Durango. Idling in a small town, drinking beers with buddies at the local high school football game, wasn't an option.

"I'll be packed up and outta here the first chance I get," Charlie declared. "If I'm offered the right job, I'll be out of Durango before sunrise."

Laura shared Charlie's dream to leave Durango. I suspected her desire was not out of financial ambition but born from a wish to be away from us. Laura dreamed of being out from under the heavy weight of our small house, out from under the suffocating blanket of bad luck. The loss of Katie and Dad's fall from grace cast a wide shadow, and Laura wanted out into the light.

CHAPTER 8

———◆———

DURANGO ARRIVED LATE TO THE 1960s. A few barefoot hippies started hanging out in Veteran's Park on sunny afternoons. Bob Dylan's music played from the record store speakers along Main Street. Toby and I spied down by the river some homeless long-haired misfits strumming guitars and rolling their own ciggies.

In an attempt to strangle the impending rebellion, the high school principal, Mr. Ginn, ruled that all tie-dye T-shirts were un-acceptable school attire and that boys' hair should never touch their shirt collars.

Mom requested that Laura and I sit down at the kitchen table. With a solemn expression, and speaking in her most serious tone, she said, "You're no longer children, but I must warn you both, it's is a godless path. Those lost souls down by the river have so pol-luted their minds with drugs and sin that they no longer can see the light."

Laura thought on it for a moment and then asked. "Some say Jesus was a hippie. Could that be?"

"Our Lord was certainly not a hippie. If the Almighty was walking on this earth today, he would be a registered Goldwater Republican."

I added, "My social studies teacher, Mr. Leon, said voting the Democratic ticket is a more loving and peaceful way,"

Mom gripped her hands, flinching from a growing frustration. "Your teacher must be a fool or a communist or both. Now that you both have grown up, it's your sole decision on how you choose to live your lives. I've done what I can to steer you in the righteous direction. It's now up to you if you want to vote Democrat or Republican." She continued, "This great country was founded on the freedom to live your own lives how you like. However, if you should decide to register as a Democrat, it is best you know God may forgive you, but I certainly will not."

Laura and I looked at one another from across the table. And with the single conversation, the 1960s were put to rest.

Every year summer's arrival was welcomed with a First Assembly of God church service on the shores of Emerald Lake. A scorching sun beat down on Pastor Barnett's freckled bald spot. He wiped the sweat from his brow with a white handkerchief, standing on a smooth rock in his black polyester suit near the water. His puffy pie face was cherry red as he delivered a blistering sermon, reading from his Bible. The Sisters' pancake makeup melted in the summer sun as they swatted at swarming mosquitos picnicking on the congregation's anointed blood.

On this Sunday the minister preached from the book of Mark, recounting the story of Jesus walking on the water's surface. The pastor told how the faithful disciples boarded a fishing boat to cross to the other side of the Sea of Galilee. Jesus left them, wandering into the wilderness.

During the apostles' passage, the vessel was caught in the arms of a storm. The boat was tossed about by strong gusts of wind and rolling, crashing waves. Then they saw Jesus out in the distance, coming toward their rocking boat, walking on the water. The Scriptures describe how Peter asked the Lord if he could join him out on the water. Jesus offered him his hand, and Peter came down off the ship. Step by careful step, he too walked on the troubled, raging water. But then Peter grew frightened of the storm whipping around him and began to sink. Jesus caught him in his arms, telling him not to be scared, reminding him that through strong faith all is possible. He then led Peter back to the vessel.

I remember as a kid longing to believe as passionately as Peter, pious and true. At night I prayed to possess his devout faith.

One afternoon, fishing Vallecito all by myself, I cast thirty yards. The line whistled as it escaped from the reel, carrying the lure soaring out over the water. I eyed the surrounding quiet forest for anyone who might be watching. Untying my ratty sneakers, I slipped them off my feet. Squeezing my eyes tight in prayer, I blindly stepped into the cold pond, hoping to be lifted, but my feeble faith couldn't sustain me atop the water's surface. Instead my useless feet sank like stones into the murky water.

After the pastor's sermon, the young folk disappeared into the woods, changing from their church best into cutoffs and tank tops. The Sisters of the First Assembly of God headed to the shade of the trees and poured themselves sweet tea. They sat around foldout tables, playing cards. Their husbands rolled up their shirtsleeves and pitched iron shoes near the white sandy shore while diapered toddlers splashed in the shallow waters.

Several local distinguished bachelors circled Betty Pilchard, who held court on a patchwork blanket under a giant oak. Betty fanned her flushed pink cheeks and sipped iced lemonade like Scarlett O'Hara picnicking at the Wilkes plantation, batting her lashes with each pledge of affection from a silver-haired beau.

The pastor's son, Ricky Barnett, and his two buds floated shirtless on inner tubes off the end of the old wooden pier. Having spiced their tin cans of Coke with Jack Daniels, Ricky and his boys whistled and catcalled at the teenage girls who sunned themselves in short shorts and tank tops.

Pastor Barnett yelled down to the end of the pier, scolding his son. "God's watching you, boys. Behave yourselves, like good Christian men!"

Ricky rolled his eyes and took a sip from his spiked cola.

Sister Combs and Momma sliced ripe red watermelon and cantaloupe. Bowls of potato salad and trays of bologna sandwiches fed the hungry Baptists.

When big ol' Nettie Bledsoe appeared from the bushes in her bathing suit, the congregation looked on, mouths agape. The sisters muttered in disbelief from behind playing cards fanned out in front of their whispering mouths.

"Yoo-hoo!" Nettie hollered. "You chillren. Auntie Bledsoe is coming to take a dip!"

Homer Bledsoe, in the midst of pitching a near-perfect game, caught a glimpse of his exposed wife. Utterly distracted, he sent an iron shoe sailing off course, nailing Brother Atkinson's bony shin. Old man Atkinson fell to his knees, clutching his right leg, writhing in pain.

Fat ol' Nettie's Lycra yellow suit fit like a sausage skin. Cut at her knees, with tight elastic bands gripping her colossal thighs, the swimsuit's fabric stretched over her belly like a well-fed ham hiding under a yellow tarp.

"Lord, have mercy," Mom whispered to Annie and elbowed her side. "Look over yonder."

Sister Bledsoe's nearly 300-pound, five-foot-five frame emerged from the trees. Like a bloated ballerina, she tiptoed through stickers and thorn patches on the forest floor.

Even with her hefty excess, Nettie never refrained from engaging in all of life's offerings. She remained more active than women half her age and carrying half her mass. She chased after six grandchildren and, with a broom in hand, shooed scavenging birds from her vegetable garden. Every season, as her plump apricots ripened on heavy branches, Nettie spent her days chasing diving birds all about the yard with a spoon and metal pot.

Sister Nettie's sheer volume required a strategy to best transport her poundage efficiently. On this particular Sunday afternoon, as she made her way onto the pier, it was clear her intention was to take a dip in the cold water of Emerald Lake.

The sisters of the church watched on from the canopy of shade trees, halting their bridge game to view the spectacle at the pier. Children splashing in the shallow water put a quick stop to their play.

"Yoo-hoo!" Nettie yodeled down to Ricky and his buds, who floated on tubes at the end of the pier. "Here I come, boys."

Starting any journey from a complete standstill required Nettie to balance her bulge and find firm footing. Safe on the pier, she gripped tight to the wood railing.

"Ready or not, here I come!" Nettie hollered, waving her fleshy white arms in the air. Onlookers gathered at the shore, holding a collective breath as Nettie started to run.

Standing alongside the other men, Homer shook his head. "Sweet Jesus, there's no way this ain't gonna end poorly."

Releasing her grip on the pier's railing, Nettie began a slow, sloth-like toddle. Step by unsteady step, she found her balance and hit her stride. Then her pace quickened, shifting into a surprisingly spry waddle. The excess pounds shifted from one massive hip to the other, and the additional velocity powered her on. After only a few yards, a brisk jaunt was well underway.

Finally ol' Nettie's pace accelerated into what could only be called a sprint. Her white thick legs and arms powered her on like a train on its tracks. Hoofing it at full speed, the bloated Baptist transformed into an engineering marvel. She chugged like the Durango Narrow Gauge, charging down the wooden pier.

Unfortunately Nettie miscalculated her escalating speed, and with the end of the pier in sight, she was about to overshoot her runway. Pumping arms and mighty legs propelled her—applying brakes for such a load was no easy task. Like those runaway gravel ramps alongside the interstate that allowed semi-trucks with faulty burning brakes to gradually come to a slow halt, Sister Bledsoe needed a longer span to bring her wide load to a safe stop, a distance the short pier simply did not provide.

Watching on with a sense of impending doom, we all winced. Momma turned her head and said a rapid silent prayer.

Sister Bledsoe tried unsuccessfully to slow her pace, but unfortunately for Nettie, the Emerald fishing pier finally ran out of pier. With the last plank behind her, Nettie went belly first into the muddy waters of Emerald Lake.

The ladies jumped up from their lawn chairs and went running. Homer dropped his horseshoe and headed to his wife's aid. The kids along the shore, laughing up a storm, splashed into the water and swam out toward Nettie's flailing arms.

Annie screamed, "Nettie!" Dropping a ripe melon, she headed toward the ruckus.

Momma was doubled over, howling, nearly wetting herself.

A frenzy of feeding carp near the pier's edge, waiting for any picnic scraps, surfaced and encircled a sinking Nettie. Like sharks toying with their prey, the carp nibbled on poor Nettie.

"Homer!" Nettie screamed, swatting at the attacking fish. "Homer, save me!" Sister Bledsoe took on more water. "I'm drowning," she hollered, struggling to tread the murky lake. "Save me, Homer!" Nettie kicked her legs and paddled her arms. "Save me."

Ricky and his buddies abandoned their tubes, tossing them in her direction.

"Mrs. Bledsoe, grab a hold!" Ricky shouted. "Take hold of the inner tube!"

Panicked and sinking fast, Nettie reached for one of the inflated rings. Coughing up lake water, she was splashing and screeching. Her once towering bouffant now formed a great wet mound, like a pile of soggy pastel seaweed.

The menfolk jumped into the water alongside Nettie, attempting to calm her hysterics. Shooing the nibbling swarm of carp, they pulled Nettie's arms through the center of each inner tube, like two giant rubber swimmies.

After a few failed tries, it became clear that even our strongest men wouldn't be hoisting big Sister Bledsoe back onto the pier. Instead Toby and I jumped in, tied ropes to her, and, like two small tugboats pulling a massive cruise ship into port, we started Nettie's journey back to shallow water.

At the shore, Homer waited for his beloved, knee-deep in the water and ready with a dry towel. Standing at the edge, Toby, me, Ricky, and his buds chuckled and reenacted Sister Bledsoe's pier plunge.

"I was scared shitless I was gonna have to perform CPR on her," I joked.

"I bet, you would have loved that." Toby teased.

Ricky gave Toby's shoulder a push. "Hey, Zane, I always knew you were crazy but I can see your nuts." Barnett pointed down to Toby's open fly. His buds had themselves a good laugh while Toby scrambled to zip up his wet cutoffs. "Come on, Toby, you can tell us, does Nance ever try mouth-to-mouth on you?" Ricky laughed.

One of Ricky's buddies piped in, "Yup, I bet you're on your back every night with Nance wanting to try out his CPR skills."

Ricky and his boys were egging him on, but Toby wasn't having it. His good eye stared Barnett down. His left eye paid no mind, looking off somewhere in the trees.

Toby pushed Ricky. "Kiss my ass, Barnett." An anger rose in his good eye.

"Come on, Toby. I'm just giving you a rough time. Besides, I'm all about queer rights. Hell, if you and Zach wanna get married, I'll give the bride away."

"Fuck you!" Toby swung hard. Ricky didn't see the punch coming, and it landed square on his chin.

Ricky's eyes crisscrossed; he was dazed by the punch. In a split second, his two buddies piled in on top of Toby. I jumped in the mix, wrestling off one of the boys. We rolled in the mud, and a flurry of wildly swinging fists and kicking feet ensued.

Toby was getting the best of Ricky, but the other guy was wailing down on his back. With a swift kick to my opponent's gut, he stumbled to the ground, and I ran to Toby's assistance.

The ladies all came running, screaming from the shade of the trees. Velma Bartlett yelled out to her husband, and the pastor and the other men headed over to break up the brawl.

"That's quite enough!" The minister pulled us apart, grabbing hold of Toby's arm. "Stop it! Stop this foolishness now!"

The five of us stood, panting like a pack of wet alley dogs, still growling at one another with tightened fists. Dripping in lake water and covered in Colorado mud, we inventoried our welts and bruises, determining who got the worst of the ass whipping.

"What in God's name do you think you boys are doin'?" Pastor Barnett demanded an answer. "We're not barbarians." Lumps of red clay twisted in our hair and were smudged across our faces, mouths, and ears.

"Toby and his boyfriend here started this!" Ricky scoffed, spitting strings of blood to the ground. The makings of a nice plump, purple shiner were swelling up around his right eye.

"Fuck you, Ricky. I'll kick your ass!" I jumped toward him, but Mom restrained me.

"Zach, hush up your mouth this instant!" She hauled off and slapped the back of my head. "This is intolerable!"

"You're all acting like a bunch of godless hooligans." Pastor Barnett tried to calm his rising anger. "This ain't acceptable. I won't tolerate this nonsense. Now clear out of here, and go directly home." The pastor pointed, directing Ricky to the parking lot.

Ricky tried to plead his case, but his father wasn't having it.

"Zach, get your shoes. We're goin' home this instant!" Mom rushed to gather up her belongings and walked off toward the car.

I called over to Toby and gestured for him to come on but he shook me off and took off into the trees. In a fury, he yelled back at me "You should go get yourself a dad-gum girl! If you went and got yourself somethin' regular, it would shut'em up. It would shut them all up!" He spoke as if a female was something that I could go buy from the shelves at Krogers.

"That's quite enough for one day." Momma announced. "Go get in the car this instant."

What Toby and I didn't know about women folk could've filled all the books in the Durango Public Library.

CHAPTER 9

IN THE LATE EVENINGS, THE sound of Pop's truck's grinding, shifting gears, making its way up the drive, announced his arrival back home, followed by the slam of the back screen door. His return to the house brought both a sense of dread and an odd relief that he'd once more come home to us. There was a time when his laughter had filled the corners of the house, and now his rage shook its foundation.

Still Mom kept Dad's dinner warm in the oven. Every night she prepared his favorite pot roast or chicken dumplings. When he was a no-show, the old yellow dog reaped the windfall with a full plate of table scraps. The less Pop came home, the fatter the old hound got. By June the mutt barely could transport his fat ass off our porch.

The threatening summer storms loomed over the San Juans in the late afternoons. Like the train's whistle sounding each morning at the depot, the August storm clouds arrived right on time every year. Rumbling in around suppertime, a heavy sky with charcoal clouds blew in from Ouray, carrying with them hard pelting rains. The deluge poured well into the night.

I lay in my bed and stared at the dark ceiling. When lightning struck outside the window, illuminating my room's interior with flashes of white, I counted down for the impending thunder.

That same summer small-town gossip of Dad's infidelity traveled like a whisper on a string stretched between tin cans. The local chatter was that Dad had taken up with Caroline Beck, a widow in nearby Grand Junction. Momma dismissed the stories as wicked slander, but incriminating evidence was mounting. I suspected she always knew the truth but wasn't ready to go poking someplace where she ought not.

"I will not abide such vicious gossip," Mom told Sister Pilchard when Caroline's name was first brought up over a canasta hand. "I'll never understand such mean-spirited wickedness."

Questioning Dad's fidelity was a battle she wasn't yet willing to wage. While Caroline's name was never spoken during my folks' quarrels, she was present in every hurled insult and accusation.

One evening, as a heavy summer rain beat down on the shingled roof, sending rivers of water rushing through the metal gutters along the porch, I listened to the ruckus downstairs. Mom's inquiries had set off Pop again. He left the house, slamming the truck door and driving off into the night. Mom finished in the kitchen and went upstairs to her room, closing the door behind her.

With the coast clear, I ventured out from my room and stepped quietly down the stairs. Outside on the porch, I found Laura alone and balled up on the front swing.

"Hey, brother." She swayed back and forth, dressed in her cotton pajamas. "It's really coming down tonight."

"Yups." I smiled. "Roof's sprung a leak directly over my pillow. Gotta climb up in the morning and go huntin' the leak."

In the glow of a streetlamp, the steady downpour created muddy pools in the yard and collected in Dad's fresh boot prints out across the drive.

Laura and I rocked side by side, listening to the rhythm of the falling rain. The old yellow dog slept at our socked feet.

Laura leaned into me. "I saw Pops with Caroline." she said. Her voice dropped to a whisper. "Charlie and I saw them out at the park two weeks ago. They were laughing and carrying on right out in public."

"Jesus Christ, what's he thinkin'? He needs some talking to, and I think I'm just the one to do it."

"Zach, you need to let this be." I heard Mom's caution in Laura's tone. "Don't go causing a stir. Just let it be."

"If he's gonna do this crap in the clear light of day, what's next? What else will he pull out from his sleeve? It's just not right, Laura."

She placed her hand on my knee. "Just let it be."

We rocked in the wooden swing under the shelter of the porch as the black rain fell in sheets from the eaves. We made a pact that night, Laura and I, to keep her discovery between us. I hid her confession so far from sight, Mom could never glimpse it in my eyes. We sat silently in the dark, knowing the telling could finally split our small white house right in two.

———◆———

It was a photograph taken the day Dad proposed to Mom. In sienna hues of sunlight, the sweethearts sat atop the hood of Pop's Plymouth, Dad's arm wrapped around Mom's shoulder and his polished shoe propped up on the chrome bumper. With her legs crossed and hands folded neatly on her lap, Mom sat demurely, smiling for the camera. She looked like Lana Turner, pretty as a picture and too young to know. Unaware of the photographer, Pop gazed at Mom like an adoring fan.

This early photograph of my parents was Laura's favorite. She placed the framed picture on her bedside table. Once cherished, the image now reminded Laura of her deepest fears. She displayed the photograph as a constant reminder of mistakes to avoid. She and Charlie swore to each other they'd beat the odds, vowing my parents' story wouldn't be theirs.

With Laura off working, attending classes, and making wedding plans, her absence echoed in the house. The small rooms filled with more shadows, and less laughter lilted through the open windows. The loose floorboards seemed louder underfoot, and the pair of songless parakeets huddled together in their wire cage, frightened by the arrival of the summer storms. The old dog disappeared out to the garage, opting not to slumber on the porch.

Mom and I missed Laura's presence and struggled at conversation. Dad's empty chair was a constant reminder that an even bigger storm was approaching. Trying to ease Mom's melancholy, Laura and Charlie included her on their trips to Farmington to help select flower arrangements and a wedding cake. The three scouted potential apartments and rental houses for the newlywed couple post-wedding day.

"I don't know why you two can't just move into this house," Mom announced to Charlie and Laura. "It's foolishness to waste all that money."

"Momma." Laura laughed. "You can't be serious. We can't move in with you and Zach."

"I don't see why not. The house is plenty big. Zach can make a room for himself downstairs, and you two can have both rooms upstairs to yourselves."

Charlie shot Laura a panicked expression.

"Momma, no. We're anxious to set up a place for ourselves, start a life of our own."

Undeterred, Mom continued, "When grandchildren come along, I can be right here to take care of the babies."

"Oh, Momma." Laura hugged her neck and calmed Charlie's nerves with a reassuring expression over Mom's shoulder. "We have to get our own place."

One evening after Charlie and she got into a lovers' quarrel, Laura questioned Mom, "When did you know for certain Daddy was the right fellow?"

Without hesitation Mom said. "It was our fourth date, when your dad showed up in his polished Chevy, its tail end loaded with fishing reels, a tackle box, and packed lunches. He took me to Navajo Lake to rent a rowboat for the afternoon. Your father arrived in his best boots and collared shirt. On the way to the lake, I knew he was a different sort. He spoke of affairs of the heart, none of the nonsense of the other boys around town. My three brothers were all spit and nails, the stuff boys are made of, but your pa was so tender. He asked me about my hopes and dreams and stole my heart in that five-dollar rowboat. I guess I'd never witnessed such gentleness from menfolk. We sat in the falling light of day with our fishing lines in the lake, and I knew then I had found someone to love."

Like the floating plastic fishing bob on the water's smooth surface, waiting for the moment when a trout takes the bait and goes swimming in the deep, Momma knew with certainty she was hooked.

When Charlie and Laura weren't working or planning wedding details, they sat at his place late into the evenings, plotting their escape from Colorado. I suspect part of Momma knew their plans to flee, but she remained quiet, understanding Laura wanted more from life.

As for me, I disappeared upstairs to my waiting room. Smuggling a six-pack in my backpack, I imagined my escape from Durango with A. J., the youngest of the roughneck McCord boys, the quiet one with broad freckled shoulders. Waiting in line to buy raw lumber or fishing lures, I watched him work behind the register at the hardware store. He seemed to pine for something more. A. J. was the closemouthed kind, and when he took my cash, for a moment I thought I caught a smile curling the corner of his mouth.

A month before the wedding, Laura and her bridesmaids traveled to Grand Junction for dress fittings. I'd worked late on a banister at the Walkers' farmhouse and walked through the back door to discover Mom cleaning up the place. A broken glass pane from the kitchen window and a wooden chair left in splinters on the floor were the last remaining hints of Dad's most recent drunken rage.

I tossed my keys on the counter and bent down to help her pick up the last shards of glass. "So he's back at it again?" I asked.

"He's just not right in the head." With a troubled sigh, she wiped the floor with a towel. "He'll come round."

Without another word passing between us, we cleared any evidence of the damage done. I tossed the pieces of the broken chair out in the garbage bin while she swept the floor of any last bits of glass.

"I'm scared what he's gonna do, Zach. I just don't know what he's capable of when he's drinking." She stood at the sink with her hands deep in the warm dishwater.

A stiff square of brown cardboard and duct tape covered the single broken pane over the sink. I ran upstairs to change from my work clothes and came back down to find Mom looking through the cardboard windowpane like there was something to see.

I walked up to Mom's side and kissed her powdered cheek. "Nothing's gonna happen. I can guarantee it."

As she washed plates, I found a dish towel and dried. From the corner of my eye, I glanced to the side in her direction. She was weary, distant from me, lost somewhere far outside the window or inside her head. Over those troubled years, I'd watched Mom's face gradually lose a subtle softness. She remained beautiful but rail thin, leaving her bone structure more pronounced. During those many months battling Dad, her features turned more exact, harsher. The moments when she smiled, her remembered youthful sweetness returned instantly, but when her smile left, when she stood at the stove or ironing or quietly contemplating Scriptures, her face appeared less supple, less soft. I hated Pops for robbing my momma of her youth.

Distracted, Mom handed off the first dripping dish. The wet plate was coated with translucent crimson-red soap. Her hands were submerged deep in a basin filled with frothy, bloody water. Scarlet suds lathered her forearms, blood-red bubbles covering her arms up to her elbows.

"What the hell? Mom, you're bleeding!" I grabbed her forearms, pulling her hands from the crimson water. "What did he do? Did he hurt you? I'll kill the son of a bitch."

"No! No. Zach, look, I cut myself! I just sliced my finger on a piece of glass from the broken window," she desperately tried to explain. "When I was cleaning the mess I must have cut my finger." She held her index finger, showing me the small slice on the tip. "Look, it's just a small cut. It's nothing." She dragged both hands up and down the sides of her housedress, staining it with streaks of red.

"If he shows up here again, I'll fuckin' kill him."

"No, I was just careless."

"I swear to God, I'll kill him."

"Zach, stop!" She hushed me, wiping her hands on a blood-stained dish towel. "Stop it now. You'll do no such thing. You stay clear of this. Do you hear what I'm sayin' to you? This is mine and your father's own making, and you just steer clear."

"Mom, you said it yourself—you're scared."

"Your father is broken."

"Stop making excuses for him. You keep making excuses, and nothin' is getting better. It's only getting worse. He's a good-for-nothin' drunk."

"Zach, that's enough! I shouldn't have said a word." She gathered herself, walked to the back door with a plate of table scraps, and yelled out to the dog.

Still stewing, I exhaled. "I'll kick his ass if—"

"Enough!" she hushed me, blunting my fire before it could reignite. "I don't need two hotheads going at it. I'll tend to your father. I need you to calm yourself," she said. "Do you understand?" As she poured the tea, Mom looked into my eyes, searching for confirmation that I understood the importance of peace and quiet.

"I understand."

She patted my shoulder. "It's a sorry state when parents put their children through this. God will strike us down for doing this to our kids."

"Mom."

"No, no. I never imagined it would come to this. I guess I never dreamt life would turn. Your father and my story has been told. Yours is just waiting to be lived."

She wiped off the counter, folded the dish towel, and draped it through the fridge door handle. I took a seat at the table and tried to steady my pulse and put out the fires in my head.

Placing her hand on my shoulder as she passed on her way to the front room, again she said, "I'm so sorry."

She flipped on the television set, and Johnny Carson was in midmonologue to the background noise of Ed McMahon's practiced laughter.

"There's a slice of pie in the fridge," she called out to me.

When Mom went off to bed, I went scavenging in the hall closet. On the highest shelf, behind boxes of Christmas ornaments, I found Dad's pistol.

———

Over the following few weeks, friends tried tempting me out to football games or to fire a few rounds at the gun range. A couple of guys wanted to roll games at the bowling alley and challenged me to some pool at Claude's Tavern. Instead I opted to stay near the house, slipping back behind the barn with a bottle of gin.

Sitting in the dark with the radio playing, I stood watch over our sleeping house, alert to any sign of Pop's headlights. With his old dog resting at my side and his gun in my lap, I waited for Dad's return.

It was a week later when I passed Phil, the local locksmith, leaving in his van from the drive. After rekeying the deadbolts, he had left three shiny keys on the counter. The new matching silver keys signified Pops was now a trespasser, an agitator to be kept at bay, a threat needing to be locked outside.

I guess I imagined that on Dad's final day with us, angry bolts of lightning would strike our small house—a black rumbling sky with massive thunderclouds would open up, sending balls of fire from the heavens. Like in some movie, I assumed he and Mom would go a final round of spilling tears and spitting anger. Instead it was a mild, sunny Saturday afternoon. The dog was barking up a storm when I heard Pop loading his last few belongings in the bed of his truck. Mom was at the church, helping with a bake sale.

The sound of shuffling feet downstairs brought me to my window. Poking my head out, I met Dad's eyes.

"Hey," I called down to him in the drive.

"Howdy, son."

"You loadin' up?"

"Yup. Just a few things." He loaded his toolbox and a few cardboard boxes from his work shed out back.

"Are you taking him with ya?" I gestured down to the old yellow dog waiting on the porch, its tail wagging at full throttle in hopes of being invited to take his rightful place in the bed of the truck.

Dad shook his head. "Naw, no place for him. Take care of him for me. Son, have you seen my gun?"

"Nope," I said, shaking my head.

"I can't find hide nor hair of it. If you come across it, let me know."

"Sure," I replied.

"Would you let your momma know I came by? I'm fixin' to send some money at the end of the week. Can you tell her that for me?"

"OK." I shrugged my shoulders and ducked back inside.

His voice sounded again from outside my open window. "You're momma was a beauty, Zach. If you could've seen us when we first met. Your momma, she was a beauty." He rubbed his unshaven gray scruff. "The way we were before it all went bad, before we lost Katie girl." Dad turned up to me, shielding his eyes with his hand from the reflecting sun. "Zach, it's not the way I thought it would be."

I stared down at the old man outside my window. "If ever you show up here again, breaking windows and causin' trouble, I'll fuckin' kill you."

He looked up to my window, examining my face. "Is that so?"

"Yup. If you ever hurt my momma, you're a dead man."

Dad's truck never again drove down the gravel drive. Laura and I looked at each other from across the supper table, each of us

mirroring the loss in the other's eyes. The finality was oddly comforting and quietly devastating. men can do, I thought. Women
stay, but men can leave.

Mom remained silent, and Laura and I followed her lead. I suppose we still waited for Dad to stumble in smelling like cheap whiskey and intoxicating regret. His well-worn path through the house
where his work boots had scuffed the floorboards and his coffee
mug hanging on a metal hook beneath the cupboard were constant
reminders he had lived there before. His prints were everywhere.

Lloyd Robert Nance would never again be known for his kindness and gentleness. Rather his legacy was the dark, ugly under-
side that shadowed him after the accident on Echo Basin Pass. I
reckon, like rotting fruit on a branch, Dad thought if he left, his
family wouldn't have to witness his inevitable fall.

On occasion I saw his pickup parked in front of the poker house
in Ignacio, where he played throughout the night and sometimes
early into the morning. His blowout brawls with the widow Beck
became local legends. Rumor had it Caroline liked her scotch,
and combined with Dad's thirst for gin, they formulated a toxic,
combustible mixture. Explosive arguments and domestic mayhem
rocked the tiny trailer park. The police department had a cruiser
assigned to pass by her mobile home on its nightly patrol.

Between binges with the bottle, Pop worked odd jobs, relying on
his skills as a handyman. A failed pursuit to open a mechanic shop
with Saul Custer in Cortez seemed to be his last attempt to aim for
something more. But arthritis set in, twisting his joints and mangling
his hands, making it nearly impossible for Dad to make a living.

A few evenings I parked down the street from Caroline Beck's
mobile home and watched the shadows behind the cotton drapes
that hung in the windows. I tried to imagine Dad and Caroline's
life in the little trailer. Were they ever joyful? Did they laugh out

loud? Was this new life far enough away from his first family on County Road 250 that he couldn't smell Mom's bacon frying in the morning or hear our laughter around the television at night?

I sat in my pickup until every window of the trailer had gone dark, and then I headed on over to Claude's Tavern.

I pushed hard through the weeks and stumbled my way through the weekends.

For the better part of a year, I dated a sweet girl named Jessie Lee Farnham, who deserved more and far better. Jessie was kind and patient with me. There were real moments, when her arm was wrapped round my waist and her finger slid through my belt loops, that I believed I could love this girl. She liked to laugh. She didn't seem to want any more from me than I had to give. It seemed that even with all my failings, I was enough for Jessie. My closed-mouth disposition didn't send her running. Content to do nothing in the evenings, we watched the sun set out beyond the Ellisons' fields. I felt safe in a way I hadn't known. In the stillness and beauty of a blue day, I yearned to tell Jessie more about me, but I hadn't the words. Still when I kissed her mouth, it was out of true desire and an earnest appreciation for her compassionate understanding. Jessie Lee was no man's consolation prize.

I knew my taking up with Jessie brought a sense of relief to Mom. She was fond of Jessie Lee and her family. When I was late coming home from work, Jessie and Mom would be on the porch waiting for my return.

"She's a keeper," Mom whispered to me. "Granted, she comes from a family of Pentecostals, but Pentecostals are just Baptists who pray too loud. We're both cut from the same cloth."

Momma kept pushing on. While grade school was in session, she and Sister Combs worked in the cafeteria, spooning lasagna and goulash onto the kids' plastic trays. My uncle Loran, Mom's brother, sent a charity check every several months.

Laura attended classes during the day and worked at the grocery store by night. Her and Charlie's wedding day was just a month away, so her attention was turned to flowers, menus, and the intricate white-lace details of her dress. Mom couldn't contribute much to the wedding costs, so Charlie's folks helped however they could.

I was pulling in good money, working long hours, mowing lawns, building barbecues and screened-in patios. I deposited money into Mom's account every week, but she remained close-mouthed on the subject.

Laura slid into the vinyl booth at the diner. "Hey, brother. Well, look at you." She smiled. "You're filling out that shirt nicely."

Blushing red, I shrugged my shoulders. "Naw, I'm gettin' fat."

"I just can't believe my Charlie. If he doesn't stop sneaking donuts and cookies, he's never going to fit into his tuxedo." She cocked her head. "So, Mom said you're seeing Jessie Lee Farnham?" She grinned.

"A little," I said.

"Good for you. I've always liked Jessie Lee." Laura opened her purse. "What is this?" She tossed a white envelope full of cash onto the checkered tablecloth.

"It's nothing. Just some cash I've been saving up for a rainy day."

"Zach." She tilted her head with smiling eyes. "You know you're the sweetest boy I've ever met, right?"

I brushed off the praise and pulled a laminated menu from behind the ketchup bottle. Handing it to her, I sensed her eyes still pinned on me.

"Charlie and I have enough money," she assured me. "We've got it all figured out."

"Good, then take the money and go spend it on yourself." I pushed the envelope back in front of her. "Go buy yourself something crazy expensive, something you've always wanted."

For a split second, I saw Laura allow herself to dream of luxury, but just as quickly her almond eyes refocused as she pushed the envelope to my side of the table.

"So, brother, have you been behaving? Are you steering clear of...?" Laura gestured like she was tipping back an imaginary bottle.

"Yes, Sister Barnett. I am."

"Hmmm." She cocked her head, with doubting eyes. "Well, I can't imagine Jessie Lee will put up with that kind of nonsense."

"You and your mother worry too much." I laughed.

"It's in our DNA. I can't help myself."

Laura waved down a waitress, whom we both knew from high school.

"Laura, how are you, hon?" The bubbly server greeted us with a big, toothy grin.

"Hey, Gail. I'm great, thanks. How's Jeffrey and the kids?"

"Jeff is as grumpy as ever. Jacob is in day care with his older sister. Now, what can I get for you?"

"I'll have the chopped salad with low-fat ranch and a Diet Coke." Then Laura added, "And no croutons."

Gail smiled. "Hon, the croutons are the best part."

"Nuh-uh. I need to lose five pounds to fit into my dress. After this wedding poor Charlie better watch out, because he doesn't know what's coming. I'm going to eat everything in sight." Laughing, Gail and Laura slapped the palms of their hands together.

"That's right, honey. As soon as you get that diamond on your finger, you can get as big as a barn if you want!" the waitress quipped. "Besides, Laura, you've always been nothin' but skin and bones. Charlie Mull is one lucky man." The waitress took my order, slid her pencil behind her ear, and disappeared into the kitchen.

"Mr. Nance, have you rented your tux?" Laura asked.

I shrugged my shoulders.

"Zach, you have to get it done."

"I will. I will," I promised.

Laura updated me on the wedding details and announced Charlie was planning on putting in a transfer request to Denver or some distant locale.

Each time Laura mentioned Charlie's name, I felt my insides tighten up—Charlie *this*, Charlie *that*. I was jealous and recognized my foolishness. Laura had Charlie, and she was his, I reminded myself. Making an unspoken promise, I swore I'd silence my silly pettiness for the sake of Laura's happiness and welcome Charlie into the fold.

Physically Charlie and Laura's pairing didn't make a lick of sense. Already resembling a balding, middle-aged man, Charlie walked small shouldered, with a belted paunch. Laura, with her sparkling eyes and long, shiny brunette hair halfway down her back, was not a match with Charlie's more pedestrian looks. But because of Mr. Mull's ambition, his promotions at the bank, and Laura's strong work ethic and no-nonsense demeanor, the townsfolk believed the two made a perfect coupling. Everyone assumed Laura would ascend to her rightful seat as one of the great Sisters of the First Assembly of God, and Charlie would excel in his position at the bank. Most of us expected the couple would end up in one of the stately Victorians on Thirteenth Avenue.

I kept telling myself Charlie was good for Laura. He was an optimistic sort. He believed opportunities abounded. He trusted life offered up a plentiful bounty to anyone who simply reached high enough and snatched it up. Charlie believed that with hard work, anything was possible.

At first glance Laura seemed to share Charlie's optimism. She had always walked proud, carrying herself with a sense of poise and confidence that was lacking in most other local girls. But sometimes I wondered if my sis was drawn to Charlie Mull because she possessed *none* of his optimism. In all of Laura's confidence, sometimes I glimpsed a reflection of doubt—a hint of sadness behind her smiling eyes. She and I had lived within the same walls. I knew what she knew.

If the truth were told, maybe Laura was drawn to Charlie because she no longer believed life willingly opened its arms to anyone who asked. Since that day on Echo Basin Pass, maybe Laura understood the world was rotten to its core, bitter to the taste. She knew full well that in the blink of a turned eye, everything sweet and good could be lost in a wicked winter freeze. I knew Laura struggled in her quiet hours to believe life still offered an abundant banquet, but with Charlie's help maybe she could still reach for the ripest fruit on the highest branches.

"Sis, I just want you and Charlie to be happy. And Mull had best be good to you, or I swear I'm coming for him," I warned. "If he don't treat you right, he'll find his ass flat on the ground." I pushed the envelope back to her, and she placed her hand on top of mine.

"He is good to me, Zach. He's a real good man."

The two of us knew something that mattered, something real, was coming to an end. I loved Laura for her patience and strong will. She was my compass in an ever-shifting world I couldn't navigate.

"Take the money. Let someone do something for you."

Laura reached across the table and cupped my chin in her hand. "Did I ever tell you you're the sweetest man I've ever met?"

CHAPTER 10

———◆———

WITH TIME MY CLUMSY, AWKWARD hands became those of an artist. I developed and honed my woodworking skills into the likes of a master carpenter. My tools became extensions of my hands. The same hands that gripped a gin bottle in the evenings held jigsaws, routers, sanders, and chisels through the day. I built intricate patios that wrapped around beautiful Victorians on Thirteenth Avenue. I constructed expansive decks and gables, carved mantels, and intricate trellises, attracting the admiration of locals and tourists who strolled through the streets of Durango.

Proud Pastor Barnett congratulated me and patted my back when I rolled up with a new walnut pulpit strapped down in the bed of my pickup.

"Son, I believe that's the finest pulpit in all of Colorado. Yes indeed, mighty fine work," he boasted, rubbing his hand along the smooth, polished wood like it was a shiny new sports car. "You're a mighty fine carpenter. You know, Zach, God not only speaks through our hearts—sometimes he speaks through our hands."

I thanked the minister for his kind words, shoving my two fists deep into my pockets, trying to hide my trembling. My eyes nervously darted down to the pavement. I wanted to get lost and needed a stiff drink.

"Zach, I know of another mighty fine carpenter," the pastor added, "who sacrificed everything for his church."

The following Sunday, when the preacher called me to the front of the entire congregation, praising my workmanship, all the hubbub made me uneasy and wishing I'd never swung a hammer.

When I wasn't crafting something from wood, I was landscaping the finest lawns around town. As soon as winter gave way to April, my phone was ringing off the wall. Some of the richest folks on 13th Avenue wanted me to cultivate their green carpets of grass and plant rows of geraniums and peonies, which bloomed vibrant until chilly September evenings arrived.

One afternoon, my pickup bed loaded with plastic trays of purple and red petunias ready for planting, I spotted Dad's truck. Waiting my turn at the Burger King drive-through, I recognized his rusted junker in the Cleveland Lumber Yard parking lot. I paid for my order and pulled into the spot adjacent to his rusted-out truck.

Through his window glass, I could see piles of empty cigarette boxes, old Styrofoam coffee cups, and scattered newspapers littering the cab. His console ashtray spilled over with ashes, butts, and bottle tops. On the splitting plastic dashboard were a pair of broken sunglasses, dozens of crinkled receipts, and fast-food wrappers. His bucket seats were soiled and torn, yellow foam squeezing from the split upholstery seams.

Leaning on his back bumper, I finished off my burger and inventoried the piles of garbage collected in the bed of his truck. Old rusted tools, gunnysacks full of plumbing fittings, and empty beer cans were strewn about. Dozens of empty motor-oil cans were scattered among the debris—Dad's attempt to delay the old truck's thirsty engine from burning up.

The scrawny old man who stepped from the doors of the hardware store, pushing a cart stacked with lumber, wasn't anyone I recognized. He was rail thin, with slumped shoulders like the homeless men who slept on the benches near the bus station. His once strong and intimidating physique was bent and limp, the broad, solid chest now weary and sunken. His thick, shiny head of hair had thinned and now grew as gray as stones. His complexion was red and pitted and puffy like a drunkard.

I watched his approach from across the parking lot. Seemingly unsteady on his feet, he tripped on his well-worn boots as he crossed the pavement. Struggling to push and guide the loaded-down cart with its wobbly rubber wheels that tried to roll their own wayward course. Dad's frayed, greasy pants were ripped across the knees and hung low on his narrow hips. Tugging on a belt loop, he attempted to pull them up higher on his waist. The seams of his soiled shirt were frayed and hung from his bony frame like the scarecrow in the Ellisons' cornfield.

Watching the raggedy man, I wondered how it could be that he'd fallen so far over the past several years. How strong must the lure of liquor be to have taken him down this road, how powerful the craving to choose poison over the warmth of our little house and the company of Mom, Laura, and me.

When Dad first spotted me leaning against his bumper, he slowed the pace of his rolling cart. His eyes darted down to the blacktop. With an unnerved expression, it seemed he was contemplating if he should turn and head back to the store or push forward to me.

His slate-blue eyes were the last remaining hint he was my father. The strong arms I remembered were scrawny, freckled with black age spots. As he approached I saw his sun-worn skin drape from the nape of his neck like thin, sagging dark leather. The whites of his eyes were yellowed, and a milky film covered any reflection.

"Hey, boy." He slowed his cart, reaching to shake my hand.

"Hey, Pops."

His unsteady hand remained extended between us like an offered gift. When my palm didn't grip his, he reached up and patted my shoulder.

"You're lookin' strong." His hand remained resting on my shoulder.

I shook my head, rubbing my abdomen. "Naw, I'm out of shape. Too many beers and not enough time in the gym."

"You look strong, like your grandpa Nance."

I surveyed the sticks of lumber on his cart. "Looks like you got yourself a nice-size job."

"Just a roof repair over in Mancos," he said. "The storm last week took the Ryans' porch cover clean off." He tossed a few boxes of nails through the open back window of the pickup cab. "Are you staying busy?"

"Yeah. Staying really busy," I said. "I've got two guys onboard with me, helping out."

"That's real good. I saw the new patio deck over at the Douglas place. Mighty fine work."

A silence suspended between us, waiting to be bridged.

"Everything OK at the house?" Dad struggled to fill the empty chasm.

I gave no response.

Dropping the tailgate of his pickup, he loaded the lumber off the cart, on top of the tools and debris. "How's Laura? Your momma? Everyone fine?"

"We're doin' just fine." I grabbed a few studs and helped him load.

"That's good."

The absurdity of our cordial chitchat caused a knot to twist and tighten in my gut. I exhaled hot air and bit down on the back of my jaw to silence my anger as I pitched two-by-fours onto his truck.

Dad murmured something I couldn't make out, shaking his head like he'd answered his own question. The sun reflected on his thinning scalp, and he swiped sweat from his brow with his forearm. His bony hands trembled like one of the old men who attempt in vain to pitch the horseshoe long after his strength had left his arms.

"You could stop by the house and find out for yourself, ya know," I quipped.

A stirring silent anger deep in my gut was now torn into small fragmented pieces like ripped pages from a book. Abandonment and disgust were the easy pieces, but with Dad standing before me in the stark light of day, a new fury raged in my chest. I was spitting angry at him for growing old, enraged because he didn't wait longer to grow feeble and frail. He was decaying and breaking down before I had time to hate him longer or love him stronger.

"I think you know I can't do that. I can't just go showing up at the house," he said, shaking his head. He picked up a few more sticks from the cart and slid them into the bed. "I reckon I've done enough damage."

"That's a crock of shit." I came back.

"I ain't doing this, Zach." He tossed the last sticks of lumber into his truck. "I ain't doing this with you today."

"You're some piece of work," I mocked. "You make me sick to my stomach."

Raising one eyebrow, he carefully considered his words. "Zach, I know you think you're better than me. I can see it all over your face. I got some news for you—you're not." He took one step closer. "I may be a disappointment, and you may think I'm a worthless piece of shit, but I'm still your father. You and your sister best remember that. I brought you into this world."

"Well, we agree on one thing—I do think you're a piece of shit." My eye began to twitch, my hate palpable.

Dusting his hands off on his dirty jeans, his squinting water-blue eyes met mine. "I'm not gonna stand here and listen to this. I won't put up with this disrespect from my own flesh and blood."

"Respect?" I scoffed. "You're fucking kidding me, right?"

"Boy, you best be careful pointing fingers. The way I see it, there's enough shame to go around." His unflinching gaze burned me like a red-hot poker. "It's a small town, and you don't have to travel too far to hear the stories."

All at once I felt young and stupid and disobedient. I was more ashamed of myself than angry at him. It was easy to wound him, like shooting fish in a barrel, but I was disgusted that he could silence me with just a word or a look.

"Go ahead, son, throw stones. Then why don't you come back and look me up in a few years? After life kicks the shit out of you, let's share a bottle, just you and me. What are you drinking now—gin, Jack?" He toyed with me. "Come on, boy, you can tell your old man. What's your pleasure? Are you a whiskey man? What do you say? Let's you and me sit down over a drink, and you can tell me how it all works. Since you've got it all figured out, come on over and show me how it's all supposed to go down." His hands were rolled up into two tight fists.

Dad looked to the sky as if he feared it might fall. Anger or hurt or both flooded his eyes. Finally his hands reached out, gripping the side of his pickup bed. "Zach, it wasn't supposed to end up this way." He dropped his head, looking down at the blacktop, slowly rocking his head, examining the pavement like he was looking for a poor man's dollar.

I'd never know his staggering loss, his waking each morning with an open wound, infected and unhealed.

"You are the better man, son." His head still hung low. "I wish it would've worked out different, but life doesn't…" He stopped himself and squeezed the edge of his truck. "I just turned round one day, Zach, and it was all gone."

"No, Dad. You gave it away—Momma, Laura, me…everything. You gave us all away."

I wasn't finished, not ready to let it go, but in his turned eyes I knew he was lost somewhere far from me. He remained silent, leaning against his truck, burrowed deep in his thoughts. I slammed the tailgate closed, bringing him back.

"You know, Laura and Charlie's wedding is coming up."

He didn't respond.

"The reception is out at Veteran's Park. She's spending every waking hour makin' plans."

"When we lost Katie, you'll never know how—" Dad stumbled on his words. "You'll never know, son. I carry it with me like a stone. There's no getting away from it. It's always here." He pressed his chest with a closed fist. "It's a heavy thing. Maybe the booze makes it easier to carry." Shaking his head, he glanced at me and then pushed the metal cart off to the side.

"Dad, you're not carrying nothin'. It's pulling you down. You're sinkin' fast, and you're pulling us down with you." I said. "We're all drowning."

He walked over to his door, squinting in the afternoon sun. "Then just cut me loose, son. You gotta cut me loose. You, your sister, and Alice Faye, just let me go."

I felt my blood leaving, spilling warm and crimson, like a slice to the jugular.

Dad opened the truck's door and climbed into the cab. An empty gin bottle lay on the floorboard and reflected like cut crystal in the afternoon sunlight. He cleared the discarded bottle to the side with a kick of his work boot and shut the door.

Cranking down his window, Dad said, "Zach, you're a good man. You and your momma and Laura deserve better than this wasted piece of shit."

I wanted the old wiry, gray-haired man to stay. "Laura would sure love it if you'd show up, Dad. It would mean a lot to her."

"You bet, I'll be there," he lied. "I wouldn't miss my baby girl's big day for the world." He grinned at me like I'd just cast my line far past his off the dock.

I watched Pop pull from the parking lot. His old truck turned onto Route 160 and disappeared into traffic. Where he was bound—a tavern, a poker table, or Carolyn's place—I didn't know.

Home means something different to whomever you ask. Maybe for Dad home was anywhere he could lay his head and shut his eyes for a spell.

———————◆———————

Laura was a beauty dressed in white. Her cheeks blushed a warm pink, and her dark, smoky eyes and lined lashes resembled those of a Hollywood starlet. She was radiant, not the pigtailed girl whose head I'd submerged in a horse trough after she had ran and told Momma I stole four dollars from her pocketbook.

Her small, soft hand folded into mine as I escorted her down the aisle. Flowering citrus trees sweetened the breeze. Dad's absence from the wedding was a surprise to no one. I reckon he didn't cross my mind for more than a bittersweet second.

To steady my trembling hand and calm my nerves, Laura squeezed with a grip and flashed me a smile. Sister Combs played the piano as we walked the carpet to where Charlie anxiously waited under a trellis of yellow roses. When Laura softly kissed my clean-shaven cheek, her wet lip gloss smelled like hard candy.

"Who gives this woman?" the minister asked.

"I do," I answered.

Charlie took Laura's hand into his.

I stepped back and found my place between Mom and Jessie Lee in the front pew. Mom patted my knee, smiling approvingly and then resting her hand on my leg.

For the years that followed, I found reasons to hate Charlie Mull for taking Laura from us, but this day he looked at her like no one had before. He held Laura's hand like something cherished.

Performing the nuptials, Pastor Barnett remarked to the congregation that he was more than amiable to baptizing any of the attending Lutherans after the ceremony. The wedding guests chuckled from the pews, but the joke was lost on Charlie—his eyes never left Laura.

In Veteran's Park, under a canopy of small white twinkling lights, Laura and I counted off our practiced steps on the dance floor. Awkward and clumsy, I stumbled through the rehearsed waltz while Laura seemed to glide across the wooden floor, her smiling almond eyes encouraging me.

Laura and Charlie stood together and toasted under streamers of crepe paper hanging from the trees. Arms intertwined, they sipped from each other's crystal glass. An occasional breeze blew through the reception, causing the white table linens to flap in the wind and sending children running across the park to chase after silver ribbons tied to escaping pastel balloons like the strings of runaway kites.

With his finger Charlie brushed a strand of Laura's hair from her face and kissed her mouth like no one was watching.

The unruly and rambunctious Lutherans outnumbered us Baptists five to one. They laughed too loud and danced like nervous chickens on the rented dance floor. The great silver-haired ladies of our church didn't acknowledge their Lutheran counterparts, who gathered across the way. The two clusters of ancient women stood segregated, huddling on separate ends of the park. The Baptist women looked over at the Lutherans, and the Lutheran ladies looked back at them. They staked their territories like rivaling packs of dogs peeing on opposite sides of the same picket fence. Watching the partying Lutherans, the Sisters of the First Assembly of God shook their heads disapprovingly. They whispered in one another's ears as the "heathens" tipped back cold beers and toasted with glasses of pomegranate wine.

The drunk groomsmen hoisted Charlie and paraded him around on their shoulders. The Lutheran ladies slipped off their dress shoes and, in stocking feet, danced together, swinging and spinning one another across the floor.

Charlie's father, who grinned incessantly, tried to pull Momma out on the dance floor, but she wasn't having any of his nonsense. She shook her finger at his attempts, running behind big ol' Nettie for cover.

Unnerved, Mom whispered to Sister Combs, "These Lutherans don't have enough sense to be unhappy."

The groom's guests partied until the full moon slid up through the pines and balanced atop the highest peak of the San Juans. The Baptist bystanders, who stood judging on the sidelines, chose not to leave the festivities and possibly miss out on any of the Lutherans' drunken debauchery.

A bonfire was stoked to warm cold hands. Beers chilled in big ice buckets, and country music played from the disc jockey's speakers.

The bride and groom slipped away early in Charlie's Buick, heading up to Boulder for a three-day honeymoon. The groomsmen had inflated dozens of condoms and tied them to Charlie's car antenna, fenders, and side mirrors. The church ladies, dismayed by the shenanigans, rushed about the newlyweds' Buick popping the swollen prophylactics with their hairpins.

Before the couple left, I loaded Laura and Charlie's luggage in the trunk. Mom and Laura were hugging near the front of the idling car, crying like two drunken cats. With a firm handshake, I wished Charlie well.

"Zach, get on over here," Laura called out, waving for me to join her and Momma.

Before I had a chance to break free, I was pulled in, locked in the clutches of their long embrace, twisted in their arms as they sobbed on my rented brown jacket. Peach lipstick smudged my collar, and pressed powder dusted my lapels.

It felt right to celebrate for a single beautiful day. Ever since the world had gotten all jacked up, there were too few of those days. Now the three of us had a memory to hold on to.

The wasted groomsmen ignited fireworks, and bottle rockets lit the sky as the newlyweds drove off into the night. Strings of tin cans tied to their bumper trailed close behind, skipping and sparking as they bounced off the black tar pavement.

Jessie and I made our way back to the fading reception. Out of sight of the crowd, I managed to sneak enough of the Lutherans' chilled beer to catch a good buzz. After drinking enough for three grown men, I drank more. Jessie Lee tried hard to manage my drunk disorder.

Toby, dressed in his least filthy shirt and pair of pants, connected with one of Charlie's drunk and horny cousins with round heels from Phoenix. She was a big-boned gal, outweighing Toby by twenty-five pounds.

Toby and the eager and inebriated cousin locked lips during a slow dance. He sucked on her tongue like he was siphoning gasoline through a hose. The messy pair swayed and stumbled on the empty dance floor, the Baptist women looking on in utter repulsion. When the song ended, Toby gave me a wink and assisted his drunk date to the parking lot. Grinning like a possum eating a sweet potato, he loaded the horny Lutheran in his car and sped off.

The party dwindled to a few laughing Lutherans when the DJ announced the final song of the night. Jessie was fed up with my drunk antics and left the reception, catching a ride home with a friend. The last guests found their way out to the parking lot, and the ladies of First Assembly of God shifted into gear. Like some unspoken ancient language or gravitational primal urge, the ladies began clearing the mess. They cleaned tables, folded linens, removed party streamers from the surrounding spruce, and stacked folding chairs. Sister Combs collected the carnation centerpieces from the tables while Sister Pilchard and Sister Ellison stacked plates. Sister Calvert emptied buckets of melting ice onto the dwindling bonfire. The struggling fire popped and sizzled and smoked until the last ember was doused.

Mom roamed the dark park, calling my name, asking around if anyone had seen me.

"I haven't seen hide nor hair of him, Alice," Sister Ellison reported.

"Zachariah," Mom called out into the night. "Where are you, boy?"

She found me just off in the trees, where I was bent over, heaving. My head spun as I struggled not to fall face first in my own vomit.

Momma kneeled down by my side. "Come on, Zach. Time to head home." She wiped the sick off my face with her white-gloved hand. "Time for you to find a pillow." She helped me up and guided me toward the car.

Sloppy and stumbling, I mumbled nonsense and tripped over shadows.

"Son, I worry 'bout you." Her small frame struggled to steady me. "What's going to become of you, Zachariah? You're in my prayers every single night."

The sweet smell of the gardenia corsage pinned to her ivory silk blouse scented the cold night air.

"I'm sorry, Momma. I'm gonna try harder."

We all knew Charlie and Laura's plan was to hightail it out of Durango, but no one expected their departure to happen a mere six months after the nuptials.

Charlie got his promotion with First National Bank, and he was finishing up his last night classes to earn his accounting degree. First National Bank offered up a transfer to him and Laura to relocate to a branch in Sioux Falls, South Dakota, and Charlie jumped.

They invited Mom and me along with Charlie's folks to a fancy dinner at the Palace Station. In the car on the way to the restaurant, Mom and I speculated Laura was going to reveal she was pregnant. But after the announcement that she and Charlie were leaving, all the air was sucked from the dining room. Everyone, including Charlie's folks, looked to Mom to gauge her reaction. She sat small in her chair, wearing a painful smile, like fat ol' Nettie had taken a seat right atop her lap. She raised her glass of tea and toasted Charlie's promotion and then looked in my direction with sad, anxious eyes, as if I could save her from sinking under the table.

On the drive home, Mom remained quiet. Her head turned, watching the passing landscape from her window. I wondered where her thoughts had taken her.

When we made the turn down our street, she abruptly pivoted in her seat, addressing me. "Zach, I've been thinkin', when you go—I mean when you leave Durango—I wanna sell the house. I won't be needing a place so big. I can get me an apartment near Annie, nearer to town."

Stunned by the pronouncement, I turned. Her silver-green eyes were determined, the decision made.

"Mom, what makes you think I'll ever leave you or that I'm planning on moving from Durango?"

She returned to the comfort of silence, reaching to place a hand on my knee.

———

May's cool days were lost to June's summer heat. I woke to Laura's final day with us in Durango. Anxious, I checked and rechecked my wristwatch throughout the morning, half hoping the day would disappear before I could make the trip over to her place. The sun's heat burned the back of my neck while I repaired a roof leak at the Gladdens'. I found reasons to dally in Mrs. Pilchard's rose garden, weeding and fertilizing.

I unloaded some raw lumber at the Walker jobsite and still had most of the late morning to stop by Laura and Charlie's place. Instead I headed over the ridge to Ouray to assemble and install an awning. By afternoon I'd worked up the nerve to make an appearance at the Mulls', worried I'd say something wrong or take the opportunity to slug Charlie square in his fat jaw.

When I drove up to their duplex, the worry knot in my gut was relieved, seeing no sign of Charlie's truck in the drive. Instead Laura's Capri was backed up to the duplex, its doors open and hatchback lifted. A rented U-Haul was parked on the street.

"Hello? Anyone here?" I tapped on the front door, which stood slightly ajar. Poking my head in, I surveyed the place. Most of her furniture was emptied from the front room. Cardboard boxes sat on the bare wood floors with stacks of Laura's books, the pair of singing parakeets perched in their cage, and a few random lamps without shades. Her clothes, still on iron hangers, lay across the kitchen counters.

"Hello! Anyone home?"

"I'm here!" Laura hollered from down the hall. "I'm in the back. Can I help you?"

"Good afternoon, ma'am," I called back in a lower octave. "I wondered if you'd be interested in learning more about the Jehovah's Witnesses faith, if I could steal just a moment of your time."

"No, sorry. I'm not interested, thank you," Laura replied from the back bedroom.

"OK, ma'am. Thank you," I called back to her. "I'll leave the literature at the door."

"That will be fine, thank you."

"Ma'am?" I called to her again.

"Yes?"

"Perhaps I can interest you in a pamphlet on the Church of Latter-day Saints?"

"No, no, no!" Losing her patience, she started down the hall in a huff. She grinned wide when she saw me standing in the open doorway. "You really are the biggest jackass!" She slugged my shoulder with her balled fist.

"Hey, sis."

Hugging my neck, she said, "You really are a piece of work, Zachariah." I liked the way my name sounded coming from her mouth.

"Sis, looks like you've almost emptied the place."

"Yup. We leave out in the morning. Charlie's treating me to a suite at the Strater for tonight, our last night."

"What?" I cocked my head. "Cheap Charlie Mull is springing for a fancy hotel?"

"Stop it," she said. "Little brother, you arrived at the perfect time. Get busy taping and loading those boxes over there." She pointed to the kitchen counters. "Those go in my trunk, and put those in the back of the U-Haul."

"Hey, I didn't come over here to work." She sharpened her look at me. "OK, OK," I relented.

"And be careful with the boxes in the kitchen. They're marked 'fragile' for a reason."

"Oh, these?" I grabbed two delicate china cups on the counter and juggled them in the air. "You want me to be careful with these?"

Laughing, she reached for the flying cups. I threw them higher, just out of her reach.

"Stop playing, and get to work!"

"Jeez, does Mull know he married such a ballbuster?"

"Just get busy, mister."

I loaded cardboard boxes into the rental truck and brought her dresses and blouses out to her car, laying them across her backseat. Within two hours everything my sister owned was boxed and loaded in her Capri or packed in the U-Haul.

Watching her pack the last items, it occurred to me Laura was always braver than I was. She was fearless, setting off thousands of miles to start a life someplace she had never been. She packed a heap of courage in her 114-pound frame.

I recalled a time I'd managed to get Laura, little Kate, and me lost in the belly of an abandoned mine near the cliffs at La Plata Canyon, and Laura was the courageous one. She and Kate followed my lead deeper into the shafts. My dim flashlight was guiding us from one dark, frigid chamber to the next when Katie whimpered, "I'm cold."

Laura spoke up. "It's time to turn around and head back."

All cocksure that I knew the way out, I resisted. My freezing fingertips felt like metal. Katie shivered in the dark, but I continued deeper down. The dim glow of my flashlight was no match against the pitch-black tunnels. I got all crossed up, forgetting which narrow vein could lead us to light.

Laura remained calm. She knew full well I was aimlessly leading us farther into peril. Going deeper into the abyss, from one dark tunnel to the next, the palms of my hands were soaked and my brow beaded wet from fear despite the frigid cold.

Laura gathered her courage and took the lead, pointing her flashlight down the dark tunnel of her choice. Katie and I followed her light. As we grew nearer to the mouth of the mine, a whisper of a cool, fresh breeze blew against our faces. Katie hugged Laura's neck at the first splinter of light.

Now Laura was starting off on her next journey, flying blind. And once again I found myself admiring her courage.

"Little brother." She came up behind me, locking her arms around my waist and laying her head on my back. "Thank you so much. You're a lifesaver. I'm not sure what I'm going to do without you."

We stood shoulder to shoulder, surveying the empty rooms.

"It's all done. I can't believe it." She smiled with a sense of satisfaction. "When Charlie gets home, he'll be in complete shock." She slapped her hands together. "Now I'm going to check in to a hotel suite and order the biggest steak from room service."

"You make sure to charge it on cheap ol' Mull's credit card."

"Why don't you come for a visit? And bring Jessie Lee."

I shrugged my shoulders.

"Uh-oh. Is that over?" She asked.

"Jessie is probably too good for me."

"Yeah, she is." Laura replied.

"Thanks a lot."

"I'm going to miss you, little brother. Promise me you'll call every week."

"Yup" was the singular response I could muster. My chest grew tight. I dismissed a passing urge to hunt down Charlie Mull and give him a good ass whipping. I wanted to unload the rental, unpack all Laura's boxes, and beg her not to leave us and tell her that she was the only sane voice inside my head. I wanted to confess that I was scared shitless and doubted I'd survive with her gone.

"I promise, Zach, we'll be back for Christmas. In the meantime," she said, squaring her shoulders with mine, "you be careful. Don't drink so much. You're not Dad, not by a long shot. You're better than our past."

Just like that her apartment seemed warm, and the room felt smaller. I wanted to squirm away. Recognizing my unease, Laura held my shoulder. "You're gonna be all right, little brother."

"You know, Laura," I replied, "it's taking all my strength to not bust up Charlie Mull for taking you so far away."

———

CHAPTER 11

CHARLIE AND LAURA SET UP house in Sioux Falls. They rented themselves a bungalow in an upper middle class neighborhood. Charlie started his new position at the bank. He cashed a nice paycheck, and Laura vowed to be a lady of leisure. She slept well into the mornings, lunched on salads with the other bankers' wives, shopped at the malls, and was home in time in the afternoon to prepare a home-cooked supper for her man. Charlie loved this new arrangement. He enjoyed this more domesticated version of Laura. But after only a year, Laura complained she was going batshit crazy. Bored out of her mind, she informed Charlie over dinner that she was going back to work. Charlie Mull knew better than to contest. Laura found herself a job in the cosmetics department at Macy's and enrolled in night classes at the community college.

Every morning Laura was at the gym by six o'clock and selling moisturizers and lipsticks from behind the department store counter by ten. Her first night class at the community college started at 4:30 p.m., and after she kissed Charlie good night at ten o'clock she studied her textbooks until midnight at the supper table.

Charlie lost his domesticated wife. The newlyweds ate microwaved dinners on TV trays. Charlie passed his bride in the hallway on the way to her next commitment. If Laura had the occasional weekend off from Macy's, she demanded plump Charlie join her on an afternoon bicycle ride or a hike on a nearby trail.

"He's a total couch potato," she complained. "The only way I can get him off the cushions and outside into the fresh air is if a box of glazed donuts is somehow involved."

One Sunday Laura phoned to tell me Pop had rung up—he was sniffing around for money. Dad's puny and sporadic paychecks never made it as far as his bank account. He squandered his earned pittance on poker tables in Cortez or swallowed it at Claude's Tavern.

With his constant boozing and a tryst with another local married woman, news arrived that Carolyn Beck had finally kicked him to the curb. I saw Dad walking the streets around town like a man with regret tied to his ankle and drowning in a pool of grievances. With his failing health, Dad's options in Durango narrowed.

Every small town has its tragic story, and the Nance family was Durango's whispered sad-luck tale. Katie's tragedy was our legacy, and Dad's roaming the streets, a broke drunkard, kept the tale alive. Our family's fall was etched in hard Colorado clay, and no matter what successes we might enjoy in the future, we'd always be the poor broken folk in the small white house off County Road 250.

Having burnt his bridges in Southwestern Colorado, Dad packed his pickup and moved eight hours north to his brother's barley farm in Sidney, Nebraska. I heard the rumor, through a cousin, that he lived in a mobile home out back of his brother's place.

Dad's story ended for us there.

By the time he left for Sidney, he was a man who had learned all he'd ever know about himself. Soaked in gin, his heart absorbed more bitterness than sweetness. He wore the stinging, rancid bitterness like a medal on his sunken chest. His grievances with God comprised a lengthy list of woes scrawled across his brow like deep-set wrinkles. He believed he had been wronged on every bend of the road and could recite his blasphemous litany by heart to any passing stranger who'd listen while he sat on a bench in the park.

His work shed out back remained untouched, like an abandoned dusty shrine. The old yellow dog moved from his spot off the front porch and took to sleeping at the shed door. Now and again I smelled a familiar scent of an unfiltered cigarette when I sat in Pop's favorite chair, or sometimes the mutt took to barking at the scarecrow fitted in a pair of Dad's old boots and hat. Occasionally, as I drove home in the late afternoons, the setting sun cast moving shadows in the fields like someone coming back to me.

One night the phone rang, and I was greeted by a familiar voice. "Zach?"

"Yes, speaking."

"It's Leland, son." The man cleared his throat. "Is your momma home?"

"Evening, Uncle Leland," I answered. "I hope Bert and the kids are well. No, Mom's out playing canasta. I'm not sure what's keeping her, but I suspect she'll be driving up any time now."

I'd met my uncle on only a few occasions in my youth, but I immediately recognized the voice on the other end of the receiver as that of my Dad's brother.

"We're all doing just fine." Uncle Leland yammered on for a few minutes concerning cousins I knew nothing of. "How's Alice and your sister?"

"Laura got married and moved to North Dakota a few months back," I replied. "I can't keep track of Mom. She stays busy at the church."

"Well, you send them both my love, and give your momma a big hug from me."

I heard a woman's voice calling out in the background. "Hi, Zachariah! Send all my love to Alice Faye."

"Zach, Bert sends her regards to you and your momma."

"Thank you," I replied. "Tell her howdy."

"I'm not sure there's any good way for me to say this, but I've got some grave news concerning your pa." My uncle's voice broke. "Your dad passed on Tuesday."

I slid up on the kitchen counter, pressing the receiver to my ear. I'd buried him a hundred times in my mind, but the news was as heavy as stone.

"I'm not sure if you knew, but I'd set him up in a small trailer out back behind the barn. Bert went out to fetch him for breakfast and found your pa."

"I understand, Leland."

"It appears he passed quietly in the night."

"How did he die?" I asked. "What was the cause?"

"Son, it appears it was a heart attack. The authorities are calling me tomorrow afternoon, and I will call you with more after I speak with them."

"Thank you."

"Zach, your father had mentioned to me he wanted to be cremated if anything ever happened to him. Now, I know that won't sit well with your momma's beliefs, but it was his wish."

"That's just fine. I'll speak with Momma. She'll be fine with your decision," I assured Leland. Cremation was taboo among Baptist folk. I knew Momma's heart would ache with the news. "Just send me the bill, Leland. I'll cover all the costs."

Leland detailed Dad's last several months in Sidney, my uncle's voice hinting that my father hadn't found any more peace in Nebraska than in Durango.

I expressed my gratitude to Uncle Leland for making the tough call. Hanging up the receiver, I turned up the volume on the radio. Neil Young's "After the Gold Rush" played while I sat on the porch and downed a six-pack of Coors.

When Mom returned home later that night, I sat her down on the couch and told her the news. She watched my mouth as I recounted Leland's story of Dad's final days. She studied my face like I was speaking a foreign language she'd never heard but yearned to understand. I watched Mom attempt to formulate a response, trying to gather words carefully, like delicately picking up shards of glass from the floor. Instead she remained silent, her eyes canvassing the room. She fidgeted with the cuffs of her sleeves and smoothed her cotton skirt with both hands.

I waited for something more from Mom, some indication of how the news from Sidney weighed upon her, but she swallowed deep and gathered herself. Standing slowly from the couch, bones stiff from sitting, she walked to the kitchen. I heard running water from the faucet as she filled the basin. After gathering silverware and dishes from the table, she washed them at the sink.

Silence was how Mom greeted disappointment. Like her mother and grandmother before her, she navigated loss in silence, sweeping useless words under the rug. Nowadays folks do so much talking that there's no telling how many wasted words are spoken over a lifetime. Fools and poets compose twisted and tangled words that spill off their tongues like poison or pomegranate wine. Talking through a thing just wasn't Momma's way. Like many times before, she remained at the kitchen sink, drying each chipped plate and placing it in the cupboard. Just out the kitchen window, in the glow of a streetlamp, a breeze corralled autumn's leaves from the cottonwood trees along the picket fence line.

From the couch in the front room, I saw her standing alone as she contemplated Uncle Leland's news. I swear if I spoke one foolish or hurtful word to her, I'd take the sharpest blade to my tongue.

Mom's voice called out too me from the kitchen. "Zachary, in the morning you need to phone your sister and let her know the news from Sidney."

When Laura answered from the other end, I smiled. Her familiar, comforting voice always reminded me of nostalgic warmer days.

"Well, hello, Brother Nance."

"Hello, Sister Nance."

Laughing about nothing special, we reminisced about the wedding, and she updated me on the new house in Sioux Falls. For the briefest moment, I'd forgotten I called with the news from Sidney. As I relayed Uncle Leland's story, Laura remained silent. She finally asked if Dad would be buried in Durango or Nebraska.

"Is Uncle Leland having a memorial or graveside ceremony?"

"No. Laura, Uncle Leland cremated dad's body."

"What?"

I knew she would struggle with the thought of burning Dad's remains to ash. "Laura, it was his wish. Leland said that's what he wanted."

With that, Laura agreed.

"I'm sending money to cover Leland's expenses," I said.

"Yes, of course. Let me know what we owe, Zach."

Our conversation turned to the weather and upcoming holiday travel plans. Any melancholy or aching sadness my sister carried was saved for her private moments.

Before hanging up the receiver, Laura added, "Well, it's done," like something inevitable had come to pass.

Life was like that for Laura. I was always twisted out of shape about one thing or the other, but it seemed my sister came at life more clearheaded. No matter what was thrown her direction, she looked hard at a situation, dealt with it, and filed it away like organizing one of her recipes on three-by-five-inch cards. Practical and precise, life seemed more matter of fact. She never tolerated folly or foolishness, and forgiveness was a hard thing for my sis. Like pushing a mountain across a prairie, Laura wouldn't budge, struggling to find a generous place in her heart for someone who had wronged her. Scriptures be damned, no clemency or reprieve was granted for those who betrayed her. When people crossed her, Laura washed her hands clean of them.

Perhaps that's why, for my sis, Pop was long gone, his name expunged. Years ago he had wronged her, and like tearing a page from one of her notebooks, Laura had tossed him away. It occurred to me that maybe I was the only one who had still been waiting for Dad's return, the only one who searched a crowd for familiar laughter.

———

CHAPTER 12

I DON'T RECALL WHEN I first noticed the old yellow dog had gone missing. When I returned home from work at night, he no longer greeted my pickup. Mom commented she'd seen him barking at a spinning summer dust devil in the pasture a few days earlier. The Ryans, down the street a ways, reported they had fed the mutt table scraps the week before but hadn't seen hide nor hair of him since.

I reckon the old hound dog was always waiting on someone to throw him a tennis ball or for Laura to come outside and tend to her roses. He waited patiently at the screen door for Mom to toss him leftovers from the supper table, or he lay in wait for Pop's truck to make its way down the drive.

For years the school bus had dropped Laura and me off where Trimble Road crossed County Road 250. She and I walked the half mile home, kicking the same rocks we'd kicked the day before. As we approached the gate, the old yellow dog came howling. He'd bark up a storm until he recognized our familiar frames. With the knowing, he turned and headed back to his well-worn spot on the shaded corner of the front porch.

I suppose the mangy mutt had sniffed out every nook and cranny of the house. Spending his days loitering on the porch, he watched us come and go. The dog spent dull, bored, and brilliant days lying in the lawn, observing Dad rake leaves from beneath the giant oak tree. Infrequent bursts of energy had him chasing squirrels up and down the porch's gutter pipes.

When he was just a pup, he explored the narrow crawl space deep beneath the house, reappearing covered in soot, with a field mouse in his teeth. He chased jackrabbits into their burrows, scratching at the hard earth in an attempt to snatch and claim one for his own.

I imagine he recognized the sound of each of our footsteps on the wooden floors. He probably memorized by heart the Scriptures Laura recited aloud while she rested on the front lawn, the mutt nuzzled close to her side. Sitting at Pop's feet, he learned the cadence of Pop's voice reciting his stories.

The old dog savored the familiar aroma of Mom's baked pies drifting on the breeze from an open window. He knew by heart the sweet sound of her singing a favorite hymn as she ironed.

Now, some weeks had passed with no sighting of the mutt. I drove up and down the interstate to see if he'd been hit by a passing car, worried I might drive up on his carcass puffing up along the roadside in the hot afternoon sun. Mom phoned Sister Combs to find out if he was bothering her shepherd bitches.

A few months later, I spotted him. He was wandering along a dirt road near the Walker farm. The long stretch of gravel scissored like a seam across a patchwork quilt of green and gold fields. I was driving east, and the old dog was plodding west along the ditch embankment. His head was dropped low, and his nose dusted the ground, sniffing his way in no particular direction. I slowed my truck and pulled to the side. Reaching over, I opened the passenger door and called for him to hop in. The old mangy mutt looked up just long enough to acknowledge me and then turned, straying between the rows of stalks, disappearing into the Walkers' crop.

I walked to the edge of the field, calling out, searching up and down long, narrow rows of green and yellow. Hopping onto the truck bed, I hollered out, but the old dog never returned. I reckon after Dad left, nothing was keeping him on our porch. Katie was long gone, Laura stolen away to North Dakota, the little house now a quiet, lonely place.

I sat cross-legged on the top of my cab; the sun slipped below the horizon as the acres of corn stalks burned a brilliant copper. I waited there, keeping watch as the fields rolled in front of me like the sea.

CHAPTER 13

———◆———

LATE ONE NIGHT AT CLAUDE'S Tavern, I swallowed scotch by the shot glass and drank enough to pay no mind to the stinging burn of the liquor as it slipped down my throat. I waited on the warm, familiar numbing to course through my veins and infect my blood until the fires burning in my head were doused. Tragically, I was my father's son.

By the time Claude's was closing up, I conjured up the courage to set off on a nine-hour drive to Sidney, Nebraska. At a truck stop in Denver, I rang up my uncle Leland and told him I was heading his way. A hint of daylight warmed the horizon when I crossed the Nebraska state line, twenty miles outside of Sidney. I found his farmhouse in the middle of a quiet barley field. He heard my truck coming up the long, narrow dirt road and met me on the front porch. With a firm handshake, Uncle Leland handed me a black urn that held the ashes of my dad.

"Zach, it sure is nice to see you."

"Good to see you, sir."

"Son, you care for a cup of coffee? Bert has the skillet heated if you'd like a hot meal."

"Much obliged, but I can't stay." I wanted to thank my father's keeper, but his face so resembled Dad's that I just nodded and turned.

I waved from my open window as I drove off, and my uncle smiled a familiar smile. In the rearview mirror, Aunt Bert came from behind the screen door and stood by his side. Their old German shepherd snapped at my tires, chasing my bumper all the way back to the interstate. Barley fields stretched as far as the violet-blue horizon.

As I crossed into Colorado, the black resin urn rested on the passenger seat. With my childhood in my rearview mirror, I confessed to my father that I was a homosexual. I had never mouthed the word. It sounded clumsy and foreign, wrong to my ears. But I didn't need to see my reflection in a glass to know who I was.

We drove over six hundred miles of blacktop together, from the thirsty prairies of Nebraska to the higher grounds of Colorado.

By the time we'd passed the La Plata County line, it was a fading afternoon. I drove to Rainbow Lake and then hiked farther up the Mancos River. The winter's snowpack had been plentiful, so the river was running strong.

I rested in the shade along the riverbank, Pop's urn at my side. The muddy waters of the Mancos had rushed through my father's veins. It was only right that I returned him back to those waters.

I used to believe all Dad ever wanted was a quiet dog and a biting whiskey. All these years later, I think maybe I was wrong.

I made it back to town and went looking for A. J. McCord. I found him at the counter, behind the register. He was checking out Mr. Marshall, who was stocking up on fishing tackle and bait. Stumbling around the shop, with my hands buried deep in my pockets, I kicked imaginary stones. Mumbling, I tried to talk myself out of the mistake of a lifetime, but sometimes life whittles a man's pride down to nothing, leaving just sawdust and shame on the floor. At the counter I stuttered through an invite, asking A. J.

if he wanted to go night fishing on Rainbow. We agreed to meet after he closed up shop.

I sat in my truck while Tammy Wynette sang on the radio. Practicing my lines, I finished off the last of a bottle. Then, at dusk, we met at a clearing near the riverbank.

In the diminishing light of day, I kissed his mouth hard. It caught A. J. off guard, and he stumbled backward. He wiped his mouth off with his shirtsleeve. For the briefest moment, I didn't know if he was going to punch me in the jaw.

"You know I ain't no fucking faggot," he declared.

"Me neither," I answered. "Just the thought makes me sick to my stomach."

A. J. came back at me, grabbing the side of my face and kissing my mouth. His unshaven beard rubbed against my mouth and face. He nibbled along the side of my neck up to my bottom lip. I pulled at his denim jacket, unsnapping the silver buttons and pulling it off his shoulders. He kissed the edges of my ear. His hot breath sent warmth up and down my spine. He kissed me again, this time sticking his thick tongue inside my mouth. My hands reached blindly, searching for the snaps of his Levi's.

We were scared boys rolling in the tall grass, trying to find something real, something true. Pulling off our boots and fighting our shirts over our heads, we groped and fumbled, searching for any way to be closer to each other.

He whispered in my ear, "My dad will cut my throat if he finds out."

I told him my dad was dead and would be floating downstream any second.

A. J. cocked his head, studying me as if I were drunker than I actually was. He then kissed my mouth again and again. We wrestled in the grass until I had him pinned under my weight. I licked his bare chest, moving up to his collarbone. My lips lingered on his neck, and when he was about to speak, I kissed his mouth hard and deep. His saliva was warm and tasted like cinnamon chewing gum. A. J. turned his head out of embarrassment or fear or both. In his telling eyes, I saw he was just a desperate kid.

He bucked, sending me flying off, and took his turn, climbing atop my chest and pinning my shoulders with his knees. He bent down and licked the ridge of my nose.

We wrestled and pulled at the buttons of our jeans. With one hand he slid off my pants, and before I knew it my boxers were off. He tossed them high in the air, and they caught on a low-hanging branch. Pushing me onto my back, he was between my legs, and I was inside his mouth.

His skills gave him away—our encounter wasn't A. J.'s first. He sucked and worked me with his hand until I came with a loud moan. He followed right behind.

We rolled onto our backs, buck naked, laughing at the fading sky. Smiling and content, we lay until the shadows fell and the cold night air chilled our bare skin. A full night sky burst open with stars spilling out before us like diamond dust.

I never ventured back to McCord's hardware store. From that night on, I shoveled my own grub worms from Mom's garden and bought my lumber from Kroeger's. When A. J. and I passed on the street, our eyes never met. Still, twice a week, we found ourselves down at the river.

Somehow A. J.'s grin assured me that one day I'd make it out of Durango. The touch of his calloused fingers on my skin soothed an aching loneliness no one before had calmed.

Once or twice a week, after a day's work, and every Saturday, we met at the riverbank to make love on a blanket in the grass and spend the rest of the late afternoon in each other's company.

A. J. didn't say much. He wasn't comfortable with words, burying them deep, someplace distant, maybe nearer to his momma. For the most part, we maneuvered around each other without wasted words, but he did speak of us buying a piece of land and moving somewhere in the deep of Wyoming or Montana. Together, with our own hands, we'd build a small cabin.

Drinking cold Budweiser along the banks of the Mancos River, we whooped and hollered in the summer sun. Splashing in the rushing water like two crazy wild men. A. J. struck a pose, flexing like a muscleman, standing on a boulder. I whistled, encouraging him. Something brave moved within us. We dreamed impossible dreams. We plotted to steal away and live quiet secret lives far from the world. Farm the land and ignore the familiar gnawing voices and all their expectations.

Our dreams were made of unbridled hope and foolish schemes, but they were ours, dreamed by two men who hadn't before thought to dream big. Until our first day at the river, we hadn't believed it possible to sit in the falling light and dream of a future together. Our plans grew bigger and more elaborate as we mouthed the words. On our weekends deep in the woods, we made love until the afternoon shadows crept closer. All that summer warm winds blew through the tops of the tallest pines, rustling the heaviest boughs, sending pinecones falling to the forest floor. All the woods felt alive, like something running free, something unafraid.

At the end of the day, we talked until we were talked out and then made love until the afternoon shadows found us. I spoke, fast and tirelessly, like I was catching up on all the lost time. If I stopped to catch my breath, A. J. jumped in and expounded on his wish list for us. When nightfall turned chilly, flashlights in hand, we hiked back to our trucks parked at the cattle guard.

I went missing back at the house, working long days and sneaking out after a quick shower and shave. I ignored Jessie Lee's phone calls, putting her off with sorry excuses. I placed her on a shelf until I needed her for some special occasion, like a double date with Toby or dinner with the family. It was only A. J. who occupied my mind.

One afternoon I picked up A. J. north of town, and we drove to the Mesa Verde Anasazi Indian cliff dwellings. A. J. stood waiting for me on the railroad tracks. Hopping in my truck, his eager smile warmed the insides of my chest. We spent the day exploring the red-clay mud huts built into the sheer sandstone cliffs. When there wasn't a tourist in sight, A. J. rested his hand on my shoulder. When I turned to him, he pulled me into his arms and kissed my mouth.

"Are you crazy?"

He kissed me again.

"You're crazy. We're gonna get caught."

With a devil's grin, he went in again. I pushed his chest, freeing my arm from his hold.

"You're a chickenshit." A. J. laughed.

With the sound of tourists entering our clay dwelling, A. J. went quiet. A mother, a father, and three kids squeezed through the tiny passageway and snapped pictures of one another standing in the tight adobe quarters.

We waited until the family moved on, and then I pulled A. J. close. Grabbing a firm hold of both sides of his face, I kissed his warm mouth. "I ain't no chickenshit."

On a warm Saturday afternoon, lying on one of the huge smooth boulders scattered along the bank, A. J.'s shirtless white, freckled chest burned red from an unrelenting hot sun. Drunk on laughter and Coors, A. J. draped his dripping wet T-shirt over his face to protect his eyes from the sun's harsh rays. We wasted the day away, comforted and content to be in each other's company.

"Hey, Zach, I had a dream last night," A. J. announced. "A crazy fucking dream." He lifted the T-shirt from his face, his watery blue eyes squinting in the sun. "There was a blazing fire burnin' out past the Webbs' farm."

"A forest fire?" I asked, running my index finger along his rib cage.

"Naw, more of a big bonfire, like the ones they burn in the Kirby citrus groves to fight the freeze. I dunno, Zach, maybe it was started by a lightning strike from a storm." He scratched his forehead. "So I'm thinkin' it was some kind of sign, some kind of crazy sign."

"A. J., were you drunk?" I laughed.

"Nope, but in my dream we was running toward it. You were there, and we were running as fast as we could. I could feel the heat burnin' my face and the smoke stinging my eyes. No matter how fast we ran, we weren't gettin' no closer."

"Crazy, A. J." I said.

"Yup. It was a big-ass bonfire." He grinned. "I got a hunch it was lit just for us."

I reached over, touching his bare shoulder. "I bet it's so, A. J. I bet it's so."

We lay in the sun, and for the briefest moment we were just two young people in love.

For nearly six months, A. J. and I hid from the rest of the world in the trackless woods, camouflaged under the cover of the forest canopy. We stashed blankets, a few towels, and a battery-operated radio in an old ice cooler hidden in a rotting tree trunk. After A. J. closed the hardware store for the day, he'd bring out bags of chips and a few six-packs of beer. I sneaked out slices of Mom's pie and any table scraps in the fridge.

A. J. scarfed down Mom's home cooking like a starving man. Sitting on a rock in the middle of the river, I watched on as A. J. gorged himself on Mom's leftovers. Butt naked, he devoured a smorgasbord of Mom's fixings sealed in plastic Tupperware bowls spread out in front of him like a king's feast.

"Hey!" I shouted to him across the water. "I'm thinkin' you're just using me for my body and my mom's meatloaf!"

He nodded, grinning with his mouth full of collard greens.

"Yups." He chewed. "If the food stops coming, I'm dumping your ass."

When A. J. spoke of his missing momma, his eyes would dart nervously, and he'd trip on words, trying to convey his life since she had skipped town. At the mere mention of his pop's name, A. J.'s chest would sink, and he'd withdraw to a place I'd never know.

While I labored through workdays, my mind often strayed to our secluded spot by the river. I waited to make love to A. J. in the afternoons, to feel his warm skin under my fingers and kiss his wet, salty mouth.

We discovered each other's bodies—the tiny black hairs on his chest, trailing down the center of his abdomen and below the elastic band of his boxers; the curve of his firm ass where it met the nape of his back.

I suppose our summer provided A. J. a respite, a hiding place far from his jacked-up life, but over the western ridge echoes of booming gunfire from approaching deer hunters seemed to be growing nearer.

One day down at the river, as we lay side by side in the sun, A. J. popped up. "Hey, I got an idea. Let's hike farther up and scale the ramparts."

"Are you crazy?"

"Come on. We can see all of Colorado. My brother said you can see as far as Arizona from up top."

"OK," I agreed. "I'm with you, but you're most likely gonna get us killed."

We set off hiking to the base of the ramparts. As I followed A. J. up the steep cliff, we reached for narrow grips in the tight crevices of the slate wall and worked our way up. Our sneakers found safe footing, hoisting us up farther. We maneuvered in and out of the narrow ridges and scaled the cliffs. When we reached the top, we stood arm in arm, sharing the last of our water.

A. J. claimed his own smooth gray-blue boulder lodged in the earth and suspended out and over the vast Hesperus Valley. Behind him, off in the distance, was a watercolor backdrop of the majestic, rugged snowcaps of the San Juans. As the day dimmed, we rested on top of the world. A tribe of two.

In the moment before dusk gives way to nightfall, he sat perched on his own ledge—shirtless and cross-legged, overlooking the canyon below. I was frightened for A. J.. I knew his old man had a mean streak a country mile wide, and I'd witnessed his worthless brothers in action around town.

I admired him as he sat silent, painted against a dying sky.

Our September turned cold, and like the echoes of rifles firing off in the distance, we understood our naïve dreams of isolated bliss were only the folly of grown men playing a dangerous game.

I began to sense A. J. was less eager when it came time to meet. His enthusiasm waned, and he turned quiet when I wanted him closer. I'm uncertain of the exact moment when we both recognized the endgame was playing out, but A. J. knew well before me.

The more I sensed his letting go, the tighter my grip held on to him. I didn't want our afternoons to end.

I guess I opted to forget what waited back home for A. J. upon his return at night—two redneck brothers and a mean pop. The local chatter was that A. J. was dating a few girls around town, but I told myself it was all a ruse, a diversion to maintain his cover. He was mine.

For those months together, I dropped any pretense. I hardly recognized how brazen I'd become. If the notion had crossed my mind, I would've crop dusted A. J.'s name across the big sky. It was only us—A. J. and me. I didn't care one bit about strutting around town and masquerading with Jessie Lee on my arm to try to hide my tracks. Instead I told myself A. J. and I could beat the cards stacked against us—that his string of random girls would fall away.

One night when he never showed down at the river, I raced home and phoned his place. Mr. McCord picked up, grumbling that A. J. was out with an Ashworth twin.

"When do you expect him back?"

"Dunno, I ain't the boy's keeper," Mr. McCord barked. "Who is this?"

"Zach Nance, sir."

"Uh-huh," he grunted.

"I really need to speak with him."

Mr. McCord sensed the urgency in my panicked voice—a part of me wanted him to hear my desperation.

"Well, like I said, he's of age. I'm not his keeper."

When A. J. didn't show the following day or next afternoon, I sat waiting with a banquet of Mom's leftovers spread out on the quilt. Like a dutiful wife whose husband never shows, I waited alone in the darkening woods, chugging Jack Daniels like it was Mom's sweet tea.

Lost in my own wishful scheming, I never considered the cumbersome weight pressing down on A. J.. I never imagined our afternoons together only made his burdens heavier. It never occurred to me I reminded A. J. of what could never be.

When I lost Dad, in a way his passing lifted a weight off of me. Confirmation of my shameful secret was never whispered in my dad's ear. A. J. wasn't so lucky.

A. J. stopped returning my calls. I drove past the hardware store and looked for his truck in the parking lot.

One afternoon, in passing Mom mentioned seeing a heartbroken Amy Ashworth at church. "My goodness, little Amy was cryin' up a storm today." Standing at the ironing board, Mom reported the church gossip. "Apparently the youngest of those rotten McCord boys broke it off with her. That sweet little girl was absolutely heartsick."

I kept my eyes on the television screen, feigning disinterest.

"Amy said the McCord boy just up and told her he was headin' back to Idaho. Just like that, without so much of a reason. That sweet little girl was absolutely sick."

"That's really too bad." I said.

"Those McCord boys are worthless. Come to find out he's had him a sweetheart back in Boise all the while."

Out of sight of Mom, I came undone. I paced a worried floor like grieving little Amy Ashworth and telephoned A. J. as many times as it took for him to finally take my call. I pleaded for him to see me.

"I promise to be cool." I said into the receiver. "Can't we just talk?"

"Zach, I gotta be careful. I got too much to lose."

The last time I saw A. J., he was loading up his pickup to head back to Idaho. A local Boise girl he'd dated in school was waiting for him, and she made it clear she wouldn't wait long. Her father was a successful construction contractor in Boise. Heading back north promised A. J. full-time work, with the possibility of moving up in her father's company.

Swinging a hammer for a meager wage was the only way A. J. knew to earn a paltry living. Without a high school diploma, the Boise opportunity was something he couldn't let pass. The big new hardware store south of town was tightening the screws on McCord's smaller store, forcing him to close within a year.

Durango was a dead end for A. J.. I suppose he knew that wasting time, walking aimlessly down the streets with his wild older brothers, was just gonna bring nothing but more trouble his way.

When I drove up to A. J.'s house, he stopped loading his pickup long enough to say good-bye. His eyes nervously darting to the payment, he mumbled something about his truck overheating.

Mr. McCord stood watch from the front window. A. J.'s brothers, working under the hood of a Chevy jacked up on cinder blocks, looked on suspiciously.

"Heading back, eh?" I asked, kicking the gravel on the drive.

"Yup. I'm hoping to leave out, make it as far as Oklahoma City tonight and into Boise by Wednesday." He avoided my gaze.

"Good traveling weather."

"Yup." He leaned against the side of his pickup, arms crossed tight to his chest. I struggled to fill the space between us. From A. J.'s expression, I knew he was already long gone from me. His mind was made up and had moved far past us.

"I wish—" Stopping myself, I remembered our onlookers. "I wish you'd said something, A. J., anything."

"I think I told you about Hailie. Sweet girl, real sweet girl. We're gonna see if we can make it work."

I shrugged my shoulders like it made no difference.

"I didn't know." I said. My eyes now couldn't meet his. "I just didn't know." The knowledge I'd become the "clinging girl" who fell too fast and too hard wasn't lost on me.

His eyes finally met mine and held for a second. "Zach, it's something I gotta do. I'm real sorry to bail on ya, but there's nothing for me here—Hailie, she's a real sweet girl."

He nervously adjusted his baseball cap, turning his back to the farmhouse, away from his dad's watching window. The faintest breath of an apology slipped from between his lips. "I'm really sorry, Zach." Then, A. J. wished me well and shook my hand like he was selling me a set of encyclopedias.

To keep him in Colorado a day longer, I wanted to lie and tell him we could beat the odds stacked against us. With balled fists, I wanted to pound my chest like a stronger man and pledge my protection from his mean pop and a jacked-up world. But it was simple foolishness thinking I could keep the wolves at bay. He took one last look at me and said, "I'm so sorry." I wanted more from the boy I loved, but I didn't fault him for not having it to give. We each travel our own road. Like me, A. J. was doing his best to find his way. It's not for me to say if his road to Boise was a shortcut or a dead end.

———————

CHAPTER 14

FOR THE LONGEST WHILE AFTER A. J. left for Boise, I escaped an aching loneliness by recalling our late afternoons by the river. In my despair I conjured up a sweeter story than what had truly been. Like Dad's far-reaching storytelling, I created in my mind a grand romance, one in which sweet confessions of love were traded instead of the foolish, clumsy words uttered riverside. In my gin-soaked dreams, I dreamed A. J. came back to me. Both the dreams and the gin sustained me. It was easier just to stay numb.

The tall glass bottle became an extension of my right hand, perfectly fitting in my palm. My fingers easily gripped its neck. Like reading braille, I memorized every smooth bend and ridge of the clear bottle. Familiar and comforting, it was like holding tight to someone's hand.

Laboring through long weeks, swinging a hammer or pushing a mower, I lost myself in my work. From dawn to dusk, I kept my head down and my nose to the grindstone. The stench of sweat and gin bled from my pores.

Jessie Lee phoned the house hunting my whereabouts, but in the evenings I hung in the garage, tweaking my mower's engine, or I'd drive up Route 160 and sit in my pickup, listening to the radio, overlooking La Plata Canyon.

When Jessie discovered I'd gotten tanked and messed with a scrawny waitress at the Narrow Gauge Train Depot Café, she arrived at one of my jobs in a fitful fury.

I was out back, breaking hard sod with a pickax, trenching footings for a brick barbecue, when Jessie Lee's Mustang tore up the drive. She got out, slammed the car door, and stomped up the sidewalk.

"Zach Nance, you're a son of a bitch!"

"Jess, what's wrong, hon?"

She pumped her fist in the palm of her hand like a nervous boxer. "You know damn well what's wrong."

Eavesdropping homeowners stirred inside, hanging near the back door.

"Baby, just settle down. Take a breath, and tell me what all this fuss is about."

"I know about you and Courtney."

"Baby, now that's just foolishness."

"Are you gonna stand here and lie to my face? Really, Zach?" Her index finger wagging at my nose, she wailed on me for thirty minutes, not stopping for a breath.

I picked through a litany of comforting words to stop her bleeding. "Baby, it ain't true. That's just people talking trash." I reached for her. "I love you, babe."

Jessie pulled away, searching my eyes, looking for something that wasn't there.

Truth and lies were easily interchangeable in my mind. I no longer could distinguish the difference.

I don't remember much of Jessie's rant that afternoon, but I recall her eyes—big, round hazel eyes welling with tears. Her angry words spilled like poison, and her gestures were rife with rage, but Jessie's eyes streamed wet with hurt and disappointment. With one hand planted on her hip and the other up in my face, she cursed like one of the foul McCord brothers. As quickly as she reached the peak of her anger, she fell into silence. Her pained expression burned into my memory. I knew how hard she had tried to make sense of my hopeless case.

"Zach, I've forgiven you all these times because I loved you. I'd heard the stories around town, but it didn't matter one whit because I thought I knew who you really were. When it was just you and me." Stopping herself, Jessie inhaled and gathered her composure. "I put up with all the drinking and all the bullshit because somewhere I saw a sweet boy. But you're no better than any of the other guys round town. You're as rotten as all the rest of them." Jessie Lee looked at me one final time and shook her head. "I thought I saw somewhere in all that bullshit a really sweet boy." She turned and walked back up to her car. She sped out the gravel drive and onto Junction Street. What Jessie Lee didn't understand was all I'd ever wanted to be was like the rest of the guys.

———

Mom worried I was putting in too many hours on the job. She complained I looked gaunt and was losing weight. Laura's concerned weekly phone calls warned that if I didn't get my act together, she was ready to step in and take hold of my predicament.

In her letters she forwarded the names of a few Christian singles social groups in Farmington and Grand Junction, attempting to put me on the road of the straight and narrow.

"You just need to meet a nice girl. That's all you need, little brother," she explained on the phone. "You need a good Christian girl who won't put up with your BS and will kick your butt into shape."

Standing at the kitchen sink, washing the last of the dinner plates, Mom reminded me of the new blue-eyed second-grade teacher recently hired over at the elementary school, earlier in September.

"Zachariah, I'll invite her over for pot roast and peach cobbler."

I grinned at her suggestion but shook my head. "Mom, I don't need your help in that department."

I didn't have the heart to tell her that Toby had quipped about the new teacher, "She's fallen from the ugly tree and hit every branch on her way down."

"Zach, you go out and get yourself a haircut and a new shirt at J. C. Penney, and I'll invite her over," Mom insisted.

"Nope, ain't happening."

Mom poured a cup of black coffee. "I won't go sticking my nose in places where it don't belong, but young ladies deserve respect. I don't claim to know what transpired between you and Jessie Lee, but I got my hunch I'd come down on her side of the matter."

"Yes, ma'am."

CHAPTER 15

—————

DRIVING RIGHT DOWN THE CENTER of Main Street, the convoy of rusted trucks and trailers loaded with crated amusement park rides announced the arrival of the La Plata County Fair. Just off the interstate, near the rodeo arena, the weary traveling carnies parked their rigs in an empty field next to Veteran's Park.

Waking well before dawn on a Wednesday morning, by Thursday night the crew had hastily constructed its own small town. It was a poor man's Disneyland with its plywood arcades, roller coasters, spinning contraptions, and giant Ferris wheel rising high above the pines.

Fried-food booths, candy apple stands, and fresh-squeezed lemonade offerings lined the midway. Strings of blinking lights were strung high in the trees, randomly flashing along the ticket booths that ran the perimeter of the fairground. A line of blue aluminum porta-potties created a makeshift divide between the fair's festivities and the small community of the carnies' camping trailers.

Every night for two weeks, a long trail of headlights slowly progressed down Interstate 160. Parked in line and at attention, cars and trucks filled the open fields surrounding the fairground. Folks from as far away as Grand Junction made the drive to take spins on a carnival wheel or taste the vendors' fried delicacies.

Led Zeppelin wailed from the stereo speakers, and tiny multicolor lights blinked along the spinning rides and rows of arcades. From their booths, toothless carnies called out to passing pushing crowds. Locals wore oversize sweaters and denim jackets to keep snug and warm against the brisk autumn Colorado night. Teenage boys battled arcade games to win stuffed animals, prized by their doting girlfriends. Giddy children ran through the crowds with caramel apples and pink piles of cotton candy. Older couples strolled with steaming-hot chocolate and black coffee in Styrofoam cups.

The first time I saw Dwight, he sat on a metal stool at the entrance of the bumper cars. Standing in the long line, I watched him as he took coupons from anxious teenagers. He was hunky and handsome, and his baseball cap sat backward on his head. He was a broad-chested, blond-haired, freckle-faced schemer. His squared-off jaw flexed when he smiled. His frayed blue jeans and muddy white sneakers were torn from the pages of *Huckleberry Finn*. When he laughed out loud, a thick vein on the side of his neck ran all the way down past his shirt collar.

I watched as Dwight measured the height of a little boy with a straight, stiff back pushed up against the measuring post. While Dwight confirmed the little rider's height, he still winked, working the swooning teenage girls waiting in line.

He was twenty-two years old when I first saw him taking coupons for the bumper cars. His broad, bulky torso was perched atop a small rusted swivel stool as he counted out the heads of the appropriate amount of riders for the next round. After collecting the tickets, he pressed a red plastic button to activate the cars. Rod Stewart's "Maggie May" played at deafening decibels. The brightly painted bumper cars followed the course around the track. Ornery boys plotted their targets, and screaming pretty girls waited for inevitable impact, like a crash 'em derby.

By the time I met Dwight, he'd already logged more miles than I'd ever see in my lifetime. Zigzagging back and forth through the Midwest, he carried in the back pocket of his worn denims more street smarts than I would ever understand.

His thick thighs and bulging biceps lifted small kids into the bumper cars. He strutted around the track, checking each rider's seat belt. His big arms reached over the drivers, tugging on their belt straps. Smudged black with oil from tweaking the cars' motors, his soiled orange Alabama State jersey had his name written across the back in bold script. Wiping his big hands on the front of his shirt, he tipped his baseball cap to a young blushing mother after pulling the rope to restart her stalled car.

Dwight's breath smelled of cigarettes and his clothes of perspiration, but his deliberate grin and strong physique attracted repeat riders in line for the bumper cars. Young women and boys like me kept coming back for another round on the track just to watch the charming, muscle-bound carny.

Even after my third trip in the long line, Dwight never gave a hint I was on his radar. He took my ticket and tossed it into the bucket without the slightest pause.

Later that night, as I roamed the rows of arcade booths looking for Toby and some friends, I spotted Dwight watching me as he leaned against a picnic table. A glowing orange cigarette burned between his thick, dirty fingers.

When he gestured for me to come over, I flushed hot and tried to steady my pulse. I stuffed my damp hands deep down in my pockets and walked in his direction.

"Hey, dude, how's it goin'?" he greeted me with a nod.

"Good, you?"

"Doing OK. It's colder than fuck here. I just spent two weeks in Phoenix workin' a rodeo, and I was able to catch rays on my days off. Now I'm freezing my balls off." He flipped his cigarette and rubbed his hands together, blowing hot air between his palms to warm them. "Is it always this fucking cold here?"

"Yeah, pretty much. It doesn't start warming up for another month or so."

"You still in school?" he asked.

"Naw." I kicked the ground with my tennis shoes. "Where are you from?"

"Kansas. You born here?" he asked.

"Yup, born and raised right here in Durango."

"Shit, no kidding?" He laughed.

"Yup. It's not too bad. Lots of great skiing," I said, although I couldn't remember the last time I'd fought the congestion of tourists on the slopes of Purgatory.

Shooting the shit with Dwight, I tried not to sound like a simple punk from another sleepy town, but Dwight was on to me. The more I spoke, the more ignorant I seemed.

He said he was from the two stoplight town of Parsons, Kansas. He boasted he had been a local high school football star. Within five minutes I knew that Dwight had figured out how to work his small-town assets. His wide, boyish grin and easy Southern flirting seemed casual and harmless enough, but his skills were practiced and honed. He worked the brawny country-boy gimmick. His dirty-blond buzz-cropped military hair, his powerful body, and his gruff and unkempt facial scruff all appeared unplanned, almost accidental, but it was all ammunition, part of his prowess. He understood the strategically unshaven shadow emphasized his strong jawline. None of it was a fluke. He knew how and when to flex his forearm and bicep when he opened the gate, letting impatient riders scatter and search for their perfect-colored bumper cars. There wasn't a single hair primped or a T-shirt pressed—he appeared to be a homegrown, rugged country boy, unaware of his own beauty. All of this, of course, made Dwight even more handsome—but because he was fully aware of his effect, it made him even more dangerous.

He felt the heat of his admirers' watching eyes. He sensed their lustful gazes. Their longing and admiration were his rewards for an orchestrated, well-played game.

Dwight said during the last semester of his senior year, he had taken to the road. Three months before high school graduation, he hatched a plan to hitchhike his way to Southern California. Dwight had never laid eyes on the Pacific Ocean, but after a few listens to The Beach Boys' *Endless Summer* on his eight-track player, the country bumpkin determined to be a professional surfer.

Dwight said the day he left home, his momma threw a frying skillet at him from the front porch, cursing his name as he sauntered down the long road leading to the interstate. He stopped long enough to wave to his pa, who sat in the garage. His old man looked up from sniffing spray paint to nod a final good-bye.

With all of his possessions packed on his back, Dwight thumbed it to Kansas City, where he bussed tables at a diner. After two weeks of washing dishes and clearing tables, he said he met a thirty-six-year-old divorcee who was passing through town. Her straw-brittle bleach-blond hair was teased and sprayed stiff. Teal eye shadow covered her lids, and heavy makeup painted her pitted skin. She scratched out a living following the state and county fair circuits, pulling an aluminum corn dog stand on wheels behind her Oldsmobile. Her home was a different hotel room for three-week stints until she packed up her wieners and moved on to the next carnival or rodeo.

After getting tossed around by Dwight back in her hotel room, the next morning she made room for him and his backpack in her wagon. Together they tracked across the Midwest, working the fair circuit.

Dwight said she stood all day over a steaming deep fryer in the cramped metal food trailer, where the bleach-blonde sold corn dogs, greeted passersby, and filled condiment tubs. Later, when the bright lights of the carnival dimmed, she returned to a dingy hotel room where Dwight waited. Without ceremony he climbed on top of her and gave her a bumpy but thrilling ride that rivaled the carnival's roller coaster.

During their encounters by the light of a glowing television, with the handsome young man on top of her, she could forget for the briefest of moments the cruel ex-husband back in Tacoma and her three babies she'd left in his care.

Never the fool, Dwight understood the trade-off. While the divorcee's skin smelled of burnt grease and she was older than Dwight preferred, he knew with each passing rodeo and carnival he was getting ever closer to the California coast.

In the meantime, she provided Dwight with a warm bed and as many corn dogs as he could stomach.

Dwight said that at a gig outside Oklahoma City, when hard rains and a tornado warning closed the county fair, the divorcee unexpectedly walked into the motel room. Dwight said she found him mounting the pretty son of a local farmer. After a few beer bottles and a handful of curse words were thrown across the room, she packed up her corn dogs in the Oldsmobile and left for Omaha without her brawny Southern boy toy. Dwight said he hopped in another carny's pickup and continued working the carnival and fair circuit throughout the Midwest.

"What kind of work you in?" Dwight asked.

"Carpentry—I build houses," I answered, conveniently omitting that I also mowed lawns and fertilized petunias. "How 'bout you?"

"A few scouts from Kansas State wanted me to play ball, but I passed. Just wanted to take some time off to travel the country."

"Are your folks still back in Kansas?"

"Yes sirree, my folks own half of Parsons." He conjured up lies as he spoke. "My old man struck it rich. That old son of a bitch has money to burn."

"Nice," I replied.

He lit another cigarette and offered me a drag. "He's a good guy, my pops," he said. "I swear to God, if he sees a homeless bum, he'll open up his wallet right there on the street and hand him a fifty note."

"Do ya make decent money working these fairs?" I asked.

"Shit no. The old geezer that runs this outfit is so fucking cheap—like tryin' to squeeze shit from a hummingbird." Dwight drew from his cig and checked me out, eyeing me from the soles of my shoes up to my chest. "You work out?" He motioned to my arms. "You look strong."

"Naw. I need to get back in the gym. But you're built, dude," I said.

"These?" Dwight flexed his guns, grinning with pride. His biceps popped on command. "I hit the gym when I can." He held his pose until some admiring girls passed by and whistled. He winked in their direction.

"Damn, it's cold," Dwight complained. "So you planning on living here forever?"

"No, I'm thinking about Tucson or Los Angeles…maybe, one day."

"Fuck yeah!" He slapped my palm with his. "Me too, dude. I'm heading to California. I've been traveling for three years, doing this same ol' shit. When I'm finished, I'm California bound. I'm gonna get me a sweet trailer and park it right on the beach and do nothing all day but work out and surf."

"Sounds cool."

"So you gotta chick? Something regular?"

"A few of 'em. Nothin' regular." I shrugged my shoulders.

"The chicks in these small towns just ain't cuttin' it. They're the same everywhere." Dwight rolled his eyes. "I'm over it."

"Yeah, I hear ya."

"It's easy to get laid, but after you fuck 'em, they hang round. They're all over you like flies on shit. You know what I mean?"

"Yup," I replied.

"You got your own place?" he asked.

"Naw, still livin' with my folks."

Dwight snickered. "I gotta piss so bad my eyeballs are floatin'. You wanna take a walk?" He motioned with a nod.

Shaking in my boots, but feeling the urgency of wanting to know what could happen next, I replied, "Sure."

"Come on, what do you say we get out of here?" The devil's charm reflected in his eye, but I was drunk enough to follow his lead. "Come on, dude, I know of a place." Dwight led, and I walked a step behind.

Making our way through the crowds and away from the flashing colored lights, I followed him into a collection of trash Dumpsters and small storage trailers. The perimeter was fenced in by chain-link. The two of us disappeared behind the gate and into the shadows.

"You wanna do this?" He motioned to his crotch.

I dropped to my knees and unbelted his jeans. In the dark I pulled at his Levi's buttons until finally his pants dropped to his ankles. My hands held on to the backs of his hairy thighs. I felt raised chill bumps running up and down his skin. He pushed himself deeper into my throat.

"Easy, boy, watch the teeth." He pumped harder and faster, his hands maneuvering my head. With a series of thrusts, he came, his body quivering under my fingertips.

Sitting on the grass at Dwight's feet, I tried not to admire his physique as he pulled up his boxers and belted his jeans.

"What's your name, kid?" he asked, offering me a cigarette from the pack of Lucky Strikes.

"Zach. Zach Nance."

Dwight reached down and, with the tips of his fingers, brushed my hair back off my face. "Hello, Zach Nance." He joined me on the ground, and we sat cross-legged on the grass.

He gave me a rundown on how he'd ended up here, exaggerating his hitchhiking adventures. I couldn't begin to match his tall tales, so I let him do the storytelling. I was still waiting for life to happen. He was already on the road living his.

When Dwight invited me back the next night and the night after that, I felt like a silly schoolgirl, flattered the popular boy liked me. On the final night of the fair, we stumbled in the dark like two drunken sailors, walking over Bankord Bridge and into Veteran's Park, a sliver of a moon lighting our path. Autumn's brittle leaves covered the ground and crumbled under our tennis shoes. We walked until we found ourselves alone. The park was still and silent except for the slowly rocking swings that swayed in a chilling November wind.

Dwight was moving on in the morning with the caravan of trucks and trailers. No promises were made that he'd phone or send postcards from his next stop. He didn't pledge to swing back around town on his way to a nearby rodeo or local carnival. Any conversations about him and me crossing paths again were only those in my imagination. Instead, on our last night we howled at the moon, drank cold Budweiser, and walked, brushing shoulders.

We came upon the stone bench dedicated to Sister Pilchard for her donation to the Durango Garden Society. Dwight stopped on the path and kissed my mouth. He pulled his sweatshirt over his head and tossed it in the grass. He kicked off his sneakers and bent me over the cold bench. I heard the unfastening of his belt, and he reached around for the snaps on my Levi's. He tugged at my pants, pulling them down around my knees. For a moment I protested, but without a word Dwight slowly slid himself inside me. I bit down on my bottom lip and struggled under his weight.

"You OK?" Dwight's hot breath whispered on my neck as he slowly pumped. "Just relax, and you'll enjoy it." He moaned, pulling my hips into his abdomen.

When Bledsoe's blinding pickup headlights flashed, I struggled to free myself. The old truck was parked forty feet away in the gravel parking lot, its high beams directed straight at us. Exposed, I turned my face as he flashed his brights again and then again and then again. I frantically pulled up my pants, trying to shield my face from the glaring light. Dwight stood in place, covering his eyes from the blinding beams.

I recognized Bledsoe's voice from inside the cab. "You boys get out of this park right now!"

I turned from the light and ran for the shadows of a nearby giant pecan tree. Dwight stood his ground, unflinching, his pants still down around his ankles. His erect penis pointed due north as he barked, "Hey, man, could ya turn off those fuckin' lights?" Shaking his head, he added, "I can't see a fucking thing."

"You heard me. You perverts clear out of this park right now," Brother Bledsoe demanded in a stern voice I'd heard when Toby and I rode our bikes across his yard, crushing his geraniums.

Impatient with the blinding light of the high beams, Dwight slowly and deliberately lifted his right arm and extended his bird finger toward Bledsoe's parked Dodge. He stood in the glare of the headlights, flipping off the voyeur behind the windshield.

I poked my head out from around the tree to steal a glimpse of the truck.

"Is that you, Zachariah?" Homer yelled from his truck.

I pulled back behind the tree and swallowed hard. A cold terror ran through my blood. Saying nothing, I stood motionless, quiet as the grave, my back pressed hard against the trunk of the old pecan tree. Warm beads of sweat gathered along my hairline, and my pulse pounded like thunder in my ears. The tree trunk's dry, brittle bark broke in my grip like burnt toast.

"Zach?" His voice hung in the air like a cold breath. "Zachariah Nance?"

I waited.

"Speak up, boy," he called out again and laid on his horn. "You boys get your faggot asses out of this park before I go fetch the police!"

Silence filled the dark park, and Dwight stood in place, framed in the bright light.

The ignition turned, and the truck's diesel engine coughed and spit, idling in place. But Dwight stood firm, his middle finger as erect as his proud cock.

I remained hidden in the shadow of the giant naked tree.

"You boys are plain filthy," he yelled from the darkness of the truck's cab. "It's an abomination against God. Disgustin'."

Dwight stood like stone before the spotlight, his bird finger aimed at the idling truck. "Fuck you," Dwight called out to the driver. "How long did you sit there watching us, you fucking old pervert?" Laughing, he shook his head and finally sat on the park bench. He lit a cig and stared unapologetically at the pickup.

My back stayed pressed against the tree. I whispered, "Shut up. Please, shut up." I pleaded with Dwight from my shadowy shelter. "He'll leave if you just shut up!"

The truck's headlights dimmed, and the gears engaged. The tires slowly rolled over crushed gravel. "Zach, your momma's heart would break," Brother Bledsoe called to me. "Son, it's a sin against nature. You gotta get right with God."

Covering my ears, I smothered his voice. Hating his words. Hating my sin.

The pickup pulled out from the parking lot, and the red tail-lights disappeared toward town.

The two of us were alone again in the dark. The burning end of his cigarette illuminated Dwight's face. He examined the night sky blanketed with stars. Even in my panic, in the glow of a low-hanging moon, I couldn't deny he was as handsome as any man had the right.

I remained paralyzed behind the tree. "It's over," I murmured, dropping my head into the palms of my hands. "It's all over." I rocked against the twisted trunk. "I'm as good as dead."

"Dude, you're just freaking out. Don't sweat it." Pinching the cigarette between his thumb and forefinger, Dwight took another drag. "Fuck 'em." He shook his head, continuing to search the night sky like he was looking for someone who never shows. "That old geezer was most likely yankin' it, sitting in his truck, watchin' us."

A panic grew larger and larger in my chest. Belting my pants, a sudden need to vomit invaded my throat. I bent over, heaving.

"Hey, man. You OK?" He came to my side.

"You, you don't understand," I stammered.

"Dude, it ain't no one's gawd-damned business. No small-minded asshole is gonna tell me nothing about my life and how I'm gonna live it."

"We shouldn't have been here, right out in plain sight." I wiped my mouth with my forearm.

"You really think that's what that old fucker's problem is with us? Man, we could be on the far side of the fucking moon, and he and his likes would still be bellyachin'. They don't want us nowhere."

"I gotta get out of here," I said.

Stumbling blindly in the dark, I left Dwight there. Running toward the strains of the music of the fair, I headed to my parked car. I heard Dwight call out behind me, but my pace turned into a full run. His voice was replaced by sounds of spinning, screaming teenagers and laughing children.

By the time I found my truck in the rows of parked cars, I was out of breath and broken into a million pieces. Waves of anxiety and exhaustion caused my muscles to go weak. I tried steadying my trembling limbs but with no relief. Sweat soaked my collar and chilled my skin in the night air. Panicked and desperate to run, I searched my pockets for my key ring and scrambled to unlock the truck with a violently shaking hand.

I sped through the parking lot and onto the interstate. My mind raced, trying to remember a place I could hide in a town where everyone knew every hiding place.

I never saw Dwight again. I never knew what became of the devilishly handsome boy from Parsons, Kansas. Even now, on sleepless nights, lying alone in my bed, I still see him standing in the blinding high beams of Brother Bledsoe's old Dodge. I remember him as clearly as any memory. While Brother Bledsoe's words will always ring in my ears, it's my memory of Dwight, fearless and unashamed, that burns brightest.

On those nights, staring up at the ceiling, covered in moving shadows like passing storm clouds, I wonder where Dwight is. To this day I carry a secret wish that he is surfing the crashing California waves somewhere along the Pacific Coast.

Years later, when I lived alone in Los Angeles and a night's sleep was hard to find, I would recall the image of Dwight standing in defiance of Cecil Bledsoe. During those same sleepless nights, I wished I loved Jesus Christ the way my mom did. I wished he were easier to find in the night sky. For me, anyway, Dwight standing there with his middle finger aimed directly between the eyes of Mr. Bledsoe's judgment was the closest thing to any God I'd ever seen.

With nowhere to run, I headed back home. Arriving in town, I found Durango sleeping soundly. Glowing streetlamps lit my way as I drove aimlessly through familiar streets I knew as well as the lines crisscrossing my open palms.

I drove up Thirteenth Avenue, which was lined with Victorians and their wraparound porches and stained-glass windows. Widow Pilchard's giant yellow gingerbread mansion was dark. The hedges and sculpted topiaries lining her sidewalks were wrapped in white cloths that protected them from night freeze.

I headed to the vacant high school, where a lone deer grazed on the frozen tundra of the abandoned baseball field. The six-point buck stood motionless, his nose to the air. He watched my truck approach and then turned his attention back to the grass. Turning onto Route 160, I blew my horn when I saw Saul Custer, working in the dark at the empty train depot, prepping for the rush of tourists later that morning. Saul had found work with the Narrow Gauge, loading up the clean dishes, polished silverware, food crates, and supplies into the first-class and dining cars.

The Durango of my childhood was disappearing brick by brick. McDonald's and Burger King and other fast-food joints lined the streets. Every passing month developers broke ground on a new hotel, office complex, or shopping plaza.

Night was lifting, and a hint of dawn arrived on the horizon. Rows of economy hotels with glowing-red neon "No Vacancy" signs lit Main Street. Cars with rental agency insignias on their back plates lined the curbs. Avid skiers, bicyclists, and hikers had discovered the San Juans; now the mountain trails and backwoods were more theirs than mine.

Traveling twenty miles on Route 160, I made the right turn at Hesperus, heading down to the Echo Basin Pass, following Dad's same route with little Kate years ago. When I reached the bend in the road where Dad's truck had drifted into the oncoming lane, I pulled off to the side. A bloated blue moon lit my path down the steep embankment. I found a rock jutting from the earth and overlooking Echo Basin valley.

I suppose a braver man would've pulled out my father's pistol buried beneath my seat and saved his family the public shame or perhaps left town in the cover of night. Instead I reached for the bottle of gin lying on the floorboard.

I reckon courage burns like a fire, fast and hot, finally burning itself out and then slipping away like an extinguished flame.

The gin sufficiently numbed my senses. I stumbled up the embankment to my pickup. Turning the truck around, I headed home. The morning sun rose above the peaks of the San Juans, shedding gold light into the deepest, narrowest part of the canyon.

When I woke the next morning, the house was no longer mine. I was a stranger in its rooms. From that night on, Mom and I lived separate lives in separate places.

My ear pressed to the thin walls of my room, I listened for her path on the floorboards. As she walked through rooms, I waited, opting for an opposite route to avoid a chance meeting.

Every morning I loaded my truck at the first hint of light and left the coffee percolating as I drove off for a long day's work. When I returned home well after the sun had set behind the San Juans, a hot dinner waited for me in the oven. Mom would be off to Bible class or playing canasta with the ladies. Sister Combs had recently fallen ill, and Mom spent nights at her bedside, nursing her back to health.

Mom and I traveled through awkward table conversations without any destinations. When the telephone rang on the kitchen wall, I strained to hear her responses, trying to decipher who was calling and what news he or she brought. On a few occasions while I watched TV in the front room, the phone rang, and Mom's voice turned to a whisper. Standing in the kitchen with the phone pressed to her ear, she turned her back and spoke in hushed tones. My mind raced. A swelling panic rose from my chest, which only a stiff drink could calm.

If Mom knew the ugly details, she never breathed a word. I wondered if Homer had told his wife what he'd seen in the park and if Sister Bledsoe had made the call to Momma. If she knew, certainly my silence was a confession. My cat-and-mouse disappearing act around the house was clear confirmation of my guilt.

There was no mistaking that the filthy particulars had made the rounds. The local gossip traveled like a wildfire. While I sat in the coffee shop, snickers from the worthless McCord brothers confirmed my fear.

"You sure look pretty today, Zach." The oldest brother smirked as they passed me at the counter.

I felt condemning eye shots around town. At the bowling alley I discovered, crudely scrawled on a metal partition in the guy's restroom, "Nance is a fucking faggot." Wearing my shame like a heavy blanket, I dodged passing glances. Walking in my dad's footprints around Durango, head hung low, I opted for the darkness of Claude's Tavern.

One afternoon, while waiting at a traffic light with my lawnmower and hedger in tow, I was heading off to tend to Mrs. Calvert's lawn when a fat-necked boy from the county baseball league hollered over to me from the open window of his Camaro.

"Hey, Nance! I heard you were with a dude playing a night game of catch over at the park."

His buddy in the passenger seat yelled, "I always thought you were a pitcher, Nance. Never knew you were a catcher!"

Tempted to silence the assholes and pump them full of lead with bullets from Pop's gun right between their eyes, I bit down on the back of my jaw until the fury subsided.

The two smirked, tearing out when the signal turned green.

"Fuck you!" I yelled at the disappearing taillights. "You fucking assholes!"

I sat fuming at the green traffic light in my idling truck until the cars behind honked their horns.

The next Sunday morning, Mom called up the stairs.

"Zach, it's time to go!" she hollered. "You ready for church? We're gonna be late."

I'd been up since sunrise, lying on my back, staring at the cracks in the plaster. I heard Mom first stirring downstairs—the fridge door closing, the smell of frying bacon drifting up the stairs.

"Zach, come along," Mom called from the kitchen. "The skillet's still hot if you want scrambled eggs."

I smothered my head under the pillow and buried myself beneath blankets.

"We're gonna be late, Zachariah," she called out again.

"Mom, I think I got a stomach bug. You go on without me."

Her footsteps traveled up the wooden treads. "That nasty bug is goin' around." She tapped at my door. "Can I get you somethin' before I leave? Maybe some warm soup?"

"Naw." I covered myself deeper in quilts.

"I keep tellin' you, you're workin' too hard, son. A body can do only so much, and then it gets tuckered out."

"I know, Mom, but I gotta strike when the iron is hot."

"You must slow down. You gotta let your bones rest up." Her church heels clicked back down the stairs.

The front door shut, and her Chrysler headed out the drive.

The following Sunday I managed to oversleep for church service. The Sunday after that, I lied when I said I needed to work at the Gauers' place.

"Sorry, Mom." I passed her in the kitchen. "I gotta get their patio deck finished before their big party next weekend."

"Pastor Barnett asked why he hasn't seen you in the pews." She shook her head disapprovingly. "Actually you didn't miss nothin' much. His sermon was as dry and unsatisfying as a slice of Betty's lemon cake."

I missed church the next month of Sundays before Mom finally stopped calling up the steps. At supper she no longer briefed me on the latest church gossip.

Some nine months later, I was constructing a new trellis for Sister Pilchard's rosebushes when she walked out the screen door onto her porch.

"Good morning, Zachariah. Isn't it a crying shame about Homer?" Betty sipped from a tall glass of iced tea. "I don't know what sweet Nettie is gonna do without him."

I looked up from my work with a lost expression.

"Your momma didn't say nothing?"

"No, ma'am."

"Yessum. He passed yesterday morning." Sister Pilchard sheltered her eyes from the late afternoon sun. "He was tending to his garden and just dropped like a stone, right there in his tomato vines. God bless his sweet soul."

"I hope Sister Bledsoe is well," I offered.

"Nettie is mighty tore up. Bless her heart. They were married fifty-three years. Homer was a good, decent man."

"Yes, ma'am. That's a shame."

"He was a God-fearing man, and the likes of those are hard to come by these days."

"Yes, he was," I added. "And he pitched a fine game of horseshoes."

Sister Pilchard strolled along her wraparound porch like a Southern belle surveying the cotton pickers out working the plantation. Blooming wisteria traveled along the picket railings and up the columns and dripped from the fascia. She sipped her tea with a slice of lemon and examined each wire basket of blossoming flowers that hung along the porch's perimeter. "His and Nettie's love was one for the ages." She plucked wilted petunia petals from the hanging baskets. "I suppose everything beautiful is destined to fall away."

I'd lost Betty to her thoughts as she meandered along the porch.

Adjusting my baseball cap, I said, "Have a nice afternoon, Mrs. Pilchard."

On the morning of Brother Bledsoe's funeral, Mom left the house wearing a black knit dress and a small black pillbox hat atop her head. Strung around her neck was a familiar string of white simulated pearls. The same necklace Dad had placed in a purple velvet box under the Christmas tree years earlier. When Mom found his gift under the lowest bough of our tree, she opened the velvet box and squealed. "Oh, Lloyd, you really shouldn't have."

He draped the strand around her neck and pinched the fastener closed. Then Pop stretched his arms around Mom's waist as she admired herself in the mirror on the foyer wall. Momma and we kids believed the plastic pearls in the purple velvet box were the most beautiful thing we'd ever seen.

On her way out the front door for the funeral service, we crossed in the narrow hallway. Mom nervously fingered the smooth pearls as she slipped by me.

"I'm heading out for a bit," she said.

"OK, Mom, sounds good."

CHAPTER 16

———◆———

I RECKON SAUL CUSTER WAS the hardest-working man I've ever known. He and Dad shared the common belief that hard work soothed a man's troubled soul like prayer nurtured a woman's worried heart.

When I saw him at the depot, he was loading crates of dishes into the dining cars of the Narrow Gauge. I watched him for a time from across the way on Main Street as he lifted the heavy aluminum crates into the train cars, prepping for the morning's ride up to Silverton. He was dressed in the green vest and starched white shirt of all the train's crew. Nodding and smiling at passing tourists, he went about his work. I shouted his way and he looked up from his clipboard and gave me a wide grin.

When he waved me over, I noticed his beard and scalp had sprouted light patches of silver hair. Still, he wore the wide grin of a young man.

"How is Loretta? The girls?" I extended my hand, but Saul pulled me into his chest, wrapping his arms around my shoulders.

"Everyone's just fine. Loretta keeps me on a short leash." He laughed. "How is life treating you? How's your momma and sister?"

"Good. Real good."

"I need to take me a break," he said. "I'm too old to be out here breaking my back." We sat on a wooden bench outside the depot's entry.

"You look good, son. Life must be agreeing with you." He unrolled the edges of a paper bag and opened it, surveying his packed lunch. "We'd love to see you at the house. I heard Laura went off and married the Mull boy." He reached in and pulled out a big red McIntosh apple from the bag and polished it on his shirtsleeve.

"Yes, sir. They moved to South Dakota."

"South Dakota? Goodness! I bet your momma had plenty to say about that." He chuckled. With a pocketknife he carved the fruit clean of its skin. The crisp red peel coiled down to the ground around his work boots.

"And you're still swinging a hammer? I see your work round town. Nice. Lloyd would be pleased."

"Thank you."

"You behaving yourself?"

"Aw, I'm thinkin' about moving to Los Angeles," I announced. "It's time for me to head out and try somethin' new."

"I suppose most young men want to spread their wings. It's the nature of things."

Shaking my head, I said, "I'm goin' nowhere here, Saul. I am gonna end up just like Dad, some worthless piece walkin' the streets."

"Son, there's not a man who doesn't have his failings, but that don't mean he's not worthy." Saul chewed a piece of the apple. "It was wrong as rain what Lloyd went off and did. He'll surely answer for it. But a man shouldn't be judged solely for his worst days."

"Well, I gotta get out of this town, or I'll end up just like him. Durango is closing in around me. Everything has gone all haywire."

"Everyone's gotta go find someplace to call home. I suppose I traveled most of the world before I settled in one place."

"I messed up, Saul. I fucked up, and people are talking."

"I wouldn't put too much weight on that. People are always talking about something or the other."

"I fucked up real bad."

Saul scratched his forehead. "Yup, it happens sometimes. It don't mean you just throw in the towel."

"I gotta try someplace different. Maybe my luck will change. I don't fit here anymore."

"Just don't run for the sake of running. That don't help no one. And son, there's nothing good comes from livin' life in dark places. You'd best not listen to those folks talking trash." He took a drink from his silver Thermos. "I'm a Bible-believing man, but folks go about quotin' Scriptures between every breath—they live their lives believing God has their backs, like the Almighty himself is watchin' them from up above." Saul cut into the meat of the apple. "From way up where the Lord is sitting, I'm guessing we're no more than ants scattered on the ground." Saul chuckled to himself and handed me a slice of the apple from the edge of the rusted knife blade. "I'm not saying a strong faith don't help good folk get through hard times, but the way I see it, the Holy Ghost don't owe nobody nothin'. He ain't got the time nor gumption to lend a helping hand to every critter that roams this here earth. You gotta make your own self happy."

Saul and I sat in silence while I tried to form any response.

"Did you get drawn for your elk or deer hunting permits this season?" he asked me.

"Naw. It seems only out-of-state folks get drawn. You?"

"Mrs. Custer has determined it's best that I retire my rifle. It appears last season's buck will be my last."

We laughed.

"Yup, I believe I saw you the season before last down by the Mancos River, when I was tracking an eight-point. I came up on you and the McCord boy enjoying some peace and quiet. It looked mighty tranquil. I didn't want to interrupt you two on such a fine day."

My mouth went dry.

"Zach, for the likes of me I can't see no shame in love." Saul didn't hesitate. "It's beyond my reckoning why there's such a dustup about such matters. If things would've worked out different for your folks, I'm certain Lloyd would've struggled with the knowing, but I suspect he'd eventually come round. And the way I see it, even Alice Faye, after all her Bible-thumpin', would've seen the light."

A rapid pulse thumped in my ears like a marching band's repeating drum. The urge to run like hell was my first inclination, but blood rushed from my limbs and left me limp. I crossed my arms, gripping my fists out of Saul's sight, trying to bring back any sensation to my numb hands. The train's morning whistle sounded, sending a riot of fluttering sparrows from the canopies of the giant elms that stood single file beside the depot. In unison the birds took flight low across the sky.

"It's gonna work out, Zach, just as it should. No need to go worrying yourself. You'll end up with gray hair, like this old man." He brushed his hand over his salt-and-pepper scalp. "Well, I best get back to work." Saul stood, extending his hand. "Son, you gotta make your own way."

I shook Mr. Custer's hand.

"If you're driving through, you make sure to stop in. Loretta and the girls would love to see ya. She'll slice you a big piece of rhubarb pie."

———

Someone had struck a match. A hurried camper perhaps neglected the last embers of a dying campfire, or maybe a stray bolt of summer lightning ignited a lone tree, but something lit the canyons of La Plata ablaze.

An unforgiving July left the forest parched. Brittle scrub brush and thirsty trees were bone-dry kindle. Twenty-five miles north, up the tracks to Silverton, the San Juan National Forest burned for eight days straight, uncontrolled and uncontained, burning the old Newberry Bridge and causing the Narrow Gauge to stay parked in its depot for an extended spell.

Momma watched from her kitchen window as ominous gray plumes of smoke bloomed in the northern sky. White ash fell on the house, covering the roof like a chalky summer rain. Firefighters fought day and night in the steep terrain. Airmen dropped red sheets of dust over the land. The warm, wicked wind whipped through the valley like God's breath stoking the flames. An unforgiving wall of fire advanced, scorching everything in its path.

On a late afternoon, Momma walked out the screen door and onto the porch, surveying the approaching fire. She found me sitting on the stoop. I sensed an uncertainty, determining if she'd turn back into the house. Holding the door an undecided second too long before letting it swing closed behind her. She came out and sat on her rocker next to me.

"This wind ain't helping matters," I said, watching the firefighters battle the blaze to the north. Copper, gold, and red reached for the blackened sky as flames consumed the groves of towering spruce. Heavy rolls of billowing smoke formed the likeness of some angry beast churning above Engineer Mountain.

Throughout the afternoon the blaze burned through the fire stops south of Silverton, jumping the lines at Purgatory, moving over the crest of the ski slopes and sweeping down into the valley toward Durango.

The radio in the kitchen window announced that state officials determined to draw a battle line fifteen miles outside of town, just on the other side of Baker's Bridge.

"The poor folks north of the fire line are plain out of luck," Momma commented.

In the distance, hilltop log mansions and sprawling vacation homes built high among the trees, nestled in the granite cliffs, were one after the next consumed in flames. They were reduced to empty, burnt-out carcasses with only spooled box springs for innards and twisted, melted copper arteries surviving the devastation. The same homes where I'd planted rows of geraniums and marigolds in flower boxes earlier that spring were all lost.

One by one propane tanks from brick barbecues and stone fire pits, some constructed by my own hands, exploded and rang out like booming gunshots. The blackened mountains were left barren and smoldering.

Mom and I sat silently watching from the front porch as the gray day dimmed. At dusk, like fireworks on the Fourth, the beautiful devastation decorated the night sky.

"I heard from Jim at the station that the ski lifts were all lost."

From her rocker, Momma spoke. "God's reclaiming what is rightfully his." She sipped coffee from a chipped mug.

"Momma, that's crazy."

A warm wind carried a silky soot that covered our clothes and skin. I rubbed the tips of my fingers together, and the ash was smooth and soft, like a pair of Momma's white church gloves slipped over my hands.

"You really think God would do something like this?"

Momma rocked to and fro. "Yessum. I reckon he struck the match."

Early the next morning, the sound of Mom going about her morning filtered upstairs, coffee percolating and the washer churning a load of whites.

"Praise the Lord!" she rejoiced. "The TV says the fire is eight percent contained. And it looks like we could see rain by Tuesday. Thank you, sweet Jesus."

By 8:00 a.m. she was driving off toward town to spend the day at the side of grieving Nettie. "I'll be back later this evening, after Bible study."

"OK. Give Nettie a big bear hug from me."

Deciding to stay around the house all day, I started up the mower and tended to the yard. Throughout the morning and into the afternoon, I kept watch for Mom's car to turn off Trimble.

By 6:45 p.m. the lawn was mowed, the planting beds fertilized and weeded. Two rows of dwarf myrtle hedges were trimmed into shape, and I sculpted Laura's wild rose trees into perfect spheres. Managing to sand down the peeling front shutters and two window boxes, I painted them a pale summer yellow. WD-40 and a few tightened screws silenced the screen door's weeping. Starting last summer our sad, tilting metal mailbox, erected near the street, had begun a slow journey toward the ground. After one sack of quickset concrete at its base, the aluminum box once again stood straight at attention.

I was painting the last white porch pickets when Mom drove up the drive. From her car window, she surveyed the house and yard and cranked down the car glass. "My goodness, Zach. I cannot believe it."

"What do ya think?" I spread my arms open to the yard.

"What has gotten into you? Did the Spirit move you?"

"You like?" I asked as I opened her car door.

"Yes sirree." She stepped from the carport and walked out front, admiring the freshly painted shutters.

"The paint is still tacky, Mom."

"I just can't believe it. Look at that!" She pointed to the rose trees, which resembled rows of lollipops.

"I figured it was time this place got some TLC."

"My goodness, you've been busy, Zach." She walked onto the porch. "It looks real nice."

"The yellow on the shutters is the same color you admired over at Betty's."

"Yes, real pretty." She sniffed the rosemary in the flower boxes. "Can you fetch the groceries out of the trunk? And there's a bucket of chicken in the backseat for supper."

My arms loaded with brown grocery bags and a tub of chicken, I pushed open the hushed screen door with my shoulder, letting Mom pass.

"Son, this was a mighty nice surprise."

At the table, Mom and I ate fried chicken straight from the cardboard bucket.

"Goodness, I was starvin'!" She licked grease from her fingertips. "Nedra brought her meatloaf casserole." Mom twisted her nose like she'd whiffed a ripe skunk. "Lord, mercy, there wasn't an edible bite on that entire table." Mom went digging in the bucket of chicken, searching for a leg. "I came home famished."

"No good, eh?"

"Just awful! Bless Nedra's heart, but that poor woman should steer clear of a kitchen." Mom sipped her iced tea. "One day she's gonna poison poor ol' Carl. Just you wait. One day it will happen." She was shaking her head with certainty as she wiped her greasy hands on a cup towel. She walked over and surveyed the fridge's contents. "I know there's a slice of pie somewhere in here."

"Momma, I'm thinking about heading out to California."

"California?" Searching behind the milk carton for the missing pie platter, she asked again, "California?"

"Yup. I'm gonna try it out there, see if I can find some good work."

"Are you sure, son?" Looking over her shoulder, she checked my expression to gauge if I was serious. "I'd imagine a soul could get mighty lost in such a place. Annie has a sister in Riverside. Remember, we met her last spring? I can ask if you could stay at her place for a spell."

"No, I'm thinking about Los Angeles. I hear there's a lot of big work, and I think I want to try livin' near the ocean."

Sensing my determination and the real possibility I was leaving, Mom grew concerned. "There's earthquakes, remember the earthquakes. I read that one day the whole of California will break clean off and drop right into the sea."

"It's time. I gotta try something new. I'm not going anywhere here. I'm pushing a damn lawn mower."

She waited.

"I'm havin' a real hard time thinking 'bout leaving you."

"That's just foolishness. I'll be fine. I want what's best for you kids. You can't live your life for me. You go find your own place in this world. I'll be right here." She folded her hand over mine.

I felt a knot tightening in my throat. "Momma, it's only a two-hour flight. I can be on a plane and back home in no time at all."

I ached to say more but covered my mouth, smothering useless words.

"Zach," she said, grabbing a hold of my wrist, "it's been so hard for so long."

"Momma—"

She hushed me with a look.

"You and Laura shouldn't have been burdened. God will strike Lloyd and I down for doin' what we did to our children."

"Mom, if it hadn't been for you, if you hadn't stayed strong, there wouldn't have been a home."

"It was wrong what Lloyd and I did—" She stopped herself before confessing regrets stored neatly out of sight. "If you need to go and find a new life, then that's just what you gotta do. Go find a nice girl in California, and start your own family. I'll be fine, just fine."

"I've saved up some money." I pulled a roll of green bills from my pants pocket and placed it in front of her. "Here's almost eighteen hundred dollars, and I'll send more as soon as I get a place and start working."

"Zachariah, that's your money."

"Mom—"

"No, no, no," she blunted me. "I get my Social Security check every month and got my own money put away." She pushed the cash back at me.

"Momma, take it. I'm thinking about heading out at the end of the month. I'm going to take a drive and check it out. Are you going to be all right?"

"Babe, I'm not made of glass. I'm not some fragile doll sitting on a mantel. You and your sister treat me like I'm something easily broken. Now, you promise me you're gonna be careful. And I'm beggin'—you gotta get this devil off your back. It's no way to live. The bottle leads down a path that is thick with trouble. That's your father's legacy and his father's before him. It doesn't have to be your burden to carry. Whatever's got you by the throat, you best get it right with God."

CHAPTER 17

———◆———

"ZACHARIAH, YOU GOTTA TIE THAT down better." Mom pointed with her scrawny index finger, barking out instructions like an army sergeant from the stoop of the porch. "Run that rope up through the blue case, and tie it down. That piece of luggage is gonna come loose and fly right out of your truck in the middle of some California freeway and kill Burt Reynolds."

I looked over my shoulder, trying to suppress a smirk. "Mom, I got this."

My two lawn mowers, hedge clippers, a few shovels, and racks were strapped down in the pickup bed. I'd crated most of Pop's tools from the shed and packed my own hardware store on wheels. Saws, routers, and belt sanders were locked in metal chests. Screwdrivers, crescent wrenches, and claw hammers were organized in four separate red toolboxes.

"You gotta run the rope up through the handle and clear over to the furthest toolbox."

"I know, Momma, I know."

She watched on nervously while I loaded the last of my luggage.

In an ice cooler, she'd frozen a month's worth of home-cooked food: barbecue ribs, meatloaf, pot roast, chili, and preserves. "You need to stop every few hours and keep everything iced."

"Yes, ma'am."

When it was finally time to depart, she stood at my truck window, reached in, and squeezed my neck.

"Zachariah, now you be careful. No speeding." She cupped my chin with her hand. "And you know you can always come back home if LA isn't to your liking."

"OK." I smiled. "As soon as I get situated, I'll fly you out and take you to Disneyland."

"Lordy, no! You'll do no such thing."

"Come on, Momma. You never know—you may like it!"

"We'll see. We'll see. Now, baby, you head out." She swatted in the air, signaling for me to move along. "And if you see Mr. Kirk Douglas, get me his autograph."

Driving out, I honked my horn, waving like some kid leaving for summer camp. "Love ya!"

"Babe, call me as soon as you get there. Be safe!"

From my rearview mirror, I watched Momma waving at the fence line until I turned onto Trimble Road.

CHAPTER 18

———◆———

THERE IS A PLACE IN the woods I remember—a path, overgrown and shaded beneath a canopy of pines, a wilderness strangled in thorned thistle, lost from sunlight and time. A whisper of a morning mist lingers like invading smoke, wrapping its way low through the groves of trees. Morning rain is collected in pools on the palm of every upturned leaf and flower. And there in the deepest burrow, below rock and mud, I buried my faith and my father's gun, left to rust and be forgotten.

CHAPTER 19

—◆—

IT WAS THE SUMMER OF 1976 when I started out to California.
Fleetwood Mac and the Eagles were on constant radio rotation.
Stevie Nicks serenaded me as I sped down Interstate 10 from
Phoenix to Los Angeles.

The Arizona deserts were wide, flat expanses of rock, dust,
and sand. For miles and miles of barren desert, only sparse vegeta-
tion sprouted from the thirsty earth. Crossing over the California
state line, it seemed the landscape had been sculpted by the strong
Santa Ana winds. The constant gusts created rows of dunes with
long ridges in the sand, as if God's own giant fingerprints pressed
into the desert floor.

The sweltering sun burned hotter than the one I'd grown under. It scorched the earth and sky white like parchment paper. My
left arm toasted, resting in the open window, and blistered a bright
spotty pink.

The freeway exits for Blythe, Indio, Palm Springs, and
Riverside whizzed past. Sailing west along Interstate 10, Jackson
Browne sang "Running on Empty." I arrived at the outskirts of Los
Angeles County, and stacked freeways widened as the countless
cars moved in and out of lanes like drunken derby drivers at the
Cortez racetrack.

Pasadena was my destination. Toby's sister, Renee, had told me about Hotel Oasis. A tiny one-room second-floor studio at the Hotel Oasis would be my new home.

I finally arrived in LA, where downtown's tall, slender high-rises rose from the center of the valley. Spiraling towers ascended into the blue sky like giant mirrored glass and steel trophies. I drove down into the San Bernardino Valley and detoured on the 405, exiting east on Santa Monica Boulevard, north toward West Hollywood.

West Hollywood was the gay district in LA, a four-square-mile suburb north of the city. I'd read a travel guide before leaving home that described the area as the "gay-friendly" part of Los Angeles.

Santa Monica Boulevard was the main artery pulsing through the West Hollywood district, a single busy street populated with clothing stores, restaurants, bars, and nightclubs. Before leaving Durango I'd imagined I'd enter a sun-drenched Sodom and Gomorrah section with a tall cinder block fence confining the entire perimeter of West Hollywood, like a gay penitentiary. I visualized raging rampant sin behind the brick wall—sodomites on the loose, hanging from tree branches and jumping nude from the bushes; heathens wearing dresses, diamond tiaras, or leather harnesses; men openly fornicating in the streets.

When I arrived to the district it was much different from what I had imagined. No restrictive fence enclosed its perimeters. The boulevard was lined with slender palm trees, glass-front boutiques, and open cafés. The area was void of my dire predictions, but most notably it was void of women—there were only men, thousands of gay men.

Behind the cover of dark sunglasses, I cruised Santa Monica Boulevard, trying to take in all the guys who were out and about. A potluck of men, some shirtless, jogged along the sidewalks, walked hand in hand, and rode bikes in the warm sun. Smiling and laughing, some sat on the patios of small bistros.

Yet even more enticing than the smorgasbord of guys were the never-ending rows of lush green lawns in the residential areas. Wide expanses of thick, manicured carpets of smooth-cut grass stretched as far as the eye could see—Tiff, Bermuda, rye, dichondra yards, and Saint Augustine—sprawling lawns needing weekly mowing, fertilizing, and hedging. Streets of bungalows, hilltop mansions, stacked condos, office parks, and shopping malls all had meticulously manicured lawns and stuffed flower beds that spilled over with geraniums, petunias, roses, and marigolds.

With no discernible change of seasons, expansive grass lawns perpetually grew under constant sun. Acres of blooming flowers and shrubs colored year-round, requiring planting and fertilizing.

Leaving West Hollywood, I traveled on to Pasadena, visions of piles of green money in my head and hot men in my arms. Every passing lawn was another bank deposit into my account, and every handsome guy was my next potential conquest.

Hotel Oasis looked nothing like its color bifold brochure. Pulling into the parking lot, I chuckled when I first laid eyes on my new home away from home.

Desperately in need of paint, the peeling apartment complex was well on its way to a state of total decay. Weeds sprouted between the cracks in the black pavement. A few loose shutters hung by their last screws. The long green-canvas awning announcing the establishment's name—OASIS VILLAS—in big gold letters was faded and ripped at the seams.

My studio apartment consisted of a tiny kitchenette with white painted cabinets and avocado Formica counters. An old sofa bed was against the wall opposite a single window overlooking the parking lot. In one corner a thrift-store television with two long, skinny antenna ears sat atop a wooden chest. Lying on my back in the center of the laminated floor, arms stretched over my head, my fingertips and big toes could reach wall to wall.

The bathroom was no more than a tiled shoe box, with a porcelain toilet, pedestal sink, and shower stall. A single white string attached to a bare lightbulb in the ceiling hung over a cracked vanity mirror. My broad shoulders barely fit into the tiny Plexiglas shower enclosure. Occasional hot water was a gift on some mornings, but an icy-cold shower greeted me most days.

With Dad's work ethic pulsing through my veins, I didn't waste any time. I drove through every parking lot in Pasadena, Azusa, and Glendale to place flyers with my name and number proudly printed in bold type. The never-ending rows of parked cars were easy pickings. I tagged every windshield wiper with a Xeroxed ad Laura had designed for me:

~Nance's Lawn Care Service~

One-stop shopping for all your lawn maintenance
and handyman needs

By the time I walked into the door of my apartment, my phone was ringing. I booked my first maintenance job, marking it on a calendar that hung from a magnet on the front of the fridge. The phone continued to ring. I returned home many nights to find a full voice recorder.

For five months straight, I pushed my mower from sunrise to sunset. At night I ate bowls of Frosted Flakes or ramen noodles. When I had extra cash in my pocket, I ordered takeout from the

Chinese restaurant on Cordova. I was able to send Mom $380 after my first four weeks on the job.

While placing flyers on car windshields in a hardware store parking lot, I met two Mexican laborers from Guadalajara. They were soliciting day work. Rodrigo and Juan were skilled masons who built cinder block fences and red brick patios around the Pasadena area. Having no reliable transportation and speaking virtually no English, the pair began working alongside me. Gesturing with our hands or using a pencil and pad, we managed to communicate. I had a pickup truck and enough ambition to keep us busy.

I picked up Juan and Rodrigo every morning on the corner of South Oak Knoll and California Boulevard in the 7-Eleven parking lot. The two hopped in the cab of my truck at sunrise, and we headed off for a day of pushing mowers, trimming hedges, and scaling palm trees until dusk.

The longer and harder we labored, the more calls waited on my voice recorder when I arrived home at night. The more work I booked, the more brothers, cousins, and nephews Rodrigo and Juan produced to work alongside us.

I had two full-time crews within four months. After buying a second pickup from a used-car lot on Glen Oaks Boulevard, I scheduled the boys all over the city.

Rodrigo's wife, Zulema, was a legal citizen and held a legitimate driver's license, so she drove the second truck for my crew. While the guys worked the lawns, Zulema sold her homemade burritos to passersby at the nearest congested intersection.

At night, when I was alone in my apartment, the voices on the television were my only company. Homesick, I wrote letters to Mom and included a check once a month.

I planned my Sunday evening around Laura's weekly phone call. The ring sounded at 6:00 p.m. every Sunday. My dinner was prepared by 5:45 p.m., and I was at the table when her call arrived promptly at six. With the phone receiver pressed at my ear, Laura updated me on her night classes and church activities. Excited for their upcoming trip to Paris in the fall, she and Charlie anxiously awaited the arrival of their passports in the mail.

"Charlie and I will be the first Nance or Mull to ever stand on the Eiffel Tower," she proudly declared.

"Sis, just get yourself home safe."

I was kept fully abreast of life back home during Mom's phone calls. High school friends and congregation members quizzed her on my marital status and the righteous condition of my soul. It seemed folks in Durango believed the entirety of the state of California consisted solely of Hollywood, the Castro District, and Disneyland. They spoke as if only raving queers, famous movie actors, and Mickey Mouse roamed the streets. Momma stayed in a constant state of worry. She concluded each telephone conversation insisting I cease sending money.

"Son, you don't know the value of a dollar," she protested.

"Business is good. I'm putting money away."

"I'm telling you now," she said, "I'll tear up your next envelope that comes in the mailbox. You need to hang on to your hard-earned money."

Still, the checks continued to be cashed, and in passing conversation, Mom mentioned that she'd gone shopping at J. C. Penney and bought herself a new dress or earrings or a pair of church shoes. I wanted her to have what she needed and more.

Mom boasted of her new pumps. "They are so pretty, Zachariah. As red and shiny as a candy apple. Betty is pea-green with jealousy."

On my occasional day off, or on the rare rain-soaked Southern California day, I explored LA's streets, traveling on the wide highways and cruising the winding boulevards. I came to know the layout of Los Angeles like I knew the familiar streets of Durango. Upon my arrival in LA, the sprawling city had seemed insurmountable. The zigzagging freeways and highways were head-spinning. Now I zipped in and out of the streets and boulevards like I had the hiking trails of the San Juans. I maneuvered through the suburbs, chartered my own shortcut routes, and entered and exited the freeways with ease.

The more I traveled the city, the clearer it became to me that with all of its wealth and excess, Los Angeles was void of any soul. Commerce and pretense powered the mighty machine. The towering high-rises stood in the stacked skyline like slender glass steeples. The millions of mirrored windows reflected color in the sun like stained glass. Cars, trucks, and buses started and stopped at a combustible pace. Congested crowds pushed forward, moving and circling but going nowhere.

At night the rapid pace momentarily idled long enough to refuel. Wannabe starlets and prostitutes, whose lips were painted the color of blood, walked the boulevards. Long black limousines stretched along the most stylish and trendy eateries and nightclubs. Come morning the crowded sidewalks pulsed again with suits, ties, and briefcases. Women as slender as scarecrows wore designer dresses, carrying shopping bags in and out of massive shopping malls. These wealthy ladies walked along ritzy Rodeo Drive with their skin pulled as tight as revival tents stretched from tree limbs. They spied their reflections in storefront windows, looking for signs of imperfections and lost youth.

Back in Durango folks honored the sanctity of marriage, vowing to stay married and miserable for eternity. In LA, husbands and wives were traded like marbles on a schoolyard. The children residing in the upscale houses where I maintained the front lawns had never washed a dish or pushed a mower in their short entitled lives. These kids sported expensive haircuts and tennis shoes and drove cars I could only dream of.

God had forsaken this land like he'd abandoned me. With all of the city's material abundance, I saw not one hint of a soul.

In a letter to Mom, I wrote that one night I had found myself lost in the streets of South Central Los Angeles. I'd crisscrossed the wrong dark street and came upon the city's underbelly—skid row, where the lost and damaged collected on sidewalks and in dark alleyways. Pretty, sad young girls walked with dirty bare feet in a city where hundred-dollar designer high heels were bought and sold like nickel candy in the Durango grocery. I told Mom I'd never seen such a pitiful place. People were lying about like yesterday's newspaper, scattered under trees and sleeping in cardboard boxes. They appeared to be thrown out and discarded, with abandoned, hollow eyes and hungry, twisted mouths. It was the first time since arriving in Los Angeles that I recognized the face of God.

When Momma received my letter in the mailbox, she wasted no time picking up the phone, worried sick, fretting about my safety. "Son, you have to watch yourself. Don't go lookin' for trouble that's not lookin' for you. And remember, if you're drinking, it's not too far of a fall to find yourself on those same dead-end streets."

"Mom, I swear, I'm behaving. When I'm not working, I'm in the gym. I'm steering clear of trouble."

A leery silence answered back.

"Why don't you let me fly you out here?" I asked. I'll take you to tour the movie studios and to Disneyland."

"No, no, no. My tomatoes are ripening. Disneyland will have to wait. In the meantime, you keep your nose clean. You understand?"

"Yes, ma'am."

Mom spent her days with the ladies. She and Annie Combs still worked alongside each other at the school. It brought a grin to my face, imagining the two ladies serving lasagna, their majestic bouffants captured beneath the nylon hairnets required by the La Plata County Health Department.

"The school administrator called Annie into his office," Momma reported, "and asked her to ease up on the lipstick, but she paid him no never mind. It only aggravated her, and the next day Annie showed up smeared with a scandalous red lipstick that would make a hooker blush," she finished. "I just don't think Annie's right in the head."

At church services Mom bragged to the ladies about her two successful children. She managed to work into every conversation that her daughter was a banker's wife and her son was a Hollywood landscaper to the stars. She paraded around church with the expensive leather purse I'd purchased for her birthday. She flaunted to Betty Pilchard the new pearl necklace I'd sent for Christmas.

"Betty's pearls don't have the luster of my strand," Mom announced. "I'm guessing hers may not be of the same quality."

I suspected the other ladies were tiring of her boasting. She and Sister Combs got in a spat when Momma compared her new winter wool coat with Annie's older well-worn fleece. I reminded Mom that Bible Scriptures warned the flames of hell were destined for those who were boastful.

"Hush up, Zach," she snapped. "I wasn't boasting. I was truth-telling."

With each delivered package postmarked from California, I sensed it brought Momma joy, so I fueled the fires of hell and sent more expensive gifts from the high-end boutiques of Hollywood, imagining her glee with the arrival of boxes at her door stoop.

A letter from home:

Dear Zachariah,

Hello, son. I woke up missing you this morning. I hope all is well in Hollywood. I felt the first winter wind last night. The cold is on its way. God and winter's arrival are the only two things you can rely on. The leaves have turned, and all the surrounding mountains are pretty as a picture.

Last week Toby came around inquiring how you were doing. He's engaged to one of the Marshall girls. I'm praying his approaching nuptials will entice that boy to take a shower.

Nettie isn't feeling well. The doctors have a close eye on her. God bless her. Her feet have swollen up to the size of cantaloupes.

The elementary school is back in session, and I swear these children are getting more rotten with every passing year. Annie and I were serving lunch when three brats threw tater tots clear over at Annie and me from across the cafeteria. Crazy Annie tried to catch the flying taters with her open mouth. Of course that just egged on the little monsters. Lord knows Annie doesn't have a lick of sense. If I'd had a sapling switch, I would've taken a few hard swipes at those little heathens' back ends.

Speaking of brats, your sister has turned into quite the Miss Bossy Pants. She got sassy with me over the phone last night. She believes I shouldn't drive after nightfall. Who in the cat hair does she think she is? I told her to tend to her own concerns. I really believe I spared the rod too often with you kids. I hope to see you this Thanksgiving. Thank you for the pretty bracelet and the blender. You shouldn't have.

I love you,
Mom

———◆———

In January of 1977, the headlines across the front page of the *Los Angeles Times* announced that President Jimmy Carter had pardoned all Vietnam War draft evaders. The bold type also reported that scientists in a laboratory had successfully identified the bacterium of Legionnaire's disease. On that same morning, on the phone, Mom reported the breaking news from Durango. Little Tara Stutsman was crowned queen at the Miss La Plata County Beauty Pageant. Her a cappella rendition of "Afternoon Delight" during the talent competition and her ample C-cup bosoms tipped the judges' votes in her favor.

Momma also conveyed the precise details of a big ruckus on Main Street. It seemed after a prayer meeting, Mom and several of the Sisters were strolling along the sidewalk, window-shopping. As the ladies perused the shops, they handed out tiny red pocket Bibles to passing strangers. When Clyde, the homeless bum who regularly slept on the curb outside of Ricky's Ice Cream Parlor, reached out and touched Sister Combs's bare ankle, Annie's blood-curdling scream triggered a considerable commotion. The gaggle of Sisters pounced on poor ol' Clyde. Like a flock of angry, attacking crows, the ladies descended, wailing down on him. Swinging black purses and white-gloved fists went a-flying, and the scrawny

beggar was lost in a plume of dust and teased hair. Momma reported that Clyde was left laid out flat on the sidewalk in an utter state
of bewilderment. The sheriff was called out to save the vagrant
from the gang of Christian women.

"Momma, you are all going to end up in prison one day," I told
her. "You can't just go about terrorizing the decent, upstanding
citizens of Durango."

"Hush up," she insisted. "Clyde got *exactly* what he had coming!"

It was a slow news day, and the story made the front page of the
Durango Herald, accompanied by a black-and-white photograph of
the lineup of women self-satisfied all standing arm in arm. The
brouhaha was the talk of the sleepy town, and the unhurried locals
paid no never mind to the world out past the La Plata County Line.

My new life moved at a rapid pace. Los Angeles raged like a rushing
river, always moving, never stopping, and time passed like a strand
unwinding on a spinning spool. For over two years, Rodrigo, Juan,
the crews, and I slaved from dawn to dusk.

At the end of a long day, I made my way through crawling traffic, swung by the gym, and returned to my apartment with takeout.
Most nights I fell asleep in front of the TV with my tennis shoes still
laced. The weekends were no different from any weekday.

Other than my crew and a chick I took to dinner once in a while,
I didn't know a soul in the city. With the four walls of my tiny studio apartment closing in around me, I said good-bye to the Oasis
and found myself a bigger condominium with a full kitchen, two
bedrooms, and a patio deck overlooking the lights of Pasadena. To
keep me company, I splurged and purchased a big color television
and a stereo system with an eight-track and cassette player.

As a boy I had spent endless hours deep in the backwoods of
the San Juans, hunting and scouting, exploring the wilderness

alone. I never gave a thought to the absence of another's voice. But lonesome is a strange thing. It's a blanket for one. After a forgiving rain washed Los Angeles clean, or when a crisp, cool breeze blew off the Pacific and the air was crisp and clear, I grew nostalgic for home. The hymns Momma sang from the second-row pew repeated in my head. Seeing a pretty, barefoot girl in patched jeans with lips the color of red licorice walking along the sidewalk or smiling children sitting cross-legged in Grant Park returned me back to Durango for the sweetest moment. Los Angeles didn't know my name. It didn't care to shake my hand or tip a hat as I passed. And so I labored all day and then curled up in my own quilt until sunlight sneaked in through the paper blinds.

———

"Please come out for a visit," I asked Laura during one of our Sunday conversations. "I have a big apartment, so there's no more excuses. I can take you around to see all of the sights. There are even buses that will take us to see all the movie stars' homes."

Her response to my invitation was left for a moment too long. "Zach, I'm not sure how you can even live there. I just don't understand it."

"Sis, you would love it here. I'll take you to the beach, and you can lie in the sun all day."

"I'm sure it's beautiful, Zach, but all the hippies and homosexuals and drugs," she continued. "And I know it's wrong, and God forgive me, but it all disgusts me."

"C'mon, I promise there are plenty of fine people here who aren't on drugs or aren't homosexuals."

"I'm not sure," she said. "I know such abominations can be forgiven, but it seems some sin, more than others, turn rancid in my stomach."

"I understand."

"Better yet," she suggested, "why don't you come here for a visit? We can hike for days. You would love it.

"Sounds terrific, sis."

I never again tried tempting Laura to the coast. Like the imaginary lines drawn across the backseat of Mom's car as we drove to church, Laura stuck to her side.

I couldn't judge her. Even I held only the slightest hope that the Lord dwelled inside men like me, hidden in the last sacred places not infected by my sin, but if I couldn't convince myself that I was worthy, I'd never convince Laura any different.

———◆———

When I woke one Friday morning in April, I pledged that later that night I'd make the drive to Santa Monica Boulevard and into the West Hollywood district.

My first day in LA, driving into town, I had permitted myself to venture into that part of the city. For reasons I couldn't square, I believed West Hollywood's beautiful men were off limits, a dream just out of my grasp, something I could never have for my own. Ever since arriving I'd banished any thought of walking among the handsome, carefree men along Santa Monica.

That Friday after work, I went to Montgomery Ward, bought myself a new pair of jeans and a nice, clean white button-down, and took myself to West Hollywood. In a Circle K, I'd found a pamphlet listing the names and addresses of all the bars along the boulevard. After each bar's name was a brief description of the type of club and its patrons. The high-gloss discos were replacing the darker dingy bars and pool halls of West Hollywood.

Sleek, slender men in tailored suits and silk shirts walked from club to club at night. Long lines of these finely chiseled, slick-haired specimens waited to be granted access into the most popular, trendy dance bars. These suave, smooth pretty boys moved like cats, stealth and discerning compared to my clumsy, brawny physique and cowlicked hair. I was a mangy mutt alongside purebreds.

From its description in the bar guide, I determined Boot Hill was the best fit—"casual, country-western music, butch guys, neighborhood crowd."

Driving through Boot Hill's parking lot on a cool April night, I felt tiny beads of sweat forming on my forehead. I sat in my car, wiping my clammy palms on the legs of my new jeans. Working up the nerve to go inside, I told myself I could do it. Sweat spotted the pits of my freshly ironed white shirt. For nearly an hour, I watched from my car the comings and goings of the men through the front door.

Finally mumbling "fuck it," I took one last look at my reflection and went inside.

Boot Hill was at full capacity. I was pressed, shoulder to shoulder, with guys who most likely had never stepped foot on a working ranch. Still, they donned expensive cowboy hats and full black-leather chaps. The packed dance floor bustled with handsome men who wore closely cropped hair; full, thick moustaches; and scruffy, shadowed jaws. An oversize pair of mirrored cowboy boots hung like a chandelier in the middle of the dance floor. Revolving from the ceiling, the boots reflected the colored spotlights, sending rays of rainbow lights around the bar.

Drag queens masquerading as Diana Ross, Cher, and Liza Minelli held court in separate corners, surrounded by laughing men who sucked drinks from straws. Wearing white cotton T-shirts two sizes too small, men strutted around the bar with overripe pumped pecs and bulging biceps.

Standing in the smoke-filled gay bar was both exhilarating and mind-numbingly terrifying. For the first time in over two years, I felt desired. I'd been putting in countless hours working and not giving much consideration to feeling attractive, but the men cruising the length of the bar reminded me of the hunting season back home—how a stealth hunter stalks his prey.

Durango girls provided us local boys with only coy, subtle hints of interest. The dance of courtship was a slow one. But the patrons of Boot Hill didn't disguise their intentions. They pursued one another with masculine vigor. Standing alone at the bar in a crowd of horny dogs, I was cruised by men of all shapes and sizes. Young twinks pranced by, batting their lashes. Elderly men glared at me from across the bar. The silver-haired geezers reminded me of the old men back home who pitched iron shoes on Sunday afternoons.

It was painfully clear I was a newbie to the West Hollywood scene. Like potent cologne, my scent gave me away—I was a closet case. A mixture of fear and excitement signaled I was prime rib to a den of hungry males. I worked up the courage to order a drink from an overly bronzed shirtless bartender. He smiled and winked.

I gripped my drink, watching men stalk the smoky club. They moved in circles, standing in one place just long enough to scout out the most promising options. They perused faces for an accomplice for a night of sex or laughs or both. The shirtless guys twisted and gyrated in rhythm on the swarming dance floor. Catching their reflections on the mirrored walls, they danced to their own images. Some men posed along the long wooden bar, waiting to catch an interested gander in another's passing eyes.

The ruggedly handsome cowboys primped more for a night out than the Sisters of the First Assembly of God working their glorious bouffants before a Sunday service.

I never felt a part of the laughing, dancing men. A thousand miles of blacktop separated me from these boys. I was the kid standing well outside the circus tent, too far removed to enjoy the three rings, too distant to laugh at the pranking clowns. I leaned on the edge of the bar through the night and watched the circus from afar.

After my first night, walking through the front doors of Boot Hill became easier. Familiar bartenders acknowledged me with friendly nods. A few regulars greeted my arrival with handshakes or pats on the back.

When the last call came from the DJ's booth and closing time arrived, the pulsing music went silent, and bright-white floodlights switched on overhead. Those of us still leaning against the bar or moving on the dance floor took one last look around with a blinding recognition that another night searching for something more was at an end. Big, bulky bar-backs herded us out the front door and onto the street. Like a hundred red-eyed mice escaping a burning mine shaft, we took in deep, full breaths of fresh air. Some boys, unwilling to let the coming daylight win, chose to loiter on the sidewalk, checking out the others who desired casual sex more than they valued a good night's sleep.

When all the world had gone home, I walked up Santa Monica Boulevard to my parked pickup. Some nights along the sidewalk, I crossed paths with a cute guy and took him to my place or went back to his. On nights I couldn't find anyone to my liking in the clubs, still wide awake with the sound of dance music pulsing in my head, I traveled by the dark city parks, cruising for the closeness of company. Closeted married men cruised the night for a place to connect. If I happened across a handsome stranger, I took him to the farthest corner of the park, where no headlights could find us. Fumbling in the dark, we got off and then walked away in separate directions like strangers who shared only the sidewalk.

Like a country mouse cliché, a Durango boy was all crossed up in a big city. All the tempting trappings of single gay life in LA was my undoing. Foolishly I confused easy sex for company, mistakenly believing getting shit-faced every night was recreation. Those first months in WeHo, my zipper was down more often than Toby Zane's and with the boozing, I fell into the same hole I'd scrambled so desperately to climb out of.

In the mornings, Rodrigo and Juan would shake their heads when I arrived, tripping onto a jobsite after a night of debauchery. I often smelled of smoke, sleep still in the corners of my eyes and my hair matted flat to my scalp on one side from a hard pillow. Too many nights I drank at the bar until the closing overhead flood-lights blinded me.

"OK, cowboy, it's time for you to call it a night," a burly bar-tender called to me. "You gonna be able to make it home?"

"Yes, sir." I tried to focus my eyes on his grin.

"You sure? You look like you're three sheets to the wind, boy."

I stood upright from my stool too fast. Grabbing hold of the bar's ledge to find balance, I navigated through the spinning room. A hunky bar-back pointed me in the direction of the front door, and I headed out toward the sidewalk and stumbled my way to the truck parked on Santa Monica. With God driving, I some-how made it back to Pasadena.

Searching my front pockets, I dug for my house keys. Finally recognizing the smooth plastic ring, I fumbled at the lock, tak-ing aim and trying to steer the tip of the key into the dead bolt. Missing after my first two attempts, I finally unlocked my front door. I stumbled into the pitch-black apartment, leaving the key lodged in the lock. I reached blindly in the dark, fumbling for the lamp switch. Tripping on the corner of the coffee table, I tumbled into the television set, knocking it from its wood console. Crashing to the floor, the television's glass and tube shattered. Tiny needles of glass pierced the palms of my hands as I hit the floor.

A neighbor yelled from somewhere outside the open door, "Can you keep it down, buddy? We're trying to sleep!"

In a drunken stupor, I lay flat on my stomach in the dark, slowly bending and twisting, testing each joint to determine any damage done. The front left side of my skull ached. I felt a line of warm blood traveling from the flesh wound on my forehead and down to the corner of my left eye. Too tanked to pick myself up off the floor, I moaned in pain. My stomach pressed on a bed of broken glass. With the front door ajar and my plastic key chain dangling from the dead bolt, I passed out.

I woke to street noises of early morning, delivery vans and garbage trucks making their rounds. Flat on my back, with an aching, splitting headache, I focused my eyes on the plastered ceiling. Slowly picking myself up, I surveyed the damage. I stumbled over the busted console. The shattered glass of the television splintered beneath my untied tennis shoes. Sharp, tiny slivers pierced the skin of my palms and fingertips like the pricks of a cactus. I picked thin needles of glass from my hands while I waited for a cup of instant coffee in the microwave.

It occurred to me that my eyeballs hurt, and I downed a handful of aspirins. My tongue was thick and swollen. The back of my throat felt like I'd swallowed gravel. I checked my reflection in the bathroom mirror. Dried blood stained my forehead and was caked in my hair. A ripe bruise on my left cheek was the souvenir from my dance with the television set. I splashed cold water on my face from the tap and cleaned my head wound with rubbing alcohol. Squeezing my temples, I tried to rub out the pounding ache in my head. In the mirror I recognized Dad's lost eyes, red and hollow. His transgressions were mine. With the open palm of my hand, I slammed the glass, shattering Pop's reflection.

"I'm a queer."

"I'm a homo."

"I'm a faggot."

Saying a thing enough times makes an ugly, awful truth more palatable, like looking hard at a painful cut or gash to the skin, gazing directly on the open wound long enough, until it looks like it's part of you. You man up, work through the pain, and carry the lesion like it's something that has always been. With the passage of time it heals, scarring over, and the nasty truth becomes as much a part of you as an arm or a leg.

For a Thursday night, Goliath's was packed. Guys cruised along the long, busy main mahogany bar. Pushing my way through the crowd, I passed the pulsating dance floor where sweating shirt-less men gyrated on a parquet-paneled floor under flashing colored lights. Finding a clear path through the maze of flesh, I walked out from the swinging doors to the back bar on the patio. Under a canopy of white lights strung from post to post, a few dozen men carried on quiet conversations, threw darts, smoked cigarettes, and drank cold beers. Three giant ficus trees along the back fence swayed in a cool breeze from the coast. For those of us loitering in the quiet back bar, the patio resembled a neighborhood barbecue under the night sky rather than a raging nightclub. Each time the wide glass double doors swung open, throbbing music escaped out onto the patio. Gradually the patio's volume decreased as the doors closed, and the casual conversations carried on.

Four giddy guys shot pool. With cues in hand, they sipped from tall, neon-colored iced drinks, laughing at one another after scratching the cue ball or misfiring, sending the balls randomly banking across the felt.

I spied two handsome guys sitting on stools at the end of the bar, the attractive pair engrossed in a private conversation. The older, muscled-up, dark-haired man leaned in close to a dirty-blond surfer type with an unshaven jawline. The two laughed between themselves, seemingly unaware of anyone else on the patio. I guessed they were a couple or making a connection for the evening. The four young queens shooting pool giggled and signaled in my direction, but I paid them no mind. I ordered another Budweiser and kept my eye on the mirror positioned above the bar. It reflected the swinging double doors, so I watched to see what men filtered out for a smoke.

I thought I caught one of the two, the surfer, checking me out, but by the time I glanced in his direction, his attention had turned back to the private conversation with the muscle head in a tank.

Several more guys walked out to enjoy the cool night air. A bloated drag queen dressed as Dolly Pardon, decked in sequins and a pink feather boa, made a grand entrance through the double doors, waving and greeting friends like she was strutting on a red carpet. Adorned with a pair of ample foam breasts, a full moustache, and a substantial beer paunch stuffed into a glistening formal gown, he greeted familiar faces, blowing kisses. Spotting me across the patio, he sauntered over. Bellying up next to the bar, he batted his long false lashes and, with the voice of a baritone, asked, "Well, hello there, big boy. Can I buy you a drink?"

"Thank you, but I'm fine." I nodded.

"What's the matter, handsome? You don't like blondes?" he asked.

"To the contrary, I am partial to pretty blondes." I replied. "I just like my women with clean-shaven faces."

Dolly grinned and continued on with her hunt.

At the end of the bar, the dark-haired muscular dude stood from his stool and hugged the surfer boy's neck. Assuming they'd leave together, I took the opportunity to take a second look at the surfer. He flashed a crooked grin, and I nodded in return. His warm blond hair flopped from side to side with no discernable part. He appeared to have left the house without the benefit of a brush or mirror. He was handsome despite himself. An unshaven scruff disguised a chiseled structure. In a wrinkled T-shirt, cargo pants, and old untied tennis shoes, he resembled a roughneck McCord brother more than a slick, well-primped WeHo boy.

His eyes were deep green like rye grass, and his arms, neck, and face displayed a warm summer tan. When he smiled, his straight white teeth looked like something from a Colgate ad. Two deep Hollywood dimples were camouflaged under his scruff. His wide grin was ever so lopsided, causing the left corner of his mouth to curl closer to his ear than the right. His crooked smile left one dimple riding higher on his cheek than the other.

With his buff companion's sudden exit, I walked my drink down to his end of the bar.

"How's it goin' tonight?" I asked.

"Great, thanks."

I extended my hand. "Zach. Zach Nance."

"Well, hello, Zach Nance. Doug Tate." He shook my hand. His tanned forearm had gold wisps of hair down to his wristwatch.

"Is it OK if I have a seat? Would I be bothering you?"

"Can I let you know after we've talked for five minutes?" He grinned.

"Now that sounds like an invitation. I just didn't want to interfere with you and your buddy." I gestured to his friend's empty Pabst bottle on the bar top.

"Kurt? No, he's a good friend. We work together." He patted the empty stool next to him. "What brings you out tonight?"

"Not sure. Bored, I guess. And that usually leads to nothin' but trouble for me."

"Ah, yes, I suppose boredom has gotten all of us in plenty of trouble. Are you new to town?"

"Is it that obvious?"

"Yup, sure is." He placed his hand on my shoulder, and we shared a laugh.

"Actually, I've been in LA for almost two years, but I'm new to the whole club scene. Been checking the bars out for the last six months and still not used to it."

"Didn't your mom warn you to stay out of places like this?" Laughing, Doug squeezed my shoulder.

"Yessum. As a matter of fact, she certainly did. You must know my mom."

Comforted by Doug's resting hand, I sensed he already knew my story. His laughter hinted he understood every sordid detail of my first few years in Los Angeles, how I stalked the darkest corners looking for any kind of connection. I sensed he left any judgment at the front door of the bar.

Later, standing in the parking lot, leaning up against his black Camaro, I kissed him. His wet mouth tasted like Coors and chewing gum.

"Wanna go back to my place?" I offered.

"No, sorry. I can't," he declined. "I have to work early."

I kissed him again, deeper, trying to make it stick. "Can I get your number?"

"Sure." Doug smiled and counted off his digits.

Over the next two weeks, I left three messages on his recorder. Rehearsing my message before speaking into the receiver, I attempted to sound casual and nonchalant. I kept my messages brief but clearly repeated my phone number. A return call never arrived.

Back at my apartment, at the end of a day's work, the blinking red light on my voicemail recorder sat like an unopened Christmas gift. But the messages never included Doug's voice. I scolded myself for coming on too hard or not hard enough.

Sitting on the couch, eating a frozen dinner, watching TV, and waiting for the phone to ring, I recalled sweet Jessie Lee and all the girls back home who had tried so hard to hold my hand for longer than a single dance. Those girls who waited by silent phones for my return call and would never hear an explanation or an apology.

I made the drive into West Hollywood for the next few weeks with the sole intention of finding Mr. Doug Tate. I walked the boulevard, poking my head in nightclubs. I perused crowds of men for any sign of his crooked grin, scoping out discos and open cafés for the surfer.

In Mickey's I ran into a few familiar faces, and we shared a few beers and shot a round of pool. On the way back to my truck, I made a final pass through Studio One, a massive dance club built in an old furniture warehouse. Studio One was patronized by pretty young guys and the older businessman types who sought them out. I circled the congested dance floor. Bolts of flashing white strobes and pumped-in fog filled the club. Walking out onto the back patio, I found a buzzing Saturday night crowd standing shoulder to shoulder. Sitting along the rail, a cute blond kid I'd connected with one night eyed me. I nodded and continued my search.

In the lounge, in a big, curved tufted-velvet booth near the corner, I spotted Doug sitting with a few other guys. He clinked glasses, toasted, and laughed with his circle of friends. Doug caught me in midsurprise, my eyes wide and mouth open. He signaled for me to come over. Scooting from the booth, he came and greeted me with a bear hug. His impossibly white smile traveled across his mouth, and every square inch of his face came along for the trip.

"Hey, guy. How's it going?" Knowing the answer, I asked, "It's Doug, right?"

His arms wrapped around my neck. "Hey, Zach. Yes, Doug Tate." His left hand remained resting on my T-shirt. I smiled, acting unaffected, but the touch of his hand warmed my chest. Speaking over the throbbing music, we struggled to hear each other. Doug's face was clean-shaven now, and a brush had made its way through his sandy hair. Wearing a beige sport coat and blue tie, he resembled a banker more than the surfer I'd met at Goliath's weeks earlier. I liked both versions of him.

"Sorry I haven't returned your call. Been in Boston for a seminar for work."

Trying to talk over the loud, pulsating music, he spoke about his business trip to Massachusetts. As he talked, an arbitrary urge to take a firm hold of both sides of his cute face and lick him crossed my mind. The random thought caused me to grin.

"Why are you smiling?"

"Nothin'. Just really glad I ran into you tonight."

"Me too. I had to fly out to our headquarters and sit through a week's worth of mindless meetings."

"Work's been crazy busy for me. Landed a really big job in Beverly Hills," I said.

"Wow, that's great, Zach. Good for you."

The DJ's decibels were deafening, and our own speaking volume was near a shout. I leaned into his ear, yelling over the music. "It's actually not a big project, and it's not in Beverly Hills. It's a barbecue out in Azusa. I'm just trying to impress you."

"Ah." He grinned. "OK, duly noted." We shared a laugh.

"What's this all about?" I tugged at the lapels of his sport jacket. "I almost didn't recognize you."

"Charity dinner. Went with some friends."

"It's a good look for you," I said. "Handsome."

"Thanks." He grabbed my hand. "Let's go!" Doug led me to the dance floor, and we moved to the music in the crowd of guys. When a horny dancing boy moved in closer to Doug, I maneuvered my way ever nearer to Doug's side. The music slowed, and the party boys exited the floor en masse. Only a few couples and the lucky pairs who'd found partners for the night remained. The bar was nearing its close, and the disc jockey played one of the few slow songs of the night.

It was the first time I'd slow danced in the arms of another man. I held Doug in my awkward arms. Trying to recall my practiced steps with Laura on her wedding day, I counted in my head. My clumsy feet stepped on Doug's polished leather dress shoes. With his arms around my waist, he guided me around the floor. As he planted kisses along my neck, I was lost somewhere between warm whispers and music.

We danced until the song ended, and Doug pulled me from the floor. Waving good-bye to his friends, we escaped from the club together. We hopped in my pickup, and I drove him up to Mount Lee and parked there, where it overlooked the lights of the city. Both of us climbed on top of my truck's cab.

Reared in the panhandle of Florida, Doug described how he had spent his childhood splashing and surfing in the warm, salty waters of the Gulf Coast. I imagined him—warm honey-blond hair, tanned chest—running on a sun-bleached Florida beach. But not unlike in my boyhood, Doug confessed the megachurches along the Bible Belt had poisoned the drinking water in his hometown of Pensacola Beach. When he was seventeen, his Momma discovered her only son was gay, and she put him out. Doug said that in that moment, she became a stranger to him. When he looked into his mother's cold stare, he didn't recognize any part of her. Like turning off the water from the tap, she shut off her affection. He was left to survive on his own, to fend for himself on the streets of Pensacola like a stray dog. He hunted for food and comfort, walking country miles, sniffing out any safe place to lay his head and fill his belly. Fending for himself, he went poking his nose into the same dark places I'd known.

His right thumb was a one-way ticket to Los Angeles; he arrived at his mom's older sister's front door in Orange County. His aunt was the black sheep in a family of Bible-thumpers, and she took in her homeless nephew. She enrolled him in a nearby high school to finish his last two years, and after Doug received his diploma, he registered at California State. Four years later he graduated with a bachelor's degree in business and secured a position with Sterling Inc., selling medical supplies.

I assumed that looking like Doug did—handsome, tanned, poster beach boy—life must've rolled out in front of him like a plush red carpet. I didn't know that even the prettiest of boys in West Hollywood had ugly bad-luck stories.

CHAPTER 20

———◆———

SOME THINGS MATTER. SOME DAYS count.

There are moments honest and true enough to carry them inside, holding them cherished and quiet in the palm of your hand until everything else falls away. Dull and ordinary days turn like so many fluttering pages and are cast aside like forgotten old photographs. Years go by waiting for those days unburdened by words, when everything that came before burns to ash and is left to scatter.

Doug and I stayed in bed all morning, taking turns drifting in and out of sleep. His body folded along mine under cool white sheets. I wrapped my arms around him from behind and held on tight as he slept, my face buried in the back of his neck. His hair smelled like shampoo, and his skin was salty like the ocean. Morning sunlight trespassed through razor-thin cracks on both sides of the blind, but the room remained more dark than light. When Doug stirred I pulled him closer into me, like life depended on it. I felt stronger, more powerful, with my chest pressed against Doug's back, like when two rivers meet and bend into one.

At one point in the early morning hours, he stirred and turned his head, looking over his shoulder to remind himself who had taken him home. Grinning at me, he scratched his unruly bed hair. "Good morning." His face smiled in all the right places.

"Good morning, sir."

When he saw it was me nestled behind him, he laid his head back down on the pillow and drifted back to sleep. Whoever had come before didn't matter now. From this morning on, it was him and me.

My beeper vibrated wildly in my discarded pants at the foot of his bed. Rodrigo and Juan would have to wait. I was content to remain there holding Doug.

When Doug finally woke, he rolled over and greeted me with a kiss. "Let's go get a huge breakfast," he announced, stretching his tan bare arms toward the ceiling. "French toast and maple syrup." He rubbed his stomach.

I brushed the hair back from his eyes with my hand. "I want waffles and bacon."

"Waffles and bacon it is, then," he announced.

After pulling on sweatpants and T-shirts, we strolled down La Cienega to the deli for a late breakfast. The morning was ripe with the sweet fragrance of blooming citrus. Laughing as we turned onto Santa Monica Boulevard, I was happy to be at his side, content to forget the rest of the world. But when Doug placed his arm on my shoulder on the public sidewalk, I pulled away. The knee-jerk twitch exposed me. Doug's expression left me feeling embarrassed and ashamed. He understood, there on the sidewalk, in a telling split second, that I was a closet case. In the shadows of a dark, smoke-filled bar, I could stand with any man—drag queens, leather-harnessed men, and glamorous twinks—but in full daylight I was a backward country bumpkin, ashamed of who I was. Now I understand the deed was done with the telling of the first lie. As a kid, I went about covering my tracks but with the first denial, a seed was planted. Buried in the deepest part of my gut, it grew and bore the most hideous crop - shame, guilt, and loathing. Like an ivy-choked field, the single lie spread unrestrained. It crept about my innards, strangling the most tender places.

We continued along the sidewalk. Uneasy and awkward, we stumbled through a conversation. I knew I'd never loved a man until now. I'd only played at love. By Doug's unsure expression, I understood that if I wanted him to stay, I'd have to find a way to let him be as near my side in the light of day as he wanted—as close to me as possible, or this new love would slip away into the bustling streets of West Hollywood. I wanted Doug to know with certainty that this loyal Durango dog could be house-trained and was willing to learn any new tricks he wanted to teach.

As we walked farther down the boulevard, I took Doug's hand in mine and kissed each knuckle one by one.

As I write this, I don't remember if I knew in that exact moment that Doug would be my only real love. I can't recall if I understood he was *the one*. But our first night at Goliath's remains as clear as any memory. His green eyes narrowed to long slivers when he smiled, shining eyes suddenly lost in laughing folds and creases, leaving only a line of dark-blond lashes. How could I have known from that day on all the missing pieces I'd lost along the way would be found somewhere in his easy laughter? I couldn't have guessed that for the next thirty-two years, with a quiet kindness, Doug would patiently go about untangling the barbwire that tripped me up.

———◆———

Momma wrote:

Dear Zachary,

I hope you are well, son. The days are still warm, but the nights have turned chilly. It's sweater weather. My tomato plants got bit from the freeze the night before last. I was so pleased to receive the magazine with all the pretty pictures of your work. I'm a proud momma!

Laura and Charlie had a nice visit. They stayed overnight at Charlie's folks' for five nights and stayed here at my place for only three nights. I really think she's converted and become Lutheran but too afraid to tell me. I just wish she'd come right out and say it. I may have to write her a note and ask. Anyway, they had a real nice trip, and took me to Denny's for a pork chop dinner on their last night.

My back spasms are acting up again. As soon as the nights turn cold, my lower back aches. Rose and I now walk up to Trimble Hot Springs and back every morning. I think it helps stretch my back out. I love Rose, but my goodness, that woman talks too much!

I've had a dry cough for a month or two and ran fever the last few days. I'm heading over to see Dr. Matos on Monday.

Thank you for the money, son, but I wish you wouldn't do that! Save your hard-earned money. You work too hard to send it to a foolish old lady in Colorado. I hope to see you this Christmas, if you can break away.

If you happen to talk to your sister, could you ask if she's Lutheran? If she is, it won't bother me a lick.

You're a good son.

Love,
Mom

CHAPTER 21

———————

DOUG AND I SPENT THE next two weekends together. We traveled up the coast to Santa Barbara and stayed in a hotel on El Capitan State Beach. The following weekend we headed farther north. Doug wanted me to see Monterey and Cannery Row. He showed me the white beaches of Carmel, and we walked until the rising tide ran us from the beach.

When Monday mornings came around, I resented his job or anything that took him away from me. Waking me at 5:00 a.m. to start the week, Doug grabbed my ankles and pulled me off the edge of his bed. I slid across his white sheets, and with a thud my bare ass hit the carpeted floor.

"Mister, if you don't get out of bed, you're going to be late." He stood over me. "You need to meet your guys, and I'm going to be late for a sales meeting."

"I'm up! I'm up!" I said, rubbing sleep from my eyes.

We showered and shaved, crowded around his small porcelain pedestal sink, sharing a single faucet. While Doug brushed his teeth, I was already quizzing him on his plans for the following weekend. "When can I see you again? Wanna catch dinner tomorrow night?"

"Nope, I can't."

"Wednesday?"

"I'll have to get back to you. I may be flying to Boston Wednesday morning."

With other men I rushed them from my apartment at the first sight of morning or crept from their places like a cat burglar, hoping to make a clean, silent getaway.

"I'm not sure I can," he answered. "Can I call you tonight, when I figure out my traveling schedule?"

Just a white cotton towel wrapped around his waist, tanned, bare-chested Doug looked like a glossy magazine ad for Gillette. Shaving cream foamed on his handsome face and down along his strong, thick neck.

He had been in love before and lived with a Los Angeles attorney for three years. More skilled in the ways of wooing, Doug shared none of my anxiety about us. He was calm and took our new relationship in stride.

I was a bulldozer, anxiously planning the next time I'd see him. Gay dating etiquette and courtship were lost on me, any subtlety abandoned. I was a wrecking ball with not a single clue how to play hard to get. I was willing and ready to be got.

Born and raised in a small town just like I was, Doug had seen the likes of me before. West Hollywood bars were populated with transplanted closeted country hicks out fishing for boyfriends but with no clue or knowledge of how to make love stick.

Luckily for me, Doug found our sex addictive and my neurotic naiveté endearing. I guess his fascination with my awkward courting techniques and carnivorous sexual appetite gave me the needed time to convince him not to toss me back in the water and go off fishing for someone else.

One night he confessed over dinner that warning bells were sounding off in his head. He wasn't sure if we were the right fit, but

I pushed for him to avoid the ringing alarm. I replaced the gnawing, loud sirens in his ears with mushy love letters and sappy songs. I was nauseatingly romantic.

My awkward and antiquated technique of courtship amused Doug. I came calling with flowers and chocolates. I rushed ahead to open his door. He quietly laughed to himself at my ways of wooing like some backwoods farmer's son hanging around outside his house, tossing stones up at his window, calling for him to come down and stroll in the cool night air. I stumbled on clumsy words, tripping over my tongue when struggling to describe my feelings for him.

After several weeks I quietly went about planting enough of my own stuff—boxer shorts, toothbrush, electric razor, change of clothes—around his place, so when he offered on the phone for me to stay the night, I was in my truck heading to West Hollywood before he had hung up the receiver.

I soon realized I'd have to share my man with the Pacific Ocean.

Having spent his youth on the beaches of Florida's Panhandle, Doug snuck off to the sea whenever he could. On weekends he escaped to Venice or Hermosa Beach, spending his days in the warm afternoon sun, swimming a long line along the shore just out past the breakers.

Along with his love of the ocean, Doug's passion for anything baseball was all-consuming. I took a backseat to his love for the Dodgers. Having played on Little League teams as a kid in Florida, he went on to play shortstop in high school, later swinging a bat for California State his sophomore and junior years in college. Now Doug channeled his obsessive passion for the game into his beloved LA Dodgers. On game days he hunkered down in front of the television at his apartment, declaring time-out from any and all conversation once the first pitch left the mound. If I hovered around the set during games, talking was prohibited for those nine sacred innings. When I made a racket, I was promptly shushed.

Doug's enthusiastic zeal for baseball was reminiscent of Mom's love for her favorite soap opera. Laura, Kate, and I had lost Mom for an hour every weekday to the TV drama. The house suddenly went as quiet as Communion except for the voices on *One Life to Live*. Dr. Michael Carlin and his alcoholic wife, Susan, always fussed and fought about something or other, whether over the millions bequeathed in an oil tycoon's contested last will and testament or about who killed the heiress to a coffee plantation fortune. The true father of the illegitimate Bryson bastard child kept Mom glued to the tube. If we kids stepped foot in the front room during Mom's holy hour, we were shooed away with quick flips of her wrists.

Like with Mom's obsession, during Doug's sacred baseball games, he griped if I spoke too loud or enjoyed potato chips too aggressively. Planted next to him on the couch, I followed the play-by-play so I could experience his joy of the game.

———◆———

"Mom, is that you?"

My phone call interrupted her sampling her way through a box of chocolates.

"Yessum. Is that you, Zach? You caught me with my mouth full."

"Yeah, Mom, it's me."

"I got chocolates caught in my teeth, son."

It was common to find a biopsied box of chocolates hidden high up in the cupboard. Truffles, mints, buds, and buttercreams, all dissected in search of caramels. She would taste a chocolate morsel, and if it wasn't to her liking, she'd squeeze it back together and then place the rejected sugary mound back in its small, round tissue cup.

"OK, keep chewing. I can wait." I held the receiver while she smacked.

"Sister Barnett brought me a box of chocolates. That woman is an angel. I've found a half-dozen caramels. Goodness, I love caramels." The sound of her continued chewing filtered through the line.

I exhaled into the receiver. "Yes, Momma, I know."

"I prefer peanut clusters, but these caramels are heaven."

"Momma, how's your fever?" I asked. "What did the doctor say?"

"Honey, he's not sure. They'll know more after Tuesday." She continued to munch. "I just know if we waste time worrying 'bout it now and find out it's nothing later, then it's perfectly good time wasted."

"Mom, I can fly in on Monday night and drive you to your appointment."

"No, no, Rose is taking me, and then we're going on to Farmington to shop for panty hose. It's just a flu or stomach bug."

She repeated the most recent church gossip with the same zeal she quoted her favorite Scriptures with and then rushed me off the telephone when Sister Millard's car horn sounded.

I found the telephone number to the nearest See's candy shop in Grand Junction and arranged for a box of chocolate peanut clusters to be delivered to Momma.

———

Laura's weekly updates became less and less about her and Charlie's travels, and instead our telephone conversations turned to Mom, fretting about how much time she spent alone. Between Mom's canasta tournaments and serving the kids at the grade-school cafeteria, Laura grew concerned Mom lost hours alone with nothing but memories for company.

"Zach, something isn't right. She seems tired every time I call." Laura's anxious voice filtered through the receiver. "She seems so sad."

"That's only because she thinks you're a Lutheran."

"Stop it, you smart aleck. I'm trying to be serious."

"I'm not kidding, sis. She's worked herself into a tizzy believing you've gone off and converted."

"That's just plain ridiculous."

"I know. I told her you could never be a Lutheran because they're always up for a good time."

"Ha ha, Zach. I'm being serious. I'm worried."

"She's getting older, Laura."

"I know. But when Charlie and I were there, she was too thin." Laura replied. "I just wish she wasn't in that house all by herself. When she called the other night, she brought up Daddy."

"I'll be heading there on the seventeenth," I said. "I will call and give you a complete update on life in Durango."

"OK. Charlie and I are flying back for a visit on Labor Day. You should join us."

"I can't take off in September, sis. All my rye lawns need to be seeded. By the way, how is Mr. Mull doin'?"

"He's getting fat, as big as a barn."

"He's always been fat."

"Be nice," she replied. "I'm fairly certain he hides donuts in his desk at the office. I caught him stashing Ho Hos in his briefcase."

I grinned, imagining poor ol' Charlie stashing sweets around the house, hiding them from his wife.

"Well, brother, I hope you're well. Has any blond California beach babe got her grips into you yet?"

I laughed. "Yup, there is one certain blond."

"What? Really? Who?"

"Yeah." I grinned into the receiver. "It's too soon to tell."

"What? Come on! Spill the beans," Laura pleaded. "You can't do that to me. Tell me more about this mystery blonde. When can we meet her? Now you must come meet us in the fall."

"No, not yet. It's too soon," I replied. "I don't wanna jinx it."

"OK, be that way," she huffed into the phone's receiver. "Call your mother. I'm worried about her. "

I shared Laura's concern. I recognized Mom's melancholy. We struggled through conversations outside of local gossip.

The herd of church ladies was thinning. Dying off like cut flowers—blooming brilliantly one day and left to dry deep in the earth the next. Mom sent word of another congregation member's funeral service. The surviving Sisters of the First Assembly of God occupied Mom's daytime hours, but I worried how her evenings unfolded. Was she lonely? What waited for her at the dimming of the day?

After Pop had packed up and left, Mom had vehemently dismissed the mere suggestion of another man. She'd shaken her head in protest, like the idea of a suitor was a blasphemous sin against God's preordained plan for her final years. When old Donald Larsen came sniffing around the house, asking Mom to share a cup of coffee, she shooed him clear off the porch and back off into the street. The widower Watson who lived up on Twelfth Street asked Momma to join him at the Friday fish fry and play a round of bingo at the hall, but she reminded him she was still a very married woman by flashing her modest wedding band.

Later, when we knew Dad was never returning, Mom still refused to grant him a divorce. The delivered legal papers found their way into the garbage pail under coffee grinds and the prior day's newspaper.

After the news of Dad's passing in Sidney, Mom declared herself forever a widow, never to remarry. I was relieved when Momma swore off other men. Laura and I wanted to keep her all to ourselves. Later I realized it was selfishness trying to keep her close. My sister and I were culpable for Mom's loneliness. We never wanted her to find another. Now, with the weight of knowing she sat alone in the house, my same selfishness and gnawing guilt left me wishing Momma had found companionship in the years following Dad.

While she never spoke his name aloud, Pop was always there. When she swayed in her rocking chair on the front porch, he was there. He resided somewhere in the sound of a summer rain slapping against the rooftop. Singing a hymn from her second-row pew could stir a passing remembrance of him. Dad was the first thought to cross her mind when she opened her eyes in the morning. He occupied her thoughts before she went to sleep and during the silence in between.

———◆———

"Hello! Hello! Can you hear me?" Mom's rising frustration with her new phone was spiking. "This dad gum phone is worthless. Zachariah, is that you?" A loud whack sounded through the receiver, as if it had been struck against a counter.

"Yes, it's me. I can hear you. Mom, I'll send you a new phone."

"These phone buttons are just too puny for my weak eyes. Did I hear it right? Laura said you went and met yourself a nice girl."

Chuckling, I answered, "Well, that didn't take long. Charlie Mull needs to keep his wife off the phone. She's got too much time to sit around and gossip."

"Hush up, now. Who is she? Who is this new girl?"

"We just met."

"She's not some silly actress or a Catholic, is she?"

"No, Momma, she's not an actress, and she's not a Catholic."

Mom covered the receiver with the palm of her hand and whispered, "Betty, she's a good Christian girl."

"Mom, say hello to Betty."

"He says hello. Now, son, tell me, have you met this young girl's folks?"

"No, no. Not yet. It's way too soon."

"Zach, it's never too soon to know about someone's upbringing."

"What's her name?"

I quickly recalled the name of the pretty young girl who worked behind the register at the nursery where I bought grass seed and mulch. "Christy," I answered. "Her name is Christy Shrub."

"Shrub? What kind of name is that? Is she a Jew?"

"I'm not sure, Mom."

"Laura said she's pretty. Is she pretty?"

"Real pretty, Momma," I said.

Mom repeated to Betty, "He says she's really pretty. Good for you, son. I'm so happy for you."

"I'm happy for you too!" Sister Pilchard hollered from the background. "Bring her here, so we can all meet her."

"Betty said you need to bring her home."

"Yes, Momma, I will."

"I'm sure you've heard your sister and Charlie are fighting like cats and dogs. I guess two nights back, she showed him the front door," Mom reported.

Betty shouted, "It was a real barn burner."

"Shush up, Betty," Mom scolded.

"Uh-oh," I replied. "Is Sister Nance on the warpath again?"

"Yessum. She just bent my ear for the better part of an hour, explaining her side of the matter, and I swear she is as wrong as a soul can be. But you can't tell her nothing nohow. Poor ol' Charlie. Your sister is a tough nut to crack. Charlie doesn't stand a chance. Lutherans fight with one hand tied behind their backs, and Baptists will gut you like a deer."

We shared a laugh.

"Poor Mr. Mull," I said. "So, it was an all-out brawl, eh?"

"A real humdinger." Mom snickered. "From the sound of it, there were plates and accusations flying. Charlie ended up sleeping at the Best Western. He cannot win against her righteous anger."

Betty added two cents from the background. "Praise the Lord!"

"I'm worried about them," Mom confessed. "I'm asking the ladies to say a prayer for Charlie on Sunday."

I asked, "How about saying a prayer for your daughter?"

"Laura don't need prayers. That child needs an exorcism."

Betty gasped. "Alice Faye!"

"She is a pistol, all right," I replied." But the apple doesn't fall too far from the tree."

"Hush up! I don't know what's to become of that girl." Momma thought on it for a moment. "Our Lord Savior is a god of abundance. He's a loving, forgiving god. Your sister's is a god of loss."

Laura was a hard one. She loved Charlie but from a distance, the kind of love always just out of his reach. Embraces were too slight to truly be felt. "I love you" was whispered in such hushed tones, it wasn't clearly heard. Charlie Mull could always claim the laurel wreath around his neck for snagging the prettiest cheerleader in Durango, but he'd never really know her. Whether it was a recipe handed down from generations or a concoction she'd cooked up on her own, Laura's love was bittersweet. She lingered just out of grasp of those of us who loved her. For years they struggled. Laura asked Charlie hard questions but never listened for his answers. Later, Charlie would find a willing ear in a secretary in his office.

———————

With Nettie Bledsoe's failing health, the ladies' table talk at the weekly canasta tournaments turned from local gossip to pills and potions. Afternoon roundtables were spent sipping coffee and complaining about their multitude of aches and pains. Between shuffles the ladies compared their long lists of ailments, symptoms, possible treatments, drugs' side effects, and concocted home remedies.

Big ol' Nettie sat propped up in a hospital bed, which the ladies had arranged to be brought over and assembled in her front sitting room. The sisters moved their weekly canasta tournament to Nettie's house to accommodate her diminishing condition. They sat around her bed and spoke of the church calendar, cake sales, and warming weather. Playing cards were dealt over a patchwork quilt draped on Nettie's lap. Rose slid into the bed right beside Nettie and held up her cards for her. Sickly and fading, Sister Bledsoe sat mute and slack-jawed, staring out the open window like someone outside was calling for her. Her skin was grayer than ash, and she sat motionless. Not saying so much as a peep, Nettie sat while the ladies carried on with their fiery canasta games. Ignoring death was sitting in the room, Rose fanned out the playing cards and held them in front of Nettie's empty eyes while the ladies laughed and cheered her on. Like a pinch hitter in one of Doug's Dodgers games, Rose played Sister Bledsoe's canasta hand.

"Lookie there, Nettie," Rose gushed. Her bulging eyes grew as round as silver dollars behind her bifocal goggle lenses. "Lookie what we got here!"

During a Tuesday canasta game, Mom happened across Sister Nettie's stash of medications. Mom had excused herself to use the toilet and made her way down the corridor. In the Bledsoes' medicine cabinet, she discovered dozens of white plastic bottles lining the shelves: morphine, Vicodin, neat rows of painkillers, sleeping pills, antidepressants, all prescribed to numb Nettie Bledsoe's final months.

When Nettie passed some four months later, the local volunteer firemen hoisted her big body from the house on a reinforced stretcher. Bob Shearer at Sunset Mortuary had an enormous pine casket brought in from Denver. Laura and I flew in for the funeral.

On a warm Sunday afternoon, the congregation crowded in the church for Nettie's funeral service - standing room only. Old-timers from the church came out of hiding to mourn Nettie's passing, sending her off to glory. On the second pew, Momma sat gripping her Bible.

"She was my dear friend," Mom reminded Laura and me. "This old world won't ever see the likes of such kindness again."

———◆———

Christmas arrived in Durango with the season's first snow. Halloween and Thanksgiving bowed to the Christmas holiday if a winter's white flurry arrived early. If snow fell in October, trick-or-treaters walked beneath twinkling red-and-green holiday lights. Spiraling garland was wrapped around the lampposts overnight. At every traffic light, plastic reindeer were suspended across Main Street. Strings of tiny white blinking lights adorned storefronts, and the Narrow Gauge's engine was dressed in sugar canes and wreaths of spruce and holly. Glowing luminaries ran the path through the park and up the steps of the old courthouse.

Icy sidewalks with shoveled muddy snowbanks became packed with tourists wrapped in ski parkas and winter scarves.

The churches along Fifteenth Avenue competed with one another's variety of nativity scenes. Their tithing-plate tallies determined the sizes, scales, and intricacies of their plastic baby Jesuses and surrounding manger scenes.

My annual pilgrimages home for Mom's Christmas ham and pumpkin pie brought both a nostalgic anticipation and a heaviness. I knew full well I was abandoning Doug for the holidays, year after year leaving him alone, choosing Mom and Laura over courage and honesty.

Eight months pregnant, Laura waddled about the house grumbling. She and Charlie stayed at his folks' place, and I slept upstairs in my old bedroom, which Mom had converted to a sewing room.

Laura was in the kitchen when I came in from the bitter cold carrying groceries. She sat alone, folding towels that were warm and fresh from the dryer.

"It's fricking freezing out there."

"There's a pot of coffee on."

"Where's Mom?" I asked.

"I suspect she'll be home anytime now. She's out with Betty."

"It's frightening, imagining those two out on these icy streets." I shook my head, calculating the calamity.

"Amen," Laura added.

"Sis, I need to talk to both of you." I emptied the last of the groceries in the cupboard and found myself a mug. "Can I pour you a cup?"

"No, I'm good."

"I almost forget how crazy cold it is here," I said, pouring myself a cup of piping-hot caffeine.

"I do believe California has made you soft, Mr. Nance. What's on your mind?"

"Just need to talk to both of you."

"All righty then." She looked at with me with an air of suspicion.

"You know, Mom is considering selling the house," I said. "It's too much upkeep."

"I guess this place is a lot for her to handle. Maybe it's time," Laura concluded.

"I'll drive around before I leave and see what's available."

"Mom said you're staying until Tuesday and then flying out?"

"Yup. I'm meeting a few friends in San Diego for New Year's Eve."

"Are you meeting your roommate?" she asked.

"Yes, Doug's driving down."

Laura looked over with a roll of her eyes and went back to sorting laundry.

"Is Charlie with his folks?"

"No. He's actually heading up to ski."

I gave a puzzled expression. "Charlie is skiing?"

"My hunch is he's heading up to the ski lodge to eat at the buffet."

I walked to check the thermostat. "It's fricking freezing. It's nearly as cold inside this old house as it is outside."

"What kind of work does your roommate do again?" she asked.

"Doug is in medical sales."

I took a seat at the table, and our conversation went quiet. Only the percolating of coffee filled the silence.

"Something has been weighing on my mind," I announced. "It's time I talk to you and Mom."

Laura was content not to respond. I watched her fold the last cotton towel. She gathered the terry cloth corners and quartered the cloth like she was wrapping a gift to go under the tree. After creasing the precise folds, she stacked it neatly atop the other freshly laundered linen.

Finally she spoke to me, but her attention stayed on the task at hand. "If you have something you need to say, some declaration, just think hard about Momma. She is not well." My sister's tone turned harsh. "Zach, Momma is my sole concern. Before you put a blinding spotlight on matters best left in the dark, think about her."

"Laura, you don't think she's my concern?" I replied. "Every waking minute she's with me. She's the first thought in the morning and my last at night."

"All I'm saying is your truth telling may allow you to sleep soundly, but it's Mom who's left tossing and turning with worry." Laura turned, addressing me like a scolding teacher. "It's Momma who I want to sleep soundly."

I suddenly felt small sitting at the table.

Standing up from the wooden chair, Laura placed the stack of towels back into the plastic hamper and lifted it up onto her hip. "We all keep things buried in places no one sees." She said, and then headed to the laundry room. She stopped short of the doorway. "Honesty is a selfish thing, Zach. Nothing good ever comes from it."

I didn't answer her, but she knew I'd heard. Unspoken words stretched between us like a string of yarn unraveling something warm.

Turning from me, Laura walked from the kitchen and left my confession unopened on the table.

———

CHAPTER 22

For Rose Millard it was arthritis crippling her joints; for Betty Pilchard it was a pinched nerve in her left ankle; and for Annie Combs, it was her spiking blood pressure. Maybe it was a sign of the times or advancing age, but the ladies of the church collected prescriptions like loose buttons—little white pills to relieve daily aches and pains. A red capsule stopped Annie's running nose each spring. A bottle of tiny round tablets reminded Sister Barnett's ticker to keep ticking. Plastic bottles were collected inside their medicine cabinets and buried deep in their purses. Pretty pink oval pills dissipated painful migraines, and a pale yellow chased away the blues. The ladies traded prescription bottles like recipes. Potions and meds were swallowed to bring smiles to the corners of their mouths or needed sleep to their eyes.

A few months after Nettie was laid to rest, the ladies of the First Assembly of God caravanned to her house to sort through closets, cabinets, and dresser drawers. The ladies boxed up the remaining belongings to be sent to Nettie's two surviving children and prepared for her antiques to be sold to the highest bidder at a charity auction for the homeless shelter in Cortez.

Mom entered Nettie's place with her famous pumpkin pie in hand. After greeting the ladies, she slipped into the small bathroom just off Nettie's bedroom, silently locking the door behind her. She powdered her face in the reflection and opened the small mirrored door to the medicine cabinet. Reaching for her bifocals, which hung from her neck by a thin silver chain, she examined the assortment of medications, carefully reading each label, selecting the bottles of choice like picking her favorite books from the shelves of a library. Quietly she placed each bottle inside her purse, tucking tissues around her stash to insulate any possible shake or rattle of the plastic bottles.

Momma was sick. I reckon she knew long before she confided in Laura and me. Maybe she decided she'd first assist Nettie Bledsoe with her own walk to the River Jordan. Tending to Sister Bledsoe was her sole focus for those several months, and when her own doctor announced Mom's breast cancer diagnosis, she simply chose not to hear him. She canceled her follow-up appointments and never returned the repeated calls from Dr. Zeidman's office. It was just like Mom to store something up in the highest shelf of her closet and bring it down only when she was good and ready. We all recognized her declining health, the weight loss, and the nagging dry cough.

"I'm just feeling poorly," she told Laura during one of my sister's visits.

"Momma, this flu bug has stuck around way too long."

"It will pass after a few good nights' rest."

Laura confided in me that she felt Mom was being less than forthcoming. "We would be the last to know if she was stricken by leprosy."

"Sis, she's gonna do exactly what she wants to do."

I can't recall when Laura next mentioned Mom's declining health in passing conversation. Spring allergies, maybe? A summer fever burning hot a few weeks too long or a stomach flu causing Mom's already thin frame to shed a few more pounds?

Standing in the Bledsoes' tiny bathroom, Mom's knees went weak, so she took a seat on the toilet lid. She dug beneath her stash of plastic prescription bottles to the bottom of her purse, feeling for a roll of Life Savers. Hoping the sweet would settle her stomach, she rested there, sucking the butterscotch candy. Using a magazine from atop the toilet tank, she fanned herself. The cool air dried the sweat on her brow and eased the anxiety. When strength returned to her legs, Mom splashed cold tap water onto her clammy hands and blunted away the last tiny beads of sweat on her upper lip with a powder compact.

As she played with the few strands of blond fringe on her fore-head, for the briefest moment she didn't recognize her gaunt reflection in the mirror. Her once thick mane of hair was thinning, revealing more and more bare pink scalp. As a young woman, her full head of gorgeous yellow locks had been her crowning glory, but with advancing age a young girl's vanity is soon forgotten, lost somewhere in the creases and folds of an older woman's skin. The shape of her bony skull could no longer be disguised by the few strands of blond and gray hair that swept across her forehead. Her mighty bouffant had been replaced in recent years with a tight bun of hair, pulled from her face and gathered with bobby pins on the back of her small noggin.

Mom collected her courage and placed the strap of the purse on her forearm. Unlocking the door, she walked from the bath-room with her score, marching straight down the short hall, right past the ladies gathered in the kitchen.

"Alice Faye, I poured you a hot cup of coffee," Rose called out. "It's already been saucered and blown!"

Mom kept walking right out the front door to her waiting Oldsmobile. She gripped her purse in her lap all the way back home. Waiting to hear the sirens of the sheriff's car chasing her, she checked her rearview mirror for Betty's or Annie's car following behind. She pulled into the carport and left her keys in the ignition with the motor idling. Inside the house she retrieved a step stool from the kitchen and headed up the stairs to her room. In the closet she reached blindly to the top shelf, stretching for the J. C. Penney shoe box hidden behind folded sweaters. Inside the box were more plastic bottles of pills. She emptied the contents of her leather clutch, filling the cardboard shoe box to the brim with her collected prescriptions.

A concerned Betty phoned, and Mom explained she'd had a weak spell.

"OK, Alice Faye, but you scared the dickens out of us. Next time you're feeling woozy, let one of us know, and we'll get you back home." Like reading Scripture from the good book, Sister Pilchard believed every word Mom said, because Momma didn't lie.

Some seven weeks later, when Laura and I visited for Easter weekend, Momma told us her prognosis. The word *cancer* spilled off her tongue like turpentine, stinging my eyes and burning my skin.

"It's just something we have to overcome." Mom shrugged her slight shoulders. "It's all in the Lord's hands."

But Laura and I knew that a piece of the sky had broken loose.

"I'll speak to your doctors in the morning." Laura shifted into gear. "I need their names and phone numbers."

"Mom, exactly how long have you known?" I asked, certain she'd hidden her prognosis out of sight like the cherished love letters from Dad in her mahogany bureau next to her bed.

"The Lord's will be done." Mom sipped her black coffee and looked past us to the blooming geraniums in the window box. "The Lord's will be done."

I kissed Doug's mouth while he slumbered someplace between sleep and waking. As I watched him resting there by my side, the quiet calm in his face reminded me of the boy I'd met years earlier in Goliath's. Even in sleep Doug's kindness remained present. I was grateful he'd saved me.

On this particular morning, I was as horny as a teen at summer camp. Doug wasn't. The alarm's snooze button gifted us ten more minutes of shut-eye, and he wasn't trading a single second of sleep just for a quickie. I was meeting the crews at the shop in forty-eight minutes to assign lawns for the day's schedule. In the meantime, though, I wanted to make love. Instead I settled for a cold shower.

In the kitchen I grumbled low to myself when he announced he was heading out of town for work. I complained often about Doug's disappearing acts. "You leave when you want a break from us, when you want to get away from me."

"Are you crazy? You really think I want to get on some plane and leave? Do you even believe most of what you say, or do you just want to start something?"

I smiled and winked. "If I start up an argument, does it mean makeup sex is involved?"

Jealous of his career and suspicious of his friends, my distrust followed us around like a brooding shadow. If Doug and I grabbed dinner or shot a game of pool at Mickey's, my suitcase of insecurities traveled along for the ride. A good-looking guy's glance at Doug from a passing car could set me off. The briefest connection between him and a handsome waiter or a flirting muscle head bartender at Roscoe's stoked a fire inside me. By the end of the night, my simmering jealousy burned to a full boil. I'd go home jealous and fuming at my own stupidity for making Doug pay the price for another man's advances.

I recalled one childhood summer when Pop and I sat fishing off the dock, and he'd described Momma's bouts with the green-eyed monster. "Your momma had a jealous streak a country mile long," he said as he slowly reeled the slack from his line. "When we first started up, if she thought another hen was pecking too close to her rooster, she'd run her clear out of the barnyard." Dad shook his head with a smirk.

Doug remained patient.

Back at the house, after one of my episodes in a bar, he rubbed my turned back in our bed. "Babe, you need to work through this stuff. I'm not going anywhere. I'm not leaving your cute ass for some waiter. I love you."

But my nagging and persistent insecurities tested Doug's calm resolve. Brought on by inexperience or immaturity, my constant fears exhausted even his understanding temperament. I felt I'd started so far behind the line that playing catch-up now seemed insurmountable. It's an odd thing, loving someone more than life itself but not having the fortitude or self-control to stop hurting him every day.

When I felt sorry for myself, I'd slip back into old habits like a pair of old work boots, finding comfort in a bottle again. I told myself I should pack my bags and head back to Durango. Like with Mom, blue days held me captive. The gin and self-pity convinced me I'd be better off staying put in Colorado, but after a few aspirins, a pot of black coffee, and some kind, soothing words, Doug would sober me up and remind me why I'd left Durango in the first place. Doug understood what I did not: if losing a thing stops you from loving again, the loss shapes the rest of your days.

"Why do you put up with all my bullshit?" I asked.

"I have no idea," he answered, grinning. "But I can't make you believe something you don't already know."

"Promise not to bail on me."

He shook his head. "Babe, I'm here. I'm not going anywhere."

"I just can't get past this gnawing in my gut that one day I'll wake up, and it will be gone. All of this—you and I, everything—will be long gone. I'm scared all my bogus bullshit will drive you away and that everything we've got will disappear."

"Babe. You're worrying about ghosts. None of it's real."

"I'm sorry I'm such a pain in the ass," I said.

"Come on, look at us. We're doing fine." He smiled. "Look at what we've got. This has nothing to do with the past. This is us."

I was scared my chickenshit confession wasn't manly, frightened I was going to send Doug running in the opposite direction. But pride shatters into the smallest pieces when the hammer comes down. Losing a cherished thing can bring a man to his knees. Even knowing that eventually everyone leaves, I wanted to hold on as long I could. To hell with pride and a god who never shows.

Doug squared my shoulders and looked directly into my eyes. "I'm staying right here."

Back home the changing seasons came and went, revolving like a carnival wheel, always turning, circling back around, reliable and repeating. Life in Los Angeles moved in a straight line, pushing me forward, leading further away from what was remembered. A long string of continual warm days passed like strangers' faces in a crowd, disappearing one into the next. My years in California moved me further from home. Looking back over my shoulder, I saw Durango far off behind me.

Business was booming, flowers were blooming, and grass kept growing. Rodrigo, Juan, and I drove new Dodge Ram trucks with chrome wheels that were polished and sparkled like Sister Pilchard's Cadillac hubcaps.

Doug's work took him to Boston twice a month for training seminars about some new medication. When he wasn't off traveling, in the afternoons he'd sneak off to Venice Beach, spending his free time in the ocean. I came home to find an indicting trail of sand through the apartment, evidence my beach boy was at play.

I flew to Durango every few months, Laura and I coordinating our trips on a calendar. She and Charlie were now a family of four, Daisy and Jon Lee demanding their mom's attention during our weekly Sunday phone calls.

"The house closes escrow on the twenty-first, but the condo is Mom's on the fourteenth," Laura said. "That gives us over a week to clear out the house."

"Yup. I'm flying in on the twelfth. I'll drive her over to the title company to sign the final papers, and I've got a few men from Grand Junction coming over to help move her into the new place."

The old house had been sold to a young family from Denver, and I'd found Mom a condominium near Rose's place. She said a final good-bye to the empty little house by running a straw broom over the wooden floorboards one last time.

"Lord knows I won't miss doing this," Mom called out from the back room. "This old place has too many loose joints. Dust finds its way through every nook and cranny."

From her empty bedroom upstairs, Laura announced, "Well, I'm going to miss this place. I think it's a crying shame we let it go."

Daisy and little John Lee played tag in the vacant rooms.

"Sis, it's just too much upkeep. This place needs a complete overhaul. Plumbing is bad. Windows don't seal."

"I know, I know. But if things would've worked out differently…" It was the first hint of nostalgia I'd recognized in Laura's voice in many years.

"Mom is going to love her new place."

Laura replied, "Yes, I'm sure she will." She attempted to convince herself.

"Laura, hon," Mom called out. "Remember, the new place has a community swimming pool, and it's close to the rec center. My grandbabies will love it."

The Sisters of the First Assembly of God orchestrated the move and settled Mom in to her new place. They kept watchful eyes on one of their own. When Laura or I wasn't there, the ladies shuttled Mom back and forth to her chemo treatments and radiation.

Mom's battle with cancer was our new normal. Bad news was always followed by good. A PET scan would show up clean, followed the next month by the discovery of some cloudy growth on her X-rays. When the most recent biopsy came back negative, we celebrated at Sizzler with steak dinners and all the fixings, and then we braced ourselves for the inevitable phone call bringing some heavy news. We learned to savor the good news when it was delivered.

When I recognized Laura's number on my phone one Tuesday morning instead of her usual Sunday, I knew the wheels had come off something.

"Zach, I got a call from Betty. Mom's back in the hospital. She took a bad fall."

"Is she OK?"

"I don't know, Zach." Laura's panic was palatable. "Betty said she was fine, but I just don't know. I guess she got a nasty cut above her left eye. They stitched her up."

Sitting across from me, Doug saw my falling expression and motioned if I was OK. "How did it happen?" I asked. "Did Betty say how it happened?"

"No, she doesn't have a clue. I'm booked to fly out in the morning," Laura replied. "Charlie and I have been talking, and we might bring her back home with me."

"OK, does Momma know of your plans yet?" I asked. "Can she travel? What are the doctors saying?"

"Nothing. I haven't spoken with anyone at the hospital."

"Have you talked to Mom yet?"

"They have her sedated, but Betty told me they aren't keeping her. They'll release her tonight or in the morning."

Laura phoned from Denver International Airport the next day. During her brief layover, waiting for her connecting flight into Durango, she stood at a pay phone in the terminal, explaining to me in detail her most recent approach to Mom's health crisis. Like so many times before, Laura stayed up through the night, researching the newest breast and lung cancer treatments. She marked pages in books, making notes in a three-ring binder, formulating her plan of attack. I pitied the unsuspecting medical staff of Durango's Mercy Medical Hospital. They hadn't a clue of the temperamental tornado flying in from South Dakota on the 2:26 p.m. flight.

Every visit Laura came prepared with list of concerns, ready to quiz Mom's doctors on their methods of treatment with questions about the many medications and potential side effects. She queried staff on new approaches to battling Mom's cancer.

Mom had inherited her weak heart from her father. After two separate operations, the insertion of three stents, and a medicine cabinet stocked with blood-thinning meds—her brittle, crusty arteries complicated any potential surgical procedures—her doctors warned that her heart condition made the removal of the breast cancer more complex. The tumor in her breast had spread to the chest wall. Despite Mom's weak heart, her oncologist determined the tumor removal warranted the risky procedure. So Momma stopped taking her blood thinners for two weeks prior to the surgery, and we prayed she wouldn't experience a heart attack on the operating table.

Her oncologist treated the remaining cancer in her breast with radiation, which kept Mom weak and sickly. The ladies of the church made it their duty to tend to her every need.

"Don't you go worry yourselves none," Betty Pilchard assured us. "We're gonna take Alice Faye to Denny's every morning for a Grand Slam breakfast and fatten her up."

Later, when her breast cancer spread to nearby lymph nodes and into the lungs, Mom's weakened heart condition eliminated any further invasive surgery as an option. Chemotherapy was declared the plan of attack, so every other week, the doctors poisoned Mom in attempt to save her.

———

When I phoned the hospital, Betty Pilchard answered the line in Mom's room. I recognized her sweet Southern drawl. "Zachariah, honey? Is that you?"

"Yes, Mrs. Pilchard. How are you?"

"I'm just fine. I'm sittin' here with your momma. She's a bit drowsy, but she's fine. The doctor said she just needs to rest. We'll get her nursed back to health. Don't you worry yourself none."

Pulling the rubber corkscrew phone cord from Betty, Mom took control of the phone. "Zach, I'm doin' just fine. I was paying no mind and fell right off the stoop."

I didn't recognize Mom's voice.

"Momma, you gotta be more careful. You've got your daughter in a frenzy."

"Aw, Laura worries too much. It happens when you have babies." Mom's breathing was labored. An occasional cough erupted from her chest, rolling like thunder. "Son, I gotta let you go." She struggled to speak between coughing fits. "Good night, baby."

Betty hijacked the receiver again. "Zachariah, your mom is going to be just fine," she again assured me. "The doctor had her on some powerful medication earlier, and she wasn't clearheaded. She insisted this morning that she saw the Virgin Mary in the white icing on a slice of cake from the hospital cafeteria. I kept telling her, 'Alice Faye, it wasn't the Virgin Mary—it was Betty Crocker.'" Betty laughed at her own joke.

I thanked Sister Pilchard for taking good care of Momma.

"Now, don't you fret. Your sister arrives later tonight, and Alice Faye is looking forward to her visit."

"Is your mom OK?" Doug asked when I hung up the receiver.

"Yeah, but she took a fall."

I paced the floor while Doug tried to watch the bottom of the seventh inning between the Dodgers and Reds. Doug looked up from the set and announced, "Babe, you might as well book a ticket, or you're going to drive me and yourself bat-shit crazy."

With that I called Frontier and purchased a ticket back home.

———

Laura and I sat around the small, round table at Mom's place, watching her struggle to bring a soup spoon to her mouth. A white bandage was taped to her forehead. Her spoon quivered in her limp grip as she labored to get a taste of the chicken broth.

"Mom, how about I arrange for a nurse to stop by and visit with you every day?" I asked.

"What would I want with a nurse? She'd mostly steal the silverware or take off with my jewelry. No. No. I just need to get my feet back under me." She dismissed my suggestion and turned to her daughter. "Laura, stop looking at me like I'm an invalid."

"Mom, if you can't feed yourself, you're an invalid." Laura's frustration grew.

"I'll get back on my feet," she insisted. "I'm just a little shaky. I'm gonna be fit as fiddle in no time at all."

"Come home with me. Stay with Charlie and me for a few weeks, until you're stronger. The kids would love it."

"It's not a bad idea." I added my two cents. "It's just for a few weeks."

"I won't hear none of it," Mom barked. "I won't be a hardship for my young'uns."

Laura turned to me, shaking her head. "There's nothing you can say to her when she's like this."

"Mom, we are just worried about you being here all alone. Laura is asking for you to stay with her for a spell, just long enough for you to build up your strength."

"Please, Momma, you're sick," Laura pleaded. "The doctor thinks you might have to start with dialysis because your kidneys are showing signs of failing."

"I want nothin' to do with staying on this earth one minute longer than the good Lord intended, not one single second longer."

"And what do you want me to do with that?" Exasperated, Laura came undone. "How can I go back home knowing I'm leaving you here alone?"

"I'm not alone," she protested. "I've got Betty and Rose. The Millards and Roberta and Velma are at a stone's throw. The Ellisons are right down the street. And Annie—I know she's gone off the rails a bit, but on her better days, she's good for a salad and sampler platter at the Sizzler."

"Laura and I would feel a whole lot better if you were with one of us."

"Zach, listen up." Mom took a hold of my forearms. "When it's my time to go, don't let me linger for one solitary second longer than necessary. Do you hear me?"

"Yes, Momma."

"Do you promise me? Your sister will keep me propped up in some chair, left to wither like a bowl of cut carnations."

"OK, I promise."

Laura was burning mad. She sat chewing a bite of turkey sandwich with vicious tenacity.

"Little lady, that bird is already dead," Momma declared. "You don't have to kill it again."

"You're impossible." Laura sighed.

Mom lowered her spoon back into the bowl of soup. With a jerking, unsteady attempt, she struggled to bring the spoonful of soup back up to her mouth. Soft noodles and broth spilled to the tablecloth and back into the bowl.

"Mom, you can't even feed yourself." Laura insisted, "You're coming home with us."

"Missy, you best go boss Charlie Mull, because I'm not havin' it here."

Laura sat brooding, and the table went quiet.

Defiant, Mom wrapped trembling hands around the entire bowl of noodle soup and lifted it up to her mouth. Resting the dish's brim on her bottom lip, she tipped it into her open mouth; soft, warm noodles and chicken broth spilled down her open throat and escaped from the corners of her mouth, drizzling off her chin and onto the floor. She lowered the empty bowl back to the table, and with the front of her blouse doused in noodles and yellow broth, she turned to Laura with a grin of complete satisfaction.

Laura bit down on her back molars, flexing her tense jaw.

"Zach, hon." Mom smiled. "I'd like a piece of cherry cobbler now."

Laura exhaled out of sheer frustration. "OK, I surrender!" Throwing up her hands in the air, she went stomping off into the back bedroom. Momma howled.

The next morning Laura walked from the bedroom into the kitchen. Mom was in bed feeling sickly, and I was tending to house repairs.

"Good morning. Where's Mr. Mull?"

"He took the babies over to his folks' for breakfast."

"I'm sorry about yesterday," I said. "I know you're always trying to help."

"It doesn't matter."

"Of course, it does."

"No, it really doesn't."

"Are you OK, sister? Are you and Charlie doing OK?"

With her back to me at the counter, she shrugged her shoulders.

"I'm worried about you."

Her eyes remained focused outside the window. "I want to get in that car and just drive." She said. "I want to keep driving so far away that no one can ever find me. Not Charlie, not Momma, not you. No one."

"You should do it, sis. Take a break and get away," I said. "When you get back, you'll feel better."

She took the clean dishes from the sink and started placing them back in the cupboard. "No. I want to keep driving and never come back. I'm sick and tired of all of it. This can't be my life." She turned to me. "Is this all there is? I'm so sick of all of you."

"You're a tough one, Laura. I don't know why you gotta be so hard."

She began readying herself to leave.

"I'm sorry," I said. "Don't go. Where are you going?"

She turned to me. "I know what I've become, Zach. I'm not blind. And don't think I can't see how you and Momma turn your eyes. Charlie walks a wide path around me too."

"No, Laura. Stop. Don't do this. I wasn't—"

"No. You stop. Don't patronize me. I may never know when or how this happened to me, but I know. Maybe it all started unraveling a long time ago. One pulled thread, and the next thing I know I woke up this person. Now I have Charlie and the babies. This don't feel like livin'."

"Sis, you try so hard for all of us—"

"No! Don't. I won't be pitied or talked down to by Charlie or Momma or you or anyone!"

She walked to the door, pulling a winter sweater over her head and gathering her long brown hair with a rubber band.

"Don't leave, Laura."

She took a seat on the stool by the door, pulled her snow boots over her wool socks, and began lacing them.

I moved to her side, kneeling near her chair. "After Katie died, after Dad, it was just you and me. Remember? Before this world got all jacked up, it was just us. Remember? I remember all of it."

She tugged at her laces. "Well, I am trying to forget. I want to forget it all."

"Not me. I remember everything, and if I could pick any one single memory, I'd choose you. I'd always choose you."

Laura stood, pulled the strap of her purse onto her shoulder, and opened the back door to a waiting winter. A bitter wind blew through the house, rustling the draperies and lifting the tablecloth. She stood facing the cold, gripping her key ring. Pretty as a porcelain doll but as tough as leather. She walked from the house without a word. I watched as her car turned onto Sixteenth Avenue. My big sister had weathered longer and harder Decembers.

———◆———

When time allowed, Doug and I went to the same spot overlooking the city where we had sat and talked years earlier. At the closing of another day, we headed up Cahuenga Boulevard to Lake Hollywood Drive and farther up to Mount Lee and parked the truck.

Tethered from the highest stars, a bloated moon watched, silent and pale, over the sleeping city. A million tiny lights blanketed the shimmering valley. Sitting on blankets in the bed of the truck, we complained about our days and then laughed at our constant bitching.

It never mattered to the moon, but it mattered to Doug. He fought hard to make us stick. He battled for us to beat the odds. In his own quiet way, he spent years trying to teach me to forget, to unlearn the whispers of the narrow-minded.

"Babe, we make a great team." He squeezed my hand. "We knocked it out of the park."

"Doug, I swear, if you're gonna talk in baseball lingo, I'll kick your ass."

He laughed. "OK, OK."

But the words never sounded sappy coming from his mouth. They rang earnest and true. He worked hard to make love stay. It might not have mattered to anyone—my folks or the faithful congregation of the First Assembly of God—but it mattered to me.

———◆———

There was no denying that Momma was dying on us.

On our first visits back home after her cancer diagnosis, Laura and I danced around the subject. It was easy to avoid something we couldn't see. But as Mom's health worsened and she wasted away to nothing and bone, my older sister and I couldn't ignore the death that waited just outside the door. Laura struggled, wanting to manage every aspect of Mom's health issues. Even from her home a thousand miles away, she tried to supervise Mom's appointments, prescriptions, and daily routines.

"Hon, let go, and let God and the doctors handle all this mess," Mom told Laura over the phone. "You're just gonna worry yourself into an early grave, missy."

Laura dismissed Mom's suggestion, unconvinced that the Almighty could juggle Mom's calendar of appointments, tests and x-rays. She kept herself in a constant exhausting tizzy, trying to keep balloons afloat that were destined to pop.

For her part, Mom's tenacity and faith sustained her. Whether trying to convince herself or comfort us kids, she proclaimed dying was a glorious bright, sunny day. Laura remained hushed on the matter, but she wasn't about to let Momma go without a fight. Laura assembled her team—the Father, Son, and Holy Ghost—and prepared for a long dragged-out fight. For me, death was a dark night, polished as black as my Sunday shoes. Whether Mom's passing would be a glorious rapture to the heavens or she simply slipped into a dark abyss of nothingness, I wanted to make the journey with her.

———◆———

The ocean belonged to Doug. It was never mine. He wanted to share his love of the sea with me. He wanted me to feel at home there, but I was born in the backwoods. The ominous ocean scared me. When we walked holding hands along its shores, the Pacific greeted us. Traveling up the sand, the water reached our bare feet and then receded back into the blue. Doug felt nurtured by the salty sea, relaxed by its repeating tides. In the same way, I found calm among the mountains. When Doug disappeared on lazy afternoons, I knew exactly where he could be found.

During those first years together, my childish jealousies had me believing Doug hung at Venice to ogle the beautiful bronze beach boys. I told myself the smooth-chested, carefree summer surfers must have been enticing to him—simple, less complicated than I was, with all my tough ridges and jagged edges.

I marveled at the ocean's beauty, its vast expanse, but when Doug called for me to join him farther in the deep, I waved him off and watched him swim out past the breakers. The longer I loved Doug, the more I learned he needed the ocean as much as he needed anything I could ever give him.

He gifted me, for my thirtieth birthday, a trip to Yosemite. It was the first time I'd set eyes on the towering sequoias north of San Francisco. Leaving from LA, we followed the 101 Pacific Coast Highway as it zigzagged along steep, perilous cliffs that overlooked the crashing Pacific. We traveled into the arms of the giant redwoods. The backwoods of my youth didn't prepare me for the majesty of the giant, soaring trees.

Doug parked the car, and I walked into the cathedral of vaulted canopies. Attempting to stretch my arms around a mammoth trunk, I leaned in and rested my head on the giant sequoia. Doug hollered for me to wait up, but I was long gone to explore the forests. Like he loved the ocean, my tranquility was hidden among trees.

I thought of Doug and our trip to Yosemite while I sat stuck in traffic in my idling truck. The morning congestion on the 110 was at a standstill. Earlier Doug had boarded a silver plane, heading to Boston for a week's stay. It was easy to work myself into a bad mood when I thought of him being gone for a week. My pickup inched along in the bumper-to-bumper gridlock. When my cell phone rang, I half expected to hear his voice.

"Zachariah, hon?"

"Yes, speaking."

"This is Rose. Rose Millard."

"Hello, Rose. Is everything OK? Is Mom OK?"

"I just got a call from Betty. She's taking your momma to the hospital. She found Alice Faye in her bed. She wasn't in good shape. Bless her heart. She's just so weak, poor thing. We're hoping they're going to give her a blood transfusion. The last time it made her feel so much better. She always comes back strong when the doctors give her blood. I've left a message on Laura's phone."

"I don't understand. I just spoke to Mom last night. She was fine," I said.

"I'm sorry."

"OK, Rose. I'm going to call the hospital now. If you hear anything, please call."

"OK, honey. I sure will."

Laura was my first call, but it rang through to her recorder. "Sis, Mom's not good. I'm flying out first thing in the morning."

Doug picked up after my first ring. "Hey, babe."

"Mom is bad. I'm flying back. I'm catching a flight in the morning."

"Damn it. I'm so sorry."

"I know. I miss you."

"I'm sorry I'm not there with you. If I get a chance to leave early, I'll catch a flight."

"Naw, don't do that. I'll call you later tonight."

"Babe, you're gonna make it through this. Do you hear me?"

"Yeah."

"You're going to be strong because that is the man your mom raised." He said. "The man I love."

I stood some three inches taller than Doug. My shoulders were broader and my thick legs were stronger, but he was kinder. His thoughtful nature calmed me. In his quiet way, he was my protector. I wanted to be Doug's hero.

"Are you going to be okay?" He asked.

"I'm gonna be fine."

It's hard to know when it will arrive, but it always comes—the moment you understand everything has changed, like a first October frost chilling a September morning. Waking to find all the leaves have fallen from the cottonwoods to scatter in the wind like children running through a schoolyard, knowing all hope for summer is gone.

CHAPTER 23

———◆———

COLORADO MORNINGS ON THE BRINK of spring begin with a deep purple reflection rising low on the horizon. The lavender glow spreads out and up as dawn slowly consumes the fading night. Darkness lifts, and a clear sky opens the morning to hint of a reprieve from the cold. The season's bitter freeze begins its gradual thaw, and the forest floor and frozen tundra welcome the new warmth. The last dusting of snow on the pines melts under a new sun, and a long winter surrenders to April.

I caught a red-eye flight from Los Angeles to Durango. Doug was in Boston, already starting his day. My plane touched down and taxied on the runway. A brief appearance by the sun, reflected off the silver wing, blinded me through the small window. The warmth lulled the passengers into futile hope that winter had departed.

When I disembarked, any thought of spring was forgotten. I stepped down the ramp onto the tarmac, and a freezing wind chilled me to the marrow, flipping my jacket's collar and wildly blowing my scarf across my face. A bitter cold burned my throat as I inhaled my first breath of winter. The night's rain had left muddy puddles dotting the tarmac, and frigid temperatures before dawn had formed the thinnest shell of ice over the small brown pools. As

I made my way to the terminal, the frozen puddles splintered and cracked under my boots like October's brittle leaves.

I waited, hands buried deep in my pockets, while luggage was unloaded from the plane's cargo bin. For the first time, the freezing reminder of the hard Colorado winters made me long for Southern California.

Clusters of red, coral, and fuchsia geraniums bloomed everywhere in Los Angeles. The palm trees along Santa Monica Boulevard shimmered in brilliant sunlight. Here in Durango the trees stood like slender bark-covered skeletons. Muddy snowbanks invaded the roadways, and black ice froze to the pavement. The columbine waited beneath the soil for any sign of summer's warmth to flower.

As I drove the rental car forty-eight miles north to town, an infrequent sun appeared through the gray haze to shed a momentary clear light on barren fields. Acres of resting, frozen soil lay dormant, only weeks away from being tilled and planted.

I made the last bend on Route 160 around Smelter Mountain, and off in the distance the familiar plume of steam rose from the Durango-Silverton Narrow Gauge. The train depot bustled with camera-toting tourists wrapped in sweaters and scarfs.

I crossed into town over the Animus River. The muddy water churned and rolled, running high from winter's snow melt. The rushing water swelled, threatening to breach its banks.

The right turn onto County Road 250 was unrecognizable. At the crisscrossing of Trimble and 250, a new traffic light created an intersection where a small shopping plaza had been constructed, housing a pizza parlor and gas station. The narrow gravel road leading to our house had been widened and paved.

I was relieved to find that the Ellison farmhouse had remained undisturbed, sitting just as it had years ago. The same knotted rope swing hung from the giant limb of the eucalyptus in the front yard, but the Ellisons' vast cornfields had been cleared and planted with rows of mobile homes.

I pulled the rental car to the curb and parked in front of our old place. The picket fence had been replaced with chain-link, but the same wooden picket railing still squared off the front porch. The oak Pop had planted in the front had grown so tall and wide that its heavy branches canopied most of the small house. Three cars were parked randomly in the gravel yard, and a snarling, snapping shepherd growled through the fence until a voice from inside the house silenced him. I half hoped to see the old yellow dog resting on the porch, waiting for my return, but instead the growling new occupant would have preferred to take a bite from my ass.

The house looked much the same. Its wooden siding was no longer painted white but rather a soft, faded yellow. The shutters and screen door were accented forest green, and the roof's wooden shingles had been replaced with asphalt roofing. Mom had warned me that the old house was in need of repair, so any sense of nostalgia was already in check. A small electric air-conditioning unit was mounted in the opening of Katie's old bedroom window, and the carport had been converted into an additional room. A child's swing set in the front yard was knee-high in yellow grass, and a sticker on one of the car's bumpers read, "My child is on the honor roll at DHS."

I drove on toward the hospital, passing the spot where the First Assembly of God had once stood. A Carl's Jr. now sat in its place. Smoke coughed from the exhaust pipes of a line of trucks and pickups that wrapped all the way to the drive-through window. Construction workers and laborers waited for cups of steaming-hot black coffee and breakfast sandwiches. Because our prayers had been ordered like combo meals in the small First Assembly of

God church, it didn't seem much of a stretch to discover a fast-food establishment standing on the hallowed ground.

I was comforted knowing that old Pastor Barnett had passed away before the little church was bulldozed to its foundation. Two years earlier Mom had written that she and Sister Pilchard had remained in vigil at Barnett's bedside for three days and nights before he'd finally succumbed in a battle with pneumonia.

I recalled Pastor Barnett preaching from behind his pulpit to an ever-listening congregation, "Nothing is louder to God's ears than a mother's prayer." He'd lean in, telling us, "A mother's sorrow is first to reach heaven's heights. Her pleas are laid nearest to the feet of our Lord."

Later I went searching for any verse or Scripture that confirmed his sentiments but came up dry. Driving to the hospital on this winter day, I wanted to believe with all my remaining faith that Pastor Barnett's words were true.

By the time I'd parked the rental car in the lot of Mercy Hospital, the sky had turned gray as ash, the dying sunlight smothered under a blanket of heavy charcoal clouds.

Back in Los Angeles, my crews, bare chested in the sun's warm rays, mowed carpets of green lawns. Farther down Santa Monica Boulevard and into Venice, children played on the beach. And somewhere in Boston, Doug sat in a conference room.

I found a pay phone in the hospital lobby and dug in my pockets for loose change. I fed quarters into the phone, and after a long series of rings, Laura's recorded voice greeted me.

"Hey, sis, I made it. I haven't seen Mom yet, but I'm heading up now. I'll call you after I've talked to the doctors. I'll let you know if you should head this way. Love you, sis."

I walked into the tiny single room to find Momma lying in bed, her eyes open. The smell of disinfectants filled the room, and the scent of a sickly sweet aerosol air freshener unsuccessfully attempted to mask them.

"Hey, you good-looking woman." I kissed her forehead.

She didn't speak a word, but the buzz of my arrival through the door seemed to trigger a coughing fit that erupted from her chest and up through her throat like a miner's lungs filled with coal dust.

I took hold of her right hand. "How are you feeling, Momma? Are they treating you well?" Ever so slightly I squeezed her fragile, bony fingers. Purple wounds spotted her forearms where needles had punctured the skin. I waited to see if she'd return my grip, but her limp hand rested motionless in my palm.

"Can you hear me?" I asked.

Mumbling incoherently, she reached, trying to locate the oxygen tubing slipped inside each of her nostrils. When she found a grip, she jerked the tube.

"No, Momma. You're gonna get us in trouble." I reinserted the breathing tube into her nose, and she mouthed something in protest.

"What, Momma? What do you want? Can I get you something?"

Her eyes momentarily closed. Her frustration eased.

"I left Laura a message," I said. "She will be here tomorrow."

Resting quietly, I ran my fingers along her forearm to lull her into a deeper sleep. When I thought she'd drifted, suddenly her head lifted clear off the pillow as she tried again to remove the oxygen supply. The lengths of plastic tubing were tangled in electric cords and draped off the edge of the bed. I again reached to position the supply back inside her nostrils.

"Sleep for a spell."

She studied me with confused eyes.

"You rest your head down here." I patted the pillow. Her eyes searched around the small room, no recognition in her lost expression.

A smiling nurse popped her head in the doorway. "Mrs. Nance, are you OK? You must've twisted up your IV. You've got our monitors sounding off like a fire alarm." The friendly nurse spoke directly into Mom's right ear, loud but comforting as she adjusted the cords and fluffed the pillow. "Are you comfy, Mrs. Nance? Will you eat anything for me?" The nurse shook her head in frustration. "We can't seem to get her to eat anything."

"Mom, you have to eat."

I turned from the bed and spoke to the nurse in a hushed voice. "I just saw her a few days ago. How did she fall so fast?"

"She's weak, and she's not eating for us."

"Momma, you have to eat if you want to get better."

She mumbled in protest and turned her head.

"You're going to waste away if you don't eat."

Her delicate collarbone pushed against her ashen skin, her undernourished frame swimming in the pile of bedsheets and blankets.

"Mrs. Nance, just press this button if you need anything at all." Knots of tangled cords and tubes kept the nurse's attention. "You must be Mrs. Nance's son."

"Yes, Zach Nance."

"Well, Zach, if you need anything at all, just call me. We're going to make your mom really comfortable."

I sat in the chair at her bedside, thumbing through the photographs in an *Us* magazine while Mom slept a disturbed sleep. England's Princess Diana had given birth to a son, Prince William, heir to the throne.

Mom's eyes twitched beneath her thin, pale lids. Monitors hummed, and lights blinked red and white and yellow. A handsome man walked into the room without acknowledging my presence. With his dark hair and fine, chiseled features, he reviewed a clipboard at Mom's bedside and then gestured for me to follow him out of the room. We stood in the corridor, and I leaned in her open doorway.

"Hello, Mr. Nance. My name is Dr. Jonathon Delany. I'm your mother's oncologist." He extended his hand.

The slightly graying hair at his temples and the black-rimmed glasses made the young man look more distinguished, more professional than his age could convey. I assumed the props were strategic.

"I understand you flew in this morning from California."

"Yes, it was an early morning."

"The weather you left in Los Angeles must be considerably better than the weather you've found here," he said with a smile.

"Well, sunshine can be greatly overrated," I answered. "A change of seasons is nice."

"I need to speak with you concerning your mother's condition. I spoke with your sister, Laura, on several occasions. She says you're aware of the recent PET scans."

"Yes, Doctor, Laura told me it wasn't good news."

"The cancer in her lungs has returned, and there's an indication it's now in the kidneys. With your mother's existing heart condition, we don't believe any surgical procedures are advisable."

"I understand."

"Dialysis is an option if we continue to see that the kidneys aren't performing. The procedure is something you and your sister should discuss."

"OK."

"Now, your sister recently expressed some interest in seeking out additional opinions and alternative treatments."

"Is that code for she's being a pain in your ass?"

Shaking his head, he laughed without smiling.

"Forgive her, Doctor. She's a good girl. My older sister means well. She's just really sad and trying hard to control things she can't."

"I understand."

"What can we expect?" I asked. "What's the next step?"

"Frankly, Mr. Nance, it's more about managing the pain at this stage. The nurses will do everything to assist with keeping her restful and free from any discomfort. I suggest you notify Laura and those you wish to be a part of this transition."

I repeated his line in my head—*those you wish to be a part of this transition.* The doctor's rehearsed line crawled under my skin. I wanted to slug his well-defined jaw and bust his designer glasses in my grip. Instead I played along, asking the expected questions: "How long can we expect? Are we talking days, weeks, months?"

"There's no way to predict these things. We promise to do our best to keep your mother free of pain. In the process it's important that you take care of yourself."

I looked back over my shoulder at Momma sleeping. Like some mock movie set in Hollywood or a scene from one of Mom's favorite soap operas, she lay in a room congested with humming machines, serious charts and graphs, and flashing monitors. The stage was set, right down to the good-looking doctor delivering the dire prognosis.

"Thank you, Doctor. I know I speak for Laura too when I say we appreciate everything you and the staff have done."

He shook my hand like a politician who wanted my vote and then took off down the corridor, disappearing into another room.

Outside Mom's window occasional sunlight slipped from behind a winter's haze of lilac clouds.

I kept vigil at Mom's bedside. She tossed and turned, struggling to rest. When she finally settled into sleep, I headed down the elevator and into the lobby to grab a cup of coffee. Every time the hospital's automatic glass doors slid open, I braced myself for another blustery gust of winter wind whipping through the lobby. I warmed both hands on the Styrofoam cup. Purchasing a stale bagel from the cafeteria, I tried to eat while waiting my turn to use a pay phone.

Exiting the elevator, walking toward me, came a nurse with a familiar face. I recognized her but couldn't recall her name. As she approached I frantically searched my memory. She walked over with a somber smile, arms spread wide open, and with her head cocked she hugged my neck.

"Well, lookie here, Zachariah Nance! Look at you. You're all grown up. It's so good to see you." Resting her hands on both of my shoulders, she said, "I'm so sorry to hear about your mother. She is going to be just fine. She's an angel." The familiar nurse squeezed my shoulders, looking at me like someone who was about to tell a lie. "You hear me, Zach? Your mom is going to be just fine. The girls are going to take good care of her. They are going to manage all her pain."

"Thank you," I replied. "I appreciate it."

"Aren't you in San Diego, making it big?"

"LA."

"Los Angeles? Wow. Are you close to Disneyland? We've been promising the kids for two years to take them."

"Yeah, about twenty-five minutes from Anaheim," I answered.

"My goodness! We will come hunt you up when we bring the kids. How's your sister? How is Laura?"

"She's good, living in South Dakota. I'm just calling her." I motioned to the phone.

"OK, Zach, send her my love. You both are in my prayers." She smiled and hugged my neck again before walking into the cafeteria.

Laura picked up on the first ring. "Zach?"

"Hey, sorry for calling so late."

"No, no. I was awake. How is she?"

"Sis, you'd best think about coming out."

"I'm on my way." Laura was breathless. "Can we get her to a specialist in Denver or Phoenix?"

"No, Laura. She can't be moved."

The silence was deafening. Finally she said, "Zach, I'm not ready to lose her."

"I know, sis."

———◆———

It was a day in March. Winter had held us kids captive behind fogged windowpanes. When the first hint of sun shone, we three set off into the San Juans. Laura, Kate, and I took to the trails, winding deep into the backwoods.

We came upon the La Plata Cliffs, the mighty Mancos River churning below. Laura motioned for Katie and me to follow her and head farther downriver to make a crossing at the Hesperus Bridge. The river rolled strong from a heavy winter snowpack melting up at the timberline, but I spotted the giant fallen aspen tree, which provided a possible path across, at the narrowest distance of the gorge. The tree lay waiting, suspended from ledge to ledge.

Laura surveyed the deep chasm and the tumbled tree. "Zach, let's just walk round and cross at Hesperus." She peered down into the chasm at the muddy, rushing rapids.

"Ain't no way," I griped. "I ain't walking clear down there when we got a perfectly fine way to cross right here."

"Zach, there's no sure way of telling if the trunk is rotted out."

"Aw, you're just a chicken. I'll head out first."

"I'm not either. You're just a fool."

Suspended almost twenty feet above the rolling Mancos, the aspen's twisted roots had been ripped from the earth, dry and exposed. The fallen tree trunk started off thick and sturdy but whittled down to a thin rail where its tip touched the other side.

"Just watch this." Flipping my ball cap backward, I started off, climbing up through the gnarly twisted maze of roots and caked mud, hoisting myself up onto the trunk's base. With untied sneakers I walked a straight line across the white trunk with my arms spread wide, like a man on a wire. The angry, churning water rolled far below my feet. Halfway across I gave it a good bounce, signaling to the girls. When I stood on the narrowest part of the tree, I gave a thumbs-up to Laura, who was waiting behind.

I hollered across to them. "See? It was nothin'!"

"You're a fool, Zachariah Nance."

"We can do it, Laura," Katie chimed in, tugging at her older sister's blouse.

"Come on across. It ain't nothin'." I flapped my arms, clucking like a chicken.

Laura shook her head in my direction, cursing my name under her breath. "I am going to beat the tar out of you when I get over there!"

Laura maneuvered herself and Kate through the knots of roots. "Hop up here, Kate." She lifted her onto the trunk. Standing atop the thick barrel, Katie grew uncertain. "Now, you wait here until I make it across. You understand me?" Laura directed Kate.

"Come on!" I yelled. "You're slower than molasses!"

"Shut up! We're comin'. We're comin'." Laura turned to Kate. "Now, don't move a muscle until I call for you."

"Hurry up!" I called. "Just put one foot right in front of the other, like you're walking on a wire."

"Save your breath!" she hollered. "You're gonna need it when I'm chokin' you."

Steady and deliberate, Laura cautiously stepped out over the water and made her way across. I reached my hand to her as she moved closer.

When Laura was clear of the tree, she hopped down and slapped the back of my head with her open hand. "You're an idiot."

Kate stood, balancing herself with a thick root.

"OK, you ready?" I hollered. "It's your turn!"

Without so much as a blink, little Kate followed right behind Laura. Holding her breath clear across, Katie used the fallen tree's last remaining branches to steady herself. When the hem of her dress got caught up on a poking stick, she wrestled the cotton skirt loose. Stumbling, she sent a pink canvas sneaker falling to the water below.

Laura kneeled at the side of the ledge and coached her across.

"Come on, Kate," Laura encouraged. "You're only a hop, skip, and jump away."

I was just a stupid kid, foolish and unknowing. Never for a single moment did I ever consider that little Kate wouldn't arrive safe and sound to us on the other side.

———

Laura called Mom's room, furious that the winter weather would delay her return a day.

"I'll get there as soon as this damn storm passes," she cursed. "I may try to drive to Omaha and see if I can fly out from there."

"No, no. Don't risk driving. Mom's not here, sis. She hasn't said a single word," I told her. "We are at the end of the road. They are just keeping her comfortable."

I paced the long, white corridors and mindlessly browsed the small gift shop with its spinning metal racks of picture postcards of the Durango-Silverton Narrow Gauge. Finding my way to the emergency entrance, I watched paramedics roll in a stretcher hauling a skier who had broken his leg on Purgatory's slopes. I walked through another room, where a newborn squealed at an ear-deafening pitch.

After I'd walked the corridors, I walked them again, passing the door to a small hospital chapel. I poked my head into the tiny, insulated square room with stained-wood paneling and dimmed sconce lighting. Pocket-size Bibles sat atop the upholstered seats of nine metal chairs lined in three rows. The altar was a simple skirted folding table with plastic racks that displayed literature and pamphlets for the taking.

For the slightest moment, I contemplated taking a seat in the makeshift chapel, but God didn't dwell there. He was a million miles away from Mercy Medical, as far away from this hospital as any old Ford could travel. I liked to imagine that God resides someplace where a narrow blacktop road turns to dirt as it winds upward to higher ground, someplace where the air is thin and clear and only strong lungs breathe and thrive. A green overgrown place where rushing, muddy rivers begin, not where they end. Somewhere high above the mountain ridge, where snowfall blankets the rugged caps and where clouds and heaven occupy the same space. Surely God was not here.

When I reentered her room, Mom seemed to be struggling with the cords and contraptions that were keeping her alive. The tiny, confining room was almost entirely occupied by her railed bed. There was barely enough room for a single chair and not much else - no room left for mourners, no room left for miracles.

"Mom, you gotta lie back, or you're going to pinch the tubes or pull a cord." But her struggle continued as she slightly lifted her head and let it collapse back to the pillow. Her eyes were glazed over with sleep and sedatives.

Where does a mind go? I wondered. She wasn't there with me but lost somewhere in the fog of death and drugs.

"What is it, Mom?" I asked. "Do you want the nurse?"

She rocked her head, like a child refusing to take a dose of bitter medicine.

"What can I get you? Are you in pain, Momma? A drink of water?" At once Mom's eyes were alert, and her mouth worked to say something. I felt an urgency of panic. I asked again, "Momma, is that it? Do you want a drink?"

She surveyed the unfamiliar surroundings as if she'd just entered her room. Her eyes landed on a small chair in the opposite corner where her sweater and purse sat.

"Momma, you want your sweater? Your purse? Is that it?" Grabbing the knit sweater and leather bag, I brought them to her bedside. Air escaped from her chest like a whimpering sigh. I opened the purse, and plastic bottles spilled out onto the bedcover. "Mom, what are you doing with these?" Her eyes focused, and she fought to lift her head from the pillow. "No. Lie back down. Rest your head," I insisted, patting her pillow.

I read each prescription—"Mrs. Elizabeth Pilchard," "Mrs. Anna Combs," "Mrs. Annette Bledsoe," and "Mrs. Rose Linda Millard."

"What are these? Momma, why do you have these?"

She said nothing, but I remembered her pronouncement: "I'll never be a hardship to you kids." I recalled her determination and my promise.

"No." I shook my head. "No." Her intention with the stash of prescribed pills and capsules was clear. "Mom, we can still try dialysis. The doctor said it's an available option."

She rested her head, letting it slip deeper into the pillow.

"Laura's gonna be here, and she wants to explore all options, other treatments. You know Laura. She never gives up. No telling what she's got up her sleeve."

Mom's eyes welled but stayed focused. She had no interest in dialysis, no interest in alternative treatments.

"Momma, this is crazy."

"How's our girl today?" Betty Pilchard strode through the door, with Annie following behind.

I scrambled to gather the plastic prescription bottles and hide them from sight.

"We aren't staying but for a second, just checking in." Betty had brought with her a big smile and a vase of yellow roses. "Hello, Alice Faye. Don't you look bright eyed," she said with a smile. "I brought you some sunny, happy flowers."

Annie spoke not a word, but with swollen, puffy eyes and teal blue tracks streaking down her over blushed pink cheeks, it was clear she'd been weeping. Annie nervously approached Mom, and bending in close, she whispered to the side of Mom's hair, "I love you, Alice Faye." She turned to me and attempted a smile but instead rushed from the room.

"Annie's just all torn up, Zach. Forgive her," Betty remarked and then walked to Mom's bedside. She went about straightening Mom's linens, tucking the white bedding under the edge of the mattress. Repositioning Momma's pillows, she asked, "Are you comfortable, honey?" But Mom said nothing as Betty continued, adjusting her white hospital gown and fashioning the last few remaining strands of Mom's hair with her fingertips. "Now, there you go, Alice Faye," she said with a satisfied smile. "Aren't you as pretty as a picture." She leaned closer and softly kissed Mom's cheek.

I suppose God moves in the souls of some men, a worthy few who strive to walk a straight line. Those men who yearn to be more and better. But I know with full certainty God resides in the heart of every last woman.

Even now, on troubled days when Doug can't lift me from my blues, I allow myself to believe God is a kind old man draped in soft, ivory linen, with sandaled feet and a mane of white hair. He sits on a gilded throne with smiling, clear eyes and the purest, cleanest heart. I envision the Almighty surrounded by laughing angels with glorious piles of ratted hair the color of candy taffy.

I escorted Sister Pilchard to the elevator.

"I wish I'd been a better man." I confessed to Betty. "Momma deserved so much more."

"Now you're talkin' plain foolishness." She smiled. "I imagine I've spent a lifetime playing cards and drinking coffee with that sweet woman. Alice Faye knows more of my dirty laundry than I care to admit, and I know hers." Betty cupped my face in her hands. "Baby, your momma loved the man you are, not the man you wanted to be."

I followed the hallway as it circled the entire fourth floor, delaying my return to the room. When I arrived Mom's fixed gaze met me at the doorway, her clear green eyes alert and determined. I took my place at her side. "Mom, I can't make any sense of this, no sense at all." But her eyes remained fixed, not turning from me.

Small numbered white lights, positioned at each room's door, lit the narrow hospital corridors. The nurse's station was silent. Mom's breathing was troubled. Fluid drowning her lungs created a low fluttering with every intake of air. Each long delay before exhaling scared me. I took my own deep breaths, trying to breathe for her. With the slightest tilt of her head, Mom acknowledged me at her bedside.

Mixed among the multicolored capsules inside the plastic bottle labeled "Mrs. Annette Bledsoe" were white morphine tablets. I counted twelve. The tiny pills spilled from the bottle into the palm of my hand like small soft pebbles. I slipped the tablets, one by one, past her thin, dry lips and into her waiting mouth. She wheezed and tried to suck air into her failing lungs. Lifting her head from the pillow, she sipped water from a paper cup and then gestured for more poison. With pleading eyes and mouth agape, Mom waited for her only son to kill her, one stone at a time.

The shuffle of the occasional nurse passing down the corridor or a beeping monitor breached the silence. When Mom recognized my fear, she'd set a determined gaze. I picked the last remaining pills from my palm as if separating grain from its chaff.

I walked to the small single window and, with one warm breath, clouded over the coming frigid morning. With my fingertip I outlined on the glass the giant, leafless tree that stood bare along the icy sidewalk below. The twisted boughs of the massive, gnarly pecan sprawled against a charcoal sky in defiance of another brutal winter. It was the sole survivor of the old Marston orchard, cleared two decades earlier for the construction of Mercy Hospital. Acres of pecan trees had been planted in precise rows over the sloping hills north of town. During the orchard's excavation, Dad had driven out with his buzz saw in hand and stocked sufficient cords of firewood to keep us warm for three cold winters. The lone giant pecan stood as a last reminder of what had been, standing bare in wait for any sign the wicked winter was loosening her tight grip.

Mom slipped in and out of troubled sleep. When she stirred I reminded her, "I'm here, Mom. I'm right here."

I kept vigil, reading her favorite verses from the book of Psalms until early morning. I reminded her of our shared story. Like Pop recounting one of his lengthy yarns, everyone in the room knew how the story ended.

Life abandons the eyes first, not the deflated lungs or quiet, motionless heart. Before the pulse ceased, it was in her eyes where I first recognized life escaping. Dull, flat eyes gazing blindly into a darkness the living cannot know. Mom's labored breathing became erratic, and she struggled to catch the shallowest of breaths.

Gripping her hand, I whispered, "It's OK, Momma."

Her face was as pale as early morning and as translucent as silence. Her drowning lungs heaved one last time, and she exhaled. I covered my face with empty palms and prayed that a lifeless soul doesn't know whether it's taken by a lone gunman or a faithful son. When I left her bedside, quiet and vacant, Momma was a million miles away.

CHAPTER 24

———◆———

I WORRIED WHERE I WOULD put this new sadness. Could I hide it someplace out of sight? Could I wrap it up in tissue paper, place it in a shoe box, and slide it under my bed?

Mom had often said, "In his own time, God tends to every sorrow." Until then, I wondered if this grief would remain so heavy and cumbersome, frightened I'd be unable to carry the weight. Would there be room enough for me and it and Doug to exist within the walls of our apartment?

The nearly fifty-mile drive back to the Durango Municipal Airport took me from the base of the San Juan Mountains to a vast prairie of rolling hills and tundra. The remote airport sat in the middle of an empty dirt field. A few scattered cottonwoods and a half-dozen mobile homes dotted the landscape. The desolate terrain with its sloping acres of sparse grass resembled the neighboring Kansas prairies more than the Colorado Rockies.

A single runway and a lone, inconspicuous stucco building comprised the extent of the regional terminal. Waiting for my flight, I sat at the Formica counter of the small coffee shop. The diner was empty except for an overly friendly waitress. The brunette server was determined to engage me in chitchat, quizzing me on my destination and the reason for my Durango visit.

"Did you enjoy your stay?" she asked.

"Yes," I replied, hoping the chatty lady would leave me be.

"Where are you from?"

"Los Angeles," I answered.

"Well, this must be as cold as all get-out." She poured a stream of piping-hot black coffee into my cup. "Was it your first visit to our quaint little town?"

"No, I've been here before," I replied.

"I'm sure it ain't much compared to LA, but it's home."

Working on no sleep and an empty stomach, I struggled to concentrate, feigning interest in her stories. Like a firm grip on an electric fence, the steaming mug of caffeine buzzed through my veins. I steadied my trembling hands with a deep breath as the waitress described her two kids, three dogs, and "good-for-nothing" husband.

Either panic or the strong coffee caused my stomach to roll. Nauseated, I worried I wouldn't last the flight—afraid I'd break down sobbing or heaving vomit midair.

Sadness swept over me in waves. I prayed the waitress would go away, but she gabbed from across the counter, her elbows bent on the bar and her chin cupped in her hands. Hoping to create a diversion, I ordered a grilled cheese, and she shuffled back to the kitchen. A tight knot of anxiety twisted in my throat. Fearing I was going to hyperventilate, I concentrated on breathing, inhaling deeply followed by a full, exaggerated exhale, pushing air from my chest.

When the waitress reappeared from the kitchen, I asked, "Could you watch my luggage? I need to use the facilities."

"Sure, hon. The restrooms are down on your right."

Splashing cold water on my face from the tap, I tried to drive the image of Mom from my mind, replacing her face with Doug's.

I imagined him in Massachusetts. I wondered if he was wearing his tweed jacket? What was he having for lunch? Did he still love me, or had he forgotten my face among the passing crowds on the sidewalks of Boston? Did he know the secret of how to make love stay? Because I hadn't a fucking clue.

In the privacy of a stall, I covered my face with the palms of my hands, calling on all my determination to keep it together for the flight. I told myself I could make sense of it later. Maybe none of it really mattered anyway. Maybe it all goes away, lost to the earth and sky, taken someplace on a summer wind like the last note of a disappearing lullaby. Maybe nothing matters in the end but the silent, secret hope that it all somehow matters.

I found a pay phone and called Laura with the news.

"She's gone, sis," I told her. "Momma's gone."

Laura didn't respond for the longest while. I could hear little Daisy's hands reaching for the phone.

After the extended silence, Laura asked, "Was it beautiful, Zach? When she passed on, was it beautiful?"

I knew my sister needed more to hold on to.

"Yes, Laura." I replied. "It was beautiful."

She thanked me like I had given her a gift. "I will tell Charlie the news." She said. "We're booked on the seven o'clock flight later tonight. I'll see you soon."

"Sis, I won't be here. I'm flying out this morning to be with Doug."

A long silence suspended between Laura and me, stretching further than the miles separating us.

"I need him, Laura."

"Of course," she replied. "I understand."

Flying on a plane in the middle of the night, the soft, constant hum of solitude is not unlike the interiors of a hospital—souls suspended somewhere between heaven and earth, and the attendants, the bad food, and the pulsing sound of engines trying to keep us all afloat.

My flight to Boston took me high above mountains and prairies. I was headed to New England to grab hold of my beach boy and never let him go.

From my window seat, all I could see below was wide expanses of black with an occasional cluster of tiny, distant lights—small towns where people lived quiet lives, not unlike those I have known. Simple, quiet folk who just barely got by and others who laughed right out loud, like they were spinning on a carnival wheel. Like all of them, I didn't belong to anyone who really knew me. From my window it all looked small and the same. From this distance even the most brilliant light was no brighter than the headlights of a rusted-out Ford.

The End

Acknowledgments

———

THANK YOU TO MY LITTLE sister, Christi. My deepest gratitude for everything you do. You are my right hand.

Thank you, Lori, for your friendship and encouragement.

Thank you to Loran and Alice—all is possible because of both of you.

Thank you, Brit, Brandon, Jessie, Court, Hailie, Lee, Kurt, Eric, Sean, and Jackson—my amazing family; Team AH.

A special thank you to Dorthe. My time in Sedona was instrumental in this manuscript coming to its fruition.

Kathie, thank you for the Camino. Each step brought me closer.

Thank you to Svend and Hjoerdis Beck—my second family.

Thank you to Jane, Karinya, Peter, Cheryl, Kelly, Eve, and CreateSpace. This was unfamiliar terrain—thank you for your guidance in navigating this journey.

Thank you to Cassie Dandridge Selleck (The Pecan Man) and Christine Ashworth for answering my constant questions.

Thank you to Tara and Renee for your early encouragement.

Thank you to Iris Dement, Rickie Lee Jones, Lucinda Williams, Jason Isbell, Robert Ellis, Stevie Nicks, Darlingside, and Johnny Cash. I was listening all the while.

And a special thank you to Patty Griffin for her "Faithful Son."

My sweet grandmothers – Beatrice & Lucille. Your fingerprints are on every page of this manuscript.

Lastly, many people helped shape this book. The faces and voices of my childhood were ever present during my four-year journey writing this manuscript. Thank you all.

Auntie Sookie & Me
By Michael Scott Garvin
Coming February 2017